SEASONS OF THE NIGHT

AMANDA ASHLEY

For Novalie and Jameson
Welcome to the world!
We love you!!!!!

Table of Contents

Heart's Desire

Chapter 1

Bethany Frasier stared at the Cupid painted on the restaurant window. As a dyed-in-the wool romantic, she had always loved Valentine's Day. The bright red hearts and flowers, the sappy movies, the heart-shaped boxes of chocolates, the sheer fairy-tale feeling of it all. It didn't even bother her that Valentine's Day decorations went up almost before the Christmas ones came down.

But that had been before Jesse Salazar swept her off her feet, made her fall head-over-heels in love with him, and then left town on Valentine's Day without so much as a word of farewell.

"Beth? Hey, Beth, where are you?"

"What? Oh, sorry. It's just…" Beth stopped mid-sentence and stared at Nicki, who worked in the office next to hers.

Nicki heaved a sigh of disgust. "Are we back to Jesse Salazar again? Honestly, Beth, it's been three years. How long are you going to mope over that guy?"

"I'm not moping," Beth protested.

"Girl, it's time you moved on. *Way* past time."

"I know." Three long years and her heart still skipped a beat every time her cell phone rang. But it was never him. "I still can't believe he left me." They had been playmates in grade school, best friends in middle school, sweethearts all through high school and practically engaged their sophomore year in college. And then he was gone, just like that. In their small town, everyone knew Jesse had dumped her. Speculation had been rampant. No one knew where he'd gone—not his best friend, Scott, not his sister, Martina, or his parents. "People don't just disappear."

"Of course they do," Nicki said. "You read about missing persons in the paper all the time."

Beth shook her head. "But Jesse didn't take anything with him. Not his Harley or his guitar or anything else. It's like he just vanished from the face of the earth. Even his mother doesn't believe he left of his own free will."

The police had searched Jesse's house, questioned everyone he knew—friends, teachers, the people he worked with. But there had been no clues, no signs of foul play. He was just gone.

"There were a lot of rumors after he left," Nicki remarked.

Beth glanced at the clock. Her lunch break was almost over. "You think I don't know that?" She'd heard the gossip. Everyone thought she was pregnant and that Jesse had left town to avoid the consequences. For the first three months after he left, everyone she'd met sent pointed glances at her stomach. Thankfully, it had remained blessedly flat. Since then, she had graduated college, found a good-paying job as a junior accountant at Simpson, Clark and Simpson, which was where she'd met Nicki. A few months later, Beth had moved into a place of her own.

Beth reached for the check. "We'd better go. Lunch is on me today."

"What's the occasion?"

"Well, I feel guilty for boring you with, you know."

"It's okay." Sighing dramatically, Nicki pressed one hand over her heart. "That's what friends are for. But, like I said, it's seriously time to move on."

Nicki was right, Beth thought as she left the restaurant. She needed to put the past behind her. She told herself she'd tried. She had dated some nice guys since Jesse left town, but her heart was never in it. Because, for better or worse, she was still deeply in love with Jesse Salazar.

Still held onto to the hope, faint as it was, that someday he would come back to her.

                     Amanda Ashley

CHAPTER 2

Jesse lingered in the shadows beneath the flowering peach tree under Beth's bedroom window. She had been in his thoughts and in his heart ever since he left Riverton three years ago. It had been thoughts of Beth that had kept him sane, that gave him hope, even though he knew the future they had once planned together was no longer possible. He had done things, seen things, that could never be forgotten or forgiven, not the least of which was leaving town without telling her goodbye. But what could he have said? Besides, he hadn't trusted himself to be alone with her after it happened. Or with anyone else, for that matter. As much as he had longed to see her, hold her, it was out of the question. He was no longer fit company for a nice girl. Or any girl.

He had read his hometown paper on his cell phone every night for the last three years, always afraid he might learn that Bethy was marrying someone else. He knew he should want her to move on, fall in love again, marry and have children, but he couldn't abide the thought of her in another man's arms.

After three hellish years of misery, he had finally succumbed to the need to see her again, even if it was just for a moment. Three years without seeing a friendly face, hearing a familiar voice, holding and being held by someone he loved, someone who loved him… Three long, lonely years. Going back home had been a risk, but it was a risk he was willing to take if it meant seeing Beth again.

Jesse tried not to think about what he'd do if she turned him away. He only knew he couldn't endure one more night of drifting from place to place, afraid to get close to anyone, or let anyone get close to him. He simply couldn't endure it. Better to end his life than spend the rest of his miserable existence alone.

Beth had always been tender-hearted, unable to ignore anything or anyone who was hurting. And he was hurting in the deepest part of his soul.

If he still had one.

* * *

On the verge of sleep, Beth had a sudden, inexplicable urge to go to the window. A glance at her bedside clock showed it was almost one a.m.

One a.m. She smiled into the darkness. How many times had Jesse shinnied up the tree outside her bedroom window when she'd lived with her parents? At least once or twice a week, she thought. Sometimes just for a quick kiss. Sometimes he'd ducked inside and they had cuddled on her bed, exchanging kisses and planning for their future. Her parents hadn't approved of Jesse. He'd been from the "wrong side" of the tracks, a rebel who wore a black leather jacket and rode a motorcycle. Jesse's father had been the town drunk, his mother had earned money by cleaning houses for some of the wealthier townspeople. Last year, his father had wrapped his car around a telephone pole. Mrs. Salazar still lived in the same house, still cleaned houses. Beth saw her from time-to-time, a small, dark-haired woman with haunted eyes.

Unable to resist the urge, Beth climbed out of bed and went to the window. Gazing into the darkness, she remembered the last night she had seen Jesse. He had been wearing jeans, boots, and his favorite black leather jacket over a blue t-shirt that matched his eyes. It had been Valentine's Day and they had been squabbling about how to spend the night. She had wanted to go out for burgers and a movie and he'd wanted to drive out to the lake. It was their secret place and she usually loved going there, but lately, things had been getting out of hand. All too fresh in her mind was the fact that her best friend, Teri, had recently given birth to a baby that nobody wanted. Beth

Amanda Ashley

had expected Teri to give the baby up for adoption but to everyone's surprise, including Teri's, she had decided to keep it. As Teri had told Beth, once she saw her son, she couldn't let him go.

"Come on, Bethy," Jesse had coaxed in his whiskey-smooth voice. "I'll be good."

"That's the problem," she'd said. "You're too good."

"Fine, we'll go to the movies. I'll pick you up at seven."

But he had never shown up and she hadn't seen him since.

A slight movement below caught her eye. Hope flared in her heart. Was that Jesse down there, by the tree? Grabbing her robe, she flew down the stairs and opened the front door.

But whoever had been standing in the shadows was gone.

* * *

Jesse cursed himself as he hurried down the street. He had wanted to see Beth so damn bad but when he saw her silhouetted in the doorway, his courage had deserted him and he'd run away like a scared rabbit.

He slowed when he was four blocks away. Hands shoved in the pockets of his jeans, he strolled down the dark street. He knew it as well as he had once known his own.

The Browns, the Hasselbecks, the Sinclair's... people he had known all his life. The Jensen's had painted their house a questionable shade of green, the Sandoval's' had added a front porch.

He paused when someone called, "Jesse, hey, Jesse, is that you?"

Turning, he saw the oldest of the Hasselbeck boys sitting on the front porch. He swore under his breath when Doug, nicknamed Hutch, stood and flicked his cigarette onto the damp grass before ambling toward him.

"Hey, man, where you been?"

Jesse shrugged as Hutch strode toward him. "Here and there." He had grown up in this neighborhood, played catch with the other boys in the vacant lot behind the Jensen's, kissed a couple of the girls under the high school bleachers.

Hutch shoved his hands into his back pockets. "Been a while."

"Three years." Jesse glanced around. He had a lot of good memories of this place. But his best memories were of Beth. He had watched her grow from a skinny Tom boy into a gangly, long-legged teen into a beautiful young woman. She was the girl he had kissed the most often, his best friend, the girl he had planned to marry.

Hutch pulled a pack of cigarettes from his shirt pocket. "Are you home to stay?"

He offered one to Jesse, who shook his head. "No, just passing through. I'd appreciate it if you wouldn't tell anyone I was here."

Hutch nodded. "You're on the run, huh? I figured that, the way you left and all."

"Yeah. So keep quiet, okay?"

"Sure, man. It's good to see ya."

"Yeah, you, too." Jesse swore under his breath as he crossed the street and made his way down the next block. He paused in front of the house he had once called home. The place was dark, shuttered against the night, and badly in need of a new roof and a coat of paint. The yard needed mowing. Once, that had been his job.

Closing his eyes, he listened to his mother's slow, even breathing and then, blinking back tears of pain and regret, he turned away from the house and headed for a rundown saloon near the outskirts of town. The place had no official name. Everyone called it Jake's because that was the name of the bartender. Jesse had spent the last few nights sitting at the bar nursing a glass of wine and pretending the last three years hadn't happened.

Stepping up to the bar, he took a seat and ordered the usual.

He stared at the blood-red drops in the bottom of his glass. *Beth.* Mi corazón. *I need you so damn bad. There hasn't been a single night when I haven't thought of you, yearned for you. Missed you. I want you so damn bad.*

* * *

Lying in her bed, sound asleep, Bethany heard his voice in her dreams.

Amanda Ashley

CHAPTER 3

Beth slept late. Rising, she took the world's quickest shower, combed her hair, brushed her teeth and dressed. Toast and coffee sufficed for breakfast. Five minutes later, she ran out of the house, climbed into her cherry-red Mustang, and made it work with two minutes to spare.

She shoved her handbag in the bottom drawer of her desk, dropped into her chair, and took a deep breath. She'd made it. Only then, as she took a moment to relax, did she remember the odd dream she'd had. It had been odd because she usually recalled all of her dreams, but the only thing she remembered from this one was the sound of Jesse's voice—soft and low and edged with pain as he whispered that he missed her, needed her, loved her.

The ringing of the phone started her day and she had no more time to think about it.

* * *

Beth sighed as she unlocked the front door and kicked off her heels. In desperate need of something chocolate, she opened the freezer, took out a pint of double fudge brownie ice cream and grabbed a spoon from the drawer. In the living room, she sank down on the sofa, turned off the voice of her conscience, closed her eyes in sheer delight as she savored the first bite. It had been a miserable day. Her first client had cancelled, the second one had left all her paperwork at home and expected Beth to be able to sort out her problems anyway.

By closing time, Beth had been more than ready to go home and put the day behind her.

She stared into the empty ice cream container with regret, thinking it was a good thing she didn't have any more in the house. She tended to be careful about what she ate, but what was the point? She didn't have a steady boyfriend, her friends didn't care if she weighed a hundred pounds or two hundred and at the moment, neither did she.

Grabbing the remote, she switched on the TV. As usual, there was nothing worth watching—just world news that grew more frightening and depressing by the day, and reruns of pointless comedies that weren't remotely funny, and cop shows, none of which appealed to her.

A station that ran old black-and-white movies was showing *Dracula* starring Bela Lugosi. A horror movie was the last thing Beth was in the mood for and yet she didn't change the channel. There was something compelling about Lugosi's portrayal of the infamous count. The dialogue was scant, most of the acting wasn't all that great, but his Dracula was compelling.

And then, to her surprise, Beth found herself imagining Jesse in the role, bending over the fair maiden, mesmerizing her with his hypnotic gaze. What would it be like to experience the bite of a vampire?

In some movies, being bitten was painful and bloody and always led to death. In others, the prey seemed to be in the throes of ecstasy. Of course, it was foolish to even think about, since there were no such things as vampires, and even if there were, it was unlikely she would ever meet one.

She was hungry by the time the movie was over. She fixed scrambled eggs, bacon and orange juice for dinner, spent thirty minutes relaxing in a hot bubble bath, and went to bed early.

* * *

The vampire hovered over her, his eyes faintly red, a hint of fang showing. He called her by name and though she knew it was dangerous, she went into his arms, a shudder coursing through her. When

      Amanda Ashley

he drew her closer, his long black cloak seemed to enfold her like the wings of some giant bird of prey.

"Don't be afraid." His voice, so deep, sent shivers of another kind down her spine.

She stared up at him, blinked, and blinked again, and now it was Jesse's face she saw, his beautiful dark eyes gazing down at her, his expression filled with love and a soul-deep sadness.

She whispered his name, heard the longing in her voice.

"I missed you." His hand slid up and down her back. "Every night, I missed you."

"Why did you leave me?"

"I had no choice. Call my name, Bethy. Call me and I'll come to you."

Filled with gladness, she opened her mouth, his name on her lips...

The shrill ringing of her alarm clock roused her with a start.

Beth jerked upright, her gaze darting around the room. "Jesse?" She felt foolish, calling for him when she knew he wasn't there. And yet the dream had been so real. She had touched him, spoken to him, felt his presence, heard his voice. How was that possible?

She didn't find it odd that she had imagined him as a vampire, not when she'd watched *Dracula* before she went to bed.

Call me and I'll come to you.

She whispered his name again, and then louder, pouring all her love into it.

But, of course he didn't come.

Throwing back the covers, she went into the bathroom. Time to stop this foolishness and get ready for work.

* * *

Beth thought about her dream in the lull between clients, during lunch, and whenever she had a few moments to herself. She was no expert in interpreting dreams but there seemed little to unravel. She had watched Dracula, she had dreamed of Jesse, and the two had merged in her subconscious mind.

There were no such things as vampires.

And Jesse was long gone.

For the first time in three years, she let herself consider the possibility that Jesse hadn't just left town, but that something terrible had happened to him.

* * *

Late that night, when she was ready for bed, she opened her bedroom window and then, feeling a little silly, she called Jesse's name.

And he stepped out from behind the tree that grew alongside the house. She closed her eyes, certain she was imagining him. But when she opened them again, he was still there, looking up at her.

It couldn't be. But it was. And he looked exactly the way he had the last time she'd seen him—black hair a little too long. Black jacket. Faded blue jeans. Boots.

"Jesse?" She leaned out the window. "Is it really you?"

He nodded. "Come down."

She hesitated only a moment, then grabbed her robe, stepped into her slippers, and flew down the stairs to the front door.

When she opened it, he stood on the porch, his hands shoved into his back pockets.

"You're here." Her gaze moved over him. "Where have you been? How long are you staying?"

"One question at a time, Bethy."

She bit down on her lower lip, then reached out to touch his shoulder, as if to assure herself she wasn't dreaming.

He grinned. "It's really me."

Beth cleared her throat. "Where *have* you been, Jesse? Why did you leave without telling me?"

"I've been traveling."

"Traveling?"

He nodded.

"I can't think of many places that don't have cell towers." She bit down on her lip. She hated the bitterness in her voice, but it spilled out. "Or phone service. Or mail delivery."

"Beth…"

"Three years! Three long years without a word and now you show up on my doorstep with no apology and no explanation except you've been traveling!"

Her words, razor sharp, sliced into him. He never should have come here. She had every right to know where he'd been, but he

        Amanda Ashley

couldn't tell her the truth. He kept his hands in his pockets to keep from taking her in his arms. "I should go."

"No, wait." She couldn't let him leave. What if she never saw him again? Taking a step back, she invited him inside.

Jesse hesitated for the space of a heartbeat, then stepped over the threshold and shut the door. He wondered if he would ever get used to the weird sensation that went through him whenever he was invited into a home. Granted, it didn't happen very often these days. He pretty much avoided being around people.

Beth waved her hand in the direction of the sofa. "Please, sit down."

He didn't miss the tremor in her voice. With a nod, he sat at one end of the couch.

She perched on the edge of an overstuffed chair, her hands tightly clasped in her lap.

For stretched seconds, they stared at each other.

Jesse tried not to notice the tantalizing scent of her blood. Instead, he focused on the familiar scent of her perfume. She looked much the same. Her hair, a rich strawberry blonde, was a little longer than he remembered, her figure a little fuller. But her eyes were the same deep green, clear and guileless as always.

Beth cleared her throat. "Three years, Jesse. I think I deserve to know why you left town, don't you? Why I never heard from you."

"I wish I could tell you what happened, why I couldn't get in touch with you, but I can't. You have to believe me when I say it's better that you don't know." He raked his hand through his hair. "I never should have come here. I'm sorry, Beth. Sorry I hurt you."

Rising, he moved toward the door.

Beth stared at his back, certain that if he walked out of her life now, she would never see him again. "Jesse! Wait!"

He paused, took a deep breath, and then turned to face her. "Beth."

She didn't remember reaching for him, but suddenly she was holding him close, his head nestled against her shoulder, his arms tight around her waist.

"I'm sorry, Beth," he said, his voice thick with unshed tears. "I missed you so damn much. Please don't ask me to explain why I left. I can't tell you. I can't tell anyone." A long, shuddering sigh wracked his body. "I've been so lonely. I had to see again." He groaned deep in his throat. "I had to hold you one more time, hear your voice, see your face."

Murmuring, "It's all right," she ran her fingers through the hair at his nape. "I won't ask you again. I missed you, too. So much."

He fell back on the sofa, carrying her with him. "Just let me hold you for a little while, and then I'll go."

She cupped his face in her hands. "Don't go," she whispered.

"Bethy."

"Please. I'm afraid you'll disappear and I'll never see you again."

"I won't leave without telling you. I promise." He ran his fingertips over her cheek, across her lips, and then, ever so slowly, he lowered his head and kissed her.

Beth pressed herself against him, felt the years melt away as he deepened the kiss. Nothing had changed. She still loved him. And she always would.

With reluctance, Jesse put Beth away from him. Surrounded by her familiar scent, intoxicated by her nearness, it took all of his hardwon self-control to keep from sinking his fangs into her throat and tasting her.

She looked up at him, her eyes cloudy with desire. "What's wrong?"

"I should go," he said, his voice thick. "It's... it's late. You have work in the morning."

She blinked at him, her whole being trembling with desire. "Stay."

"I'd better not. I'll see you tomorrow night around seven," he said, rising. "If that's okay."

"You promise?"

"I promise."

Bending down, he kissed her again. "Good night, *mi corazón*."

She stared after him as he left the room, flinched when she heard the front door close behind him.

Had he really been here, she wondered as she climbed the stairs to her bedroom. Or had she fallen asleep on the sofa and imagined the whole thing?

     Amanda Ashley

CHAPTER 4

Beth thought the day would never end. She found herself constantly looking at the clock, counting the hours and the minutes until she would see Jesse again. When she wasn't checking the time, she wondered if he had really been there last night. It all seemed so dreamlike, his unexpected appearance, the way she had practically fallen into his arms. She had mentally rehearsed what she would say to him if she ever saw him again. She had planned to tell him that she never wanted to see him again, that she hated him, that she had never loved him, but those lies had vanished at the sight of him. Why wasn't she more angry? He had left her without a word and now he refused to tell her why or where he'd been for the last three years.

And she really didn't care. All that mattered was that he was back and she would see him tonight.

* * *

Beth hurried out of her office, ran down the stairs because she was too impatient to wait for the elevator, blithely exceeded the speed limit as she drove home.

Inside, she quickly kicked off her shoes, changed out of her skirt and blouse and into a pair of soft black pants and the green sweater that had been his favorite - a sweater she hadn't worn since he left town.

She brushed her hair and her teeth, applied her lipstick and a dash of perfume and then took a deep breath.

Too nervous to eat, she poured herself a glass of orange juice. She drank it slowly, telling herself to be calm. Still, she nearly jumped out of her skin when the doorbell rang.

Closing her eyes, she took three slow, deep breaths, and then went to let him in.

* * *

Jesse felt like a kid on his first date as he waited for Beth to open the door. He heard the rapid beat of her heart as she put her hand on the latch, felt a rush of excitement when she invited him in.

He crossed the threshold then just stood there, looking at her. Three long years he had yearned for her, dreamed of her, and now she was here looking up at him, as speechless as he.

He didn't know who moved first, but suddenly they were reaching for each other. Jesse kicked the door closed with his heel and then they were in each other's arms, mouths fused together. It felt so right to hold her close. Her perfume teased his nostrils, the scent of her blood aroused his hunger and he fought it back. This wasn't prey. This was his Beth.

Still locked in each other's arms, they crab-walked to the sofa. Jesse dropped onto the cushions, carrying her with him, reluctant to let her go for even a moment.

"Beth..." He rained kissed on her cheeks, her brow, the tip of her nose. "Do you know how much I missed you? I thought of you every waking moment."

"Why did you stay away so long? I missed you like crazy. I thought..." She sucked in a deep breath. "At first I thought I'd done something wrong, and then I was afraid you were dead."

To her astonishment, he laughed softly.

"It isn't funny!"

"No," he said, his voice laced with pain. "It sure as hell isn't."

She stared at him, confused by the tone of his voice, the look of distress in his deep brown eyes. "You can tell me," she said. "Whatever is tormenting you so, you can tell me."

He shook his head.

 Amanda Ashley

"We never used to have secrets from each other."

"I know." His gaze searched hers. "Believe me, I'm dying to tell you." He laughed again but there was no humor in it.

Beth's eyes widened. "You're not sick, are you?" she asked anxiously.

"No, I'm not sick." I'll never be sick, he thought bleakly. I'll never grow old or weak. I'll never marry the woman I love.

"Jesse, you're scaring me."

"I'm sorry. Maybe I should go?"

"No! I mean, please don't leave."

"All right. Do you want to go out? See a movie? Take a walk?"

"Can't we just stay here?"

He nodded. He couldn't tell her that scent of her blood was driving him crazy, or that her nearness was torture of the worse kind. To be so close, yet so afraid he might hurt her. It was that fear that had kept him away for so long.

He grinned when her stomach growled. "Am I keeping you from your dinner?"

"I was too excited to eat."

"I've already eaten, but I think you should go fix yourself something. I don't want you wasting away."

"Well, since you wanted to go out, I'd love a burger and fries."

Yeah, me, too, he thought. "Let's go."

"Just let me get my coat!"

* * *

They went to Manny's Grill. It had been their favorite hangout back in the day and it hadn't changed a bit. Same old album covers on the walls, same black-and-white tile floor, the same booths covered in fake red leather. How many times had they come here for burgers, he wondered—or simply just for a place to be together?

They slid into the booth in the corner, the one where he'd asked her to marry him.

From her expression, she was remembering that night, too.

A waitress took her order and left, and suddenly Beth couldn't think of anything to say.

"We had some good times, didn't we?" he said quietly.

Beth nodded. "They were all good times, Jesse. Until you left. I know I said I wouldn't ask again, but why did you leave? Was it something I said or did?"

Reaching across the table, he took her hands in his. "Don't ever think that, sweetheart." But of course she was the reason he left. Once he'd been changed, he was afraid to be near her. Afraid to be near anyone he cared for. Even now, he didn't trust himself to be alone with her.

"Then why?"

"Let it go. I'm here now. We're together. Can't you let that be enough?"

Beth nodded reluctantly. She was relieved when the waitress arrived with her order.

Jesse took a deep breath. Aside from his mother's cooking, he missed a good cheeseburger most of all.

"Do you want a bite?" Beth asked.

More than you can imagine, he thought, even as he shook his head.

Beth was almost finished with her meal when Jason and Dina stopped by their booth. Dina and Jase had married right out of high school. And had a baby girl eight months later.

"Well," Jason exclaimed, punching Jesse on the shoulder. "Look at the two of you together. It's just like old times. Where you been, Jess?"

"Seeing the world. You still working for your old man?"

"Yeah. Mind if we join you?"

Jesse glanced at Beth.

"Not at all," Beth said, sliding over to make room for Dina. "Where's Brook?"

"My mom's watching her," Dina said. "I needed a night out."

Beth nodded. It *was* just like old times, she thought, the four of them together. They had double-dated frequently before Jesse went away.

Not surprisingly, they were soon reminiscing about the good old days—like the time Jesse and Jase painted the boys' bathroom pink, or the day Beth added a quarter of a cup of salt to Dorothy Sutton's cake batter in homemaking class, or the time when Jesse snuck into the girls' shower and stole all their underwear.

"I got suspended from school for a month for that one," Jesse said.

   Amanda Ashley

"Good times," Jase remarked, slugging him on the shoulder. "We should get together one of these nights, take in dinner and a movie."

"Sounds like fun," Beth said.

"I'll call you," Dina said, "but right now we've got to go. I promised my mom we'd be home before ten."

"It was good to see you guys again," Jesse said.

Jase nodded. "You, too."

"That was fun," Beth remarked as Jase and Dina headed for the door. She glanced at her watch. "We should go, too," she said, though she hated to see the night end. "I have to go to work in the morning."

They walked hand-in-hand to the parking lot. Jesse opened the driver's side door for her, then went around to the passenger side.

Beth was acutely conscious of Jesse's presence beside her. She wondered if she would see him tomorrow night. How long he would be in town. But she didn't ask. "Do you want me to drive you home?"

"No, I think I'll walk."

"All right. Are you staying at your Mom's?"

"Yeah, for now."

"I'll bet your mom was surprised to see you."

Jesse grunted softly. No doubt she would be, if he decided to risk seeing her.

A few minutes later Beth pulled into the driveway. Ever the gentleman, Jesse walked her to the front door.

"Thanks for tonight," he said. "I had a good time."

"Me, too."

"Beth."

She looked up at him, felt her heart skip a beat when he reached for her. His kiss, when it came, was achingly tender, stirring memories of other nights, other caresses.

"Goodnight, *mi corazón*," he murmured.

"Night."

He waited until she was safely inside and he heard the door lock behind her, then whistling softly, he went in search of prey.

CHAPTER 5

Jesse stood on the front porch of his mother's house later that night. He'd told himself coming home would be a mistake, but he had to see her, had to know she was all right. He'd read about his father's accident on his cell phone. He had tried to summon a sense of loss, but all he'd felt was relief that the old man was gone. Never again would his mother be the victim of his father's bad temper. Never again would she have to lie about the bruises the old man had inflicted on her. On both of them.

He took a deep breath, let it out in a long, slow sigh, and knocked on the door.

With his preternatural powers, he heard the soft scuffling sound of his mother's familiar footsteps as she made her way to the front door, the increased beat of her heart as she wondered who had come calling at eleven o'clock at night. The slight tremor in her voice, as she called, "Who's there?"

"It's me. Jesse."

He heard the quick intake of her breath as she unlocked the door, the hope in her voice as she whispered, "*Mijo?*"

"Si, Madre."

The door opened and she stood there, as beautiful as ever, her long black hair in its customary night-time braid. "Jesse! Is it really you?"

Before he could answer, the door flew open and she reached for

Amanda Ashley

him, her slender arms wrapping around him as she pulled him closer, her tears wetting his shirtfront.

"Mama, don't cry. Please don't cry." He patted her on the back. "Come on, let's go inside."

She clung to him as he crossed the threshold and closed the door. Inside, she took both of his hands, her gaze moving over him from head to foot.

He shifted uncomfortably beneath that all-knowing gaze. He had never been able to hide anything from her, never been able to lie while looking into those deep brown eyes.

"What's wrong, *mijo?*" she asked. "You have changed."

"I'm fine."

She shook her head. "No." Letting go of his hands, she went into the living room and turned on the lights. Sitting on the sofa, she beckoned for him to join her.

He followed reluctantly. How many times had he sat beside her on that very couch? How many times had the lies he prepared morphed into the truth beneath that all-knowing stare? But this time— ah, this time there was no way she could know what he was hiding.

She clasped one of his hands in both of hers. "Tell me, *mijo,*" she said quietly. "Tell me what has happened to you? I see my boy's face, but he is not the same boy that left me three years ago."

"You're right. I am different, but for your own good, I can't tell you why."

"Are you in trouble?" He'd been arrested once. She had always feared it would happen again.

"No, mama. At least not the way you mean."

"You can tell me," she said, squeezing his hand.

"I wish I could. How's Marti?" Martina was his older sister. She'd been the smart one. Married a handsome lawyer and moved to Vermont. He hadn't seen her since the wedding eight years ago. "Does she ever come home?"

"Not since your father's funeral. She calls once a week."

Jesse nodded. That was more than he'd done.

"Can I get you something to eat?"

He shook his head.

His mother took a deep breath and released it in a long, weary sigh. Then, as if fearing the answer, she asked, "Are you home to stay?"

"I don't know."

"I have missed you." She blinked back her tears. "I wish you would stay, *mijo*, at least for a while."

Jesse nodded. She was lonely, he thought, but no more than he was. "Okay, for a while," he agreed. Now that the excitement of seeing him again had faded, she looked worn out, defeated. He blamed himself for that. They had always been close, the two of them finding comfort against his father's abuse. He never should have left home. But how could he have stayed? "Are you all right, *Madre mio?*"

Patting his hand, she said, "I am now. Welcome home, *mijo.*"

Leaning forward, he kissed her on the cheek. "There's just one thing."

She looked at him askance.

"I won't be here during the day and I can't tell you why or where I'll be."

"You are in trouble, aren't you? You can tell me."

He shook his head. "I can't explain it to you now, but if it's going to be a problem, then I'll go."

"No! No. Stay. Your room is just the way you left it."

"*Gracias, Madre.* I'm sorry I woke you."

"*De nada.* Sweet dreams, *mijo.*"

"You, too, mama."

Giving him a quick hug before heading for her bedroom, she said, "Don't stay up too late."

Jesse grinned. Going to bed late at night wasn't the problem. It was waking too early in the morning that was dangerous.

Rising, he went to the window and drew back the faded yellow curtains. It was hours until dawn and he had nothing to do. He had fed earlier. Beth was asleep. His mother had gone back to bed.

Going into his room, he looked around. It was just as he'd left it—the same twin bed with the bookcase headboard, the same dark blue spread, the same U2 posters on the wall.

It felt good to home again, but he couldn't spend the night, couldn't have his mother trying to wake him in the morning. Still, he needed to make it look like he'd spent the night here.

With that in mind, he rumpled the covers on the bed and punched the pillow a few times so it would look like he'd slept there.

When he was satisfied that the bedding looked rumpled enough, he went to his closet to find a change of clothes, felt his heart twist

     Amanda Ashley

when he saw his old guitar leaning against the back wall. He had missed it almost as much as he'd missed Beth and his mother.

He took off his boots and socks, shucked his pants, jacket, shirt and underwear and tossed them on the chair in the corner. He found some clean underwear in his dresser, then grabbed a pair of jeans and a shirt from the closet. When he was dressed, he sat on the edge of the bed, pulled on a pair of socks and stomped into his boots.

Suddenly restless, he went out the kitchen door and ambled toward the run-down shed located in the far corner of the back yard. He had nothing better to do. Might as well pull out the old push-mower. It didn't make much noise and he doubted if his mother, who slept in the front bedroom, would hear it. He could cut the grass and pull a few weeds until the sun came up.

CHAPTER 6

A flood of excitement swept through Beth when she answered the phone after dinner Friday night and heard Jesse's voice on the other end.

"Hey, beautiful, what are you doing?"

"Nothing much. I just finished doing the dishes and I was thinking of watching a movie."

"No hot date tonight?"

Or any night, she thought, though she didn't say so. "No." She was tempted to add, *Not unless you come over*. She might have said that once, but not now, when things were so uncertain between them.

"What movie?"

"*The Avengers*."

"One of my favorites. Mind if I come by and watch it with you?"

"That would be great."

"Okay. See you in a few."

When the call ended, Beth couldn't stop smiling. It was Friday night and Jesse was coming over. Just like old times.

* * *

In his room, Jesse shrugged into his old black leather jacket, ran a comb through his hair, and all the while he wondered if seeing Beth

     Amanda Ashley

again was a good idea. He couldn't offer her any kind of a future. Didn't own anything except the clothes in his closet, an old Harley with a flat tire, and an even older guitar.

Muttering that he was a damn fool for insinuating himself into Beth's life, he went into the living room and asked his mother if he could borrow the car.

She looked up from the dress she was mending. "Where are you going, *mijo?*"

"Just over to Bethy's place to watch a movie."

Smiling from ear-to-ear, his mother nodded, then picked up the key ring from the table beside her chair and tossed it to him, accompanied by the same four words that had always followed him out the front door. "Be a good boy."

* * *

Beth's heart skipped a beat as she went to answer the door. Strange as it seemed, it was almost as if the last three years hadn't happened. It was Friday night and Jesse was coming over to watch a movie. She told herself not to get her hopes up. He'd said nothing about staying in town. Better to take each day as it came and take nothing for granted. If he stayed, maybe they would get together again. If not, well, she had best be prepared for that, too.

But he was here now. Excitement fluttered in the pit of her stomach as she opened the door.

Only it wasn't Jesse standing on the porch, but a tall woman with spiked blonde hair and ice blue eyes heavily lined with kohl. She wore black pants and a sleeveless black vest. A faint scar ran down the left side of her face; a stark white skull-and-crossbones had been tattooed on her impressive biceps. Her lipstick was a dark red, so dark it was almost black.

Disappointment washed over Beth like a splash of cold water. "May I help you?"

"I'm looking for Jesse," the woman replied in a deep, sultry voice. "Is he here?"

An odd chill ran through Beth. Who was this scary woman and why was she looking for Jesse? "Who are you?"

"An old friend."

Beth took a step back and eased the door forward a little,

narrowing the gap. "I'm sorry, I don't know where he is." The lie fell easily from her lips.

"I know he's been here."

Beth recoiled when the woman leaned forward and sniffed her. Sniffed her!

"He hasn't bitten you," the woman remarked, looking amused. "I'm surprised. You look very tasty. When you see Jesse, tell him Zelina is looking for him."

The woman's narrow-eyed gaze ran over Beth from head to foot and then, with a shake of her head, she spun around on her high heels and walked away, hips undulating.

Shutting the door, Beth wondered how Jesse and Zelina knew each other and how Zelina had known Jesse had been here.

She hesitated when the doorbell rang, peered out the peephole to make sure it was Jesse before opening the door. "Hi. Come on in."

"Has someone been here?" he asked, following her into the living room.

"Yes, some dreadful woman. How did you know?"

Jesse muttered an oath. "You didn't invite her in, did you?"

"Heaven's no. She said to tell you she's looking for you. She was..." Beth shuddered. "Creepy."

"You have no idea. Just don't ever ask Zelina to come inside."

Beth frowned. "How did you even know who I was talking about? I never told you her name."

Jesse swore again. How the hell was he going to get out of this without revealing the truth?

Beth tilted her head to one side. "Well?"

Thinking quickly, he said, "I recognized her perfume."

"I didn't smell anything."

"It's very subtle. I'm ready for a little *Avengers* action. How about you?"

Beth led the way into the living room, went into the kitchen to make popcorn while Jesse turned on the TV. And all the while she wondered what he wasn't telling her. And just how well he knew that tattooed woman.

He had made himself comfortable on the sofa by the time she returned to the living room with a bowl of hot buttered popcorn and two cans of soda.

She sat down, the bowl between them. "Who is she, Jesse? How did she know you were here? And how do *you* know *her?*"

"You're not going to let this go, are you?"

"No. Is she the reason you left town?"

"In a way." He ran his hand through his hair, his mind racing as he rejected one lie after another. What could he tell Beth that wouldn't put her life in jeopardy, send her running from his presence, or dashing outside screaming for the police?

"I'm waiting."

"Bethy, you have to trust me. The night I left town... after I left your house, I ran into Chad and Joey on my way home. They were going out to Jake's for a drink and I went with them."

"And she was there? At the bar?"

He nodded. "I guess I drank too much, I don't know. I don't remember much of what happened that night. It's all..." He shrugged. "I woke up the next night in some town in Los Angeles with no memory of how I'd got there..."

"Los Angeles! That's thousands of miles from here. What did she do, kidnap you?" Beth asked, her voice thick with skepticism.

"In a manner of speaking." He really didn't remember much of that night. It had happened pretty much as he'd said. He'd been drunk, Zelina came on to him, and like a fool, he had followed her home. What had happened next was little more than a blur. She had seduced him, then turned him, and pretty much kept him at her side until a few months ago. He'd been shocked when she told him she had tired of him and he was free to go—with one stipulation. If he told anyone what had happened, she would drain them dry and then rip out his heart.

He hadn't wasted any time putting as much distance between them as he could.

And now she was here.

"Are you telling me that she kept you locked up for *three* years!"

"I can't tell you any more, Beth. I'd tell you if I could, I swear it. But I can't. Bethy?"

"I don't know what to say." Rising, she paced the floor, back and forth, before settling on the edge of the sofa. "It sounds so far-fetched."

"I know."

"I have to think about it."

Nodding, he stood, intending to go home.

"Don't go. The movie's going to start in a few minutes. It's more fun to watch with someone else."

"Are you sure?"

Beth nodded. She didn't want him to leave. She wasn't sure she wanted him to stay. She just knew she didn't want to be alone.

Surprised, Jesse resumed his seat. He was wondering how to explain why he didn't eat or drink anything, but it wasn't necessary. Beth seemed focused on the TV but he knew she wasn't seeing the movie. She was thinking about everything he'd told her and trying to decide whether to believe him or not. He knew how improbable his story sounded. On the surface, it was quite a stretch to believe he couldn't have overpowered Zelina and escaped. But then, Beth didn't have all the facts. And he couldn't tell her the whole truth.

A glance at the screen showed that Thor and Iron Man were in serious trouble.

Well, hell, Jesse thought glumly. *The Avengers* weren't the only ones.

* * *

"So," Jesse asked, "where do we go from here?" The end credits were playing and Beth still hadn't said a word. "Beth?"

"I need to know where we stand," she said slowly. "Where *I* stand? Are you here to stay? Do you want to have a relationship? Is that woman important to you? I just need to know what's going on."

"I love you. I never stopped. I never will. What happened in the last three years can't be changed and it can't be undone." He shook his head as he searched for the right words and even as he did so, he knew he couldn't ask her to stay with him unless he told her the whole truth. Beth had a right to know what she was getting into, but telling her the truth could put her life in danger. How was he supposed to make a choice like that? Revealing what he'd become could be dangerous for both of them.

He scrubbed his hands up and down his thighs. Dammit. There was always a chance Zelina's threat had been just empty words, but what if it wasn't?

Beth cleared her throat. "What did she mean when she said you hadn't bit me?"

The question caught him completely off guard. "She said that?"

     Amanda Ashley

Beth nodded. "She sniffed me. Like I was a… a piece of meat. Then she said I looked very tasty."

Well, damn, Zelina might as well have just said *vampire*. "What do you think she meant?"

"I don't know. Why would she think you'd bitten me…?" Beth frowned as she remembered the woman's clothing and her tattoo. "You're not caught up in some scary Goth cult, are you? Tell me you haven't turned into one of those people who go around drinking each other's blood and pretending to be vampires."

"I'm not pretending."

Beth stared at him, eyes wide. "What are you saying? That you're a vampire? There's no such thing."

"I wish."

"Jesse, this isn't the least bit funny."

"No, it's not."

She knew him well enough to know when he was teasing her and this wasn't one of those times. He meant what he said. But that was impossible. Vampires didn't exist.

"I'm afraid they do. And it's dangerous for you to know that. And for me to tell you."

She blinked at him. Was he reading her mind?

"Yes, I am."

Feeling suddenly light-headed, she fell back against the seat cushions, too stunned to speak. Jesse was a vampire? She stared at him. If vampires were real, did that mean other paranormal creatures also existed? It was beyond comprehension. If he hadn't looked so serious, she might have thought he was lying.

"I knew I shouldn't have come back here, but I missed you so damn much. I'd hoped, hell, I don't know what I hoped. I should have known we couldn't have a life together. Not now. I'm sorry, Bethy."

"I don't know what to say."

"Try goodbye," he said, gaining his feet. "And whatever you do, don't invite Zelina into your house."

Jumping up from the sofa, Beth grabbed his arm. "Wait a minute! You can't leave, just like that. Not now."

"It's for the best."

"I don't care. I waited three years for you and now you show up out of the blue and tell me you're a vampire. I want to know everything. How it happened. Where you've been. What you've been doing."

Jesse shook his head. He had expected her to freak out, send him away while cursing his name, not ask for a rundown of the last three years.

Sitting on the sofa again, Beth tugged him down beside her. "What's it like, being a vampire? Start from the beginning. I want to know everything!"

Chapter 7

Jesse settled back on the sofa. "Everything, huh? Do you think you can handle it?"

"Try me."

"Well, like I told you, I was at Jake's with Chad and Joey. I was feeling pretty good when Zelina showed up. Everything after that is kind of hazy." He shook his head. "I think maybe she mesmerized me. All I remember is that she took me home, and drained me to the point of death, then, just like in the movies, she gave me her blood. When I woke up the next night, I had a ravenous thirst. She gave me a little of her blood to ease the hunger, then took me hunting…" He paused at the look of horror on Beth's face. "Hunting," he repeated. "It's just what it sounds like. You track your prey and drink their blood."

Beth swallowed hard. "Isn't it… like, really gross?"

"You'd think so. But I craved it the way an addict craves his drugs. And as disgusting as I thought it was the first few times, going without isn't an option. The pain of not feeding is horrendous. And after a while…" He shrugged. "You learn to like it."

"Do you…?" She worried her lower lip between her teeth. She couldn't imagine Jesse murdering some poor soul for their blood, but wasn't that what vampires did?

"I haven't killed anyone yet." Unlike Zelina, he thought, who relished the chase, who enjoyed toying with her prey before the kill.

Beth shuddered. "So you don't eat or drink anything but blood?"

"Right. You realize you can't tell anyone about this."

She nodded. "Have you told your mother?"

"No. All I told her was that I wouldn't be around during the day and I couldn't tell her why."

"And she was okay with that?"

"Not really."

"Your mother's a wonderful cook. Doesn't she wonder why you don't eat?"

"So far, I haven't been home at meal times."

Beth nodded slowly. It was a lot to take in. Trying not to stare, she studied him. He looked the same as always and yet, now that she was really looking, she noticed that his hair seemed thicker, his eyes darker. He'd always been light on his feet, but she'd noticed earlier that his movements seemed more fluid.

He shifted under her scrutiny. What was she looking for? Fangs? He could have read her mind, it was remarkably easy, but he wasn't sure he wanted to know what she was thinking at that moment.

"Do you have feelings for that woman? Zelina?"

"Only hatred. Remember what I told you, don't ever invite her inside. Vampires can't enter a home without being asked."

"Have you ever turned anyone into a vampire?"

"No!"

Beth was quiet for several moments. Then, to his surprise, she reached for his hand. "In spite of everything, you still seem like the man I fell in love with. My feelings for you haven't changed." She took a deep breath. "Is there a chance for us?"

"I honestly don't know, *mi vida*, but I'm willing to give it a try if you are."

Blinking back her tears, she nodded, and then she was in his arms and nothing else mattered.

Jesse held her close, unable to believe that in spite of everything he'd told Beth, she wanted to stay with him. Maybe life wasn't so bad after all.

* * *

Beth smiled as she got ready for bed that night. She and Jesse had

     Amanda Ashley

spent the evening cuddling in each other's arms, sharing kisses in-between reminiscing about the past. Content to be together in the present, they hadn't speculated about the future, except to agree that Jesse would come over the following night as soon as the sun went down.

She knew that, eventually, they would have to discuss where they were going from here, whether to stay in Riverton or move to a new town where no one knew Jesse.

Still awash in the afterglow of his kisses, she slid into bed and closed her eyes, only to bolt upright moments later.

Why was that woman—that vampire—looking for Jesse?

That thought, and others, even more troubling, kept her awake far into the night. Why had Jesse left so early? He didn't need to seek his daytime rest until the sun came up, yet he had left a little after midnight. Where had he gone?

Beth tried to dismiss the first suggestion that came to mind, but it refused to go away. Every time she closed her eyes, she pictured him stalking some pretty young thing, taking her in his arms, bending over her neck… She slammed the door on that train of thought, only to have it replaced by another, more insidious one. Had he gone to meet Zelina?

She turned onto her side and punched her pillow. When Jesse was with her, his being a vampire didn't seem to matter, not when he was holding her close and kissing her. Not when just hearing his voice made her insides flutter with desire. But now, alone in the dark, she wondered if his being a vampire created a gulf between them that she could never cross.

CHAPTER 8

Zelina strolled through the downtown area's main street. Life had changed drastically in the five hundred years since she had become a vampire. She recalled shopping in open-air markets for the fruits and vegetables that they hadn't grown at home. They had raised and butchered their own meat, made their own furniture and clothing, washed in a wooden tub, relieved themselves outside.

Yes, times had changed. Now, you could buy anything you wanted with a few clicks of a mouse.

She loved modern technology. Many of the ancient vampires had trouble acclimating to a rapidly-changing world, but she found it fascinating.

She paused in front of a jewelry store window bedecked with valentines, fake red roses, and heart-shaped lockets and pendants crafted of fine gold and silver. She supposed love was the one thing that remained constant, though matters of courtship and marriage had undergone remarkable changes in the last few centuries. What had once been considered immoral was now the norm, not that she cared one way or the other. She couldn't bear children, had no need for a husband or a house or any of the trappings of civilization. She grimaced. No doubt Jesse's pretty little mortal dreamed of those things.

Zelina snorted. If so, the woman was in for a big disappointment.

     Amanda Ashley

And then she frowned. Was it possible Jesse was planning to settle down with that tasty-looking female? Since he had not yet bitten the girl, Zelina assumed the female meant more to him than prey. She found the idea strangely troubling. She didn't love him. She had never loved anyone.

Turning away from the window, Zelina continued down the street. She had come to this dreary little town to take Jesse home with her. She had been surprised by how much she missed him. Of course, she had known he wouldn't want to go with her, but she'd been certain she could persuade him. Until she saw him with the girl. If she took him away by force, he would hate her for it, she thought. But then, he already hated her. Of course, a little hate sometimes added an extra zing to a relationship.

Still, humans didn't live long. She could let him spend the next thirty or forty years with the girl. After all, three or four decades was nothing to a vampire.

Yet it rankled that he had returned home to the girl he left behind. She laughed softly. Was it possible she was jealous of a mortal female?

The idea surprised her even as she admitted, reluctantly, that it was true.

Why should she give Jesse up for some puny woman?

She couldn't think of a single reason. It had been a mistake to let him go. Jesse was hers. She had turned him. She wanted him. And she always got what she wanted, one way or another.

He wouldn't come with her of his own free will, of that she was certain. But there were ways to change his mind.

Chapter 9

Sitting on the edge of his bed, Jesse strummed a few chords on his guitar. He had gone hunting after leaving Beth's house. After releasing his prey from his thrall, he had wandered the streets, lost in thought. When a police car pulled up alongside him, he had decided the smart thing to do was head for home. The cops hadn't stopped him or questioned him, just drove alongside, keeping pace, until he turned down his street. Once he reached home, he had decided he might as well stay until the sun drove him to his lair.

His mother had left a light on for him, something she had always done. He had looked in on her before going to his room, thinking that he really needed to spend more time with her.

His thoughts returned to Beth as he tried, without success, to imagine a future for the two of them. Maybe coming back here had been a mistake. He had no place of his own, no job, no income. How was he going to support a wife? Granted, she had a good-paying job and a nice house. Granted, his needs were few. Even if she was willing to let him move in with her, how would he feel, letting her pay the rent and all the other bills while he contributed nothing? It was bad enough that he was sponging off his mother.

Feeling the approaching dawn, he put his guitar away, rumpled the bedding, and headed for the abandoned building east of Main Street where he spent the daylight hours.

For once, he didn't regret it when the dark sleep carried him away.

CHAPTER 10

After going to church on Sunday, Beth went to visit her mom and dad. She enjoyed going home. Like all teenagers, she'd had problems with her parents when she lived under their roof. Nothing too horrible, just the usual arguments about what time she had to come home and cleaning her room, that kind of thing. The biggest argument they'd ever had was over her dating Jesse. Her father hadn't approved of him at first, but Jesse wasn't like so many of the other boys she knew. He didn't smoke, he didn't drink, he didn't swear. He respected his mother and her folks. It had been her father who had comforted her the most when Jesse left town.

Beth spent the rest of the day with her parents, chatting, watching TV, playing Scrabble. She was thinking about leaving when her mother mentioned that they were having Beth's favorite chicken and broccoli casserole for dinner, and homemade lemon meringue pie for dessert.

It was late when she finally returned home.

As she unlocked the door, Beth wondered why she hadn't heard from Jesse. Going inside, she closed the door behind her, let out a shriek when an arm went around her neck and a hand covered her mouth.

"Don't fight me," rasped a voice in her ear. "And don't scream. I'm not going to hurt you as long as you do what I say. Understand?"

    Amanda Ashley

Trembling from head to foot, Beth nodded.

Beth almost fell to her knees when the intruder released her. She took several steps away from him before turning around. "What do you want?"

"I'm looking for a friend of yours."

Stiffening her spine, she said, "I doubt if we have any mutual acquaintances."

The man snorted. "I think we do. Does the name Jesse Salazar ring a bell?"

"You're a hunter."

"So you know what he is. Good." He turned on one of the table lamps, then pulled a wicked-looking knife from the sheath on his belt. "Just sit down and relax."

Beth gave him a wide berth as she moved toward the sofa where she perched on the edge of one of the cushions. "He's not coming here tonight."

"I think he will. He's been here every night."

She clasped her hands in her lap. Knowing that this man—this hunter—had been spying on her and Jesse, sent an icy chill slithering down her spine.

"You some kind of wanna-be vampire?" he asked with a sneer.

Beth shook her head, praying that Jesse wouldn't stop by.

"So, why are you hanging around with a dirty blood-sucker?"

She glared at him. What right did he have to spy on her? To question her?

The man cocked his head to the side. Eyes narrowed, he studied her as if she was a bug under a microscope. "Did he hypnotize you? Is that it? You're under some kind of vampire hocus-pocus?"

Again, Beth refused to answer. If she ignored him, maybe he would go away.

The hunter fell silent.

Folding her arms across her chest, Beth stared at the floor. The ticking of the clock on the mantel sounded very loud in the stillness.

A quiet knock on the front door sounded like a gunshot.

Beth's head snapped up. She opened her mouth to warn Jesse away, but the hunter was on her, his hand trapping the words in her throat.

Whispering in her ear, he said, "Tell him to come in or I'll slit your pretty neck."

"Come in." She forced the words through a mouth gone dry.

But the door remained closed.

The hunter's gaze was fixed on it.

A faint movement to her left caught Beth's eye. She turned her head slightly, gasped when she spied a silver-gray mist hovering near the side window. A mist that gradually took on a familiar, human shape. Jesse!

Her startled gasp must have warned the hunter.

Beth let out a scream as he spun around and threw the knife still clutched in his hand. But Jesse ducked out of the way and the weapon fell harmlessly to the floor.

The hunter pulled a wooden stake from his coat pocket. "Come on, blood-sucker!" he called, tossing the stake from hand to hand. "Come and get it!"

Heart pounding, Beth hastened out of the way as Jesse and the hunter came together. They struggled over the stake for what seemed like hours but was only moments.

Beth glanced around, looking for a weapon, something she could use to defend Jesse—or herself—if it came to that.

She was reaching for the fireplace poker when Jesse's eyes went red and his lips peeled back to reveal a pair of very white, very sharp fangs. She smothered a harsh cry of denial when he sank those fangs into the man's throat.

Certain she was going to be sick, Beth closed her eyes and turned away, her hands clasped over her ears to shut out his last, anguished cry.

When she opened her eyes, she was alone in the living room.

* * *

Jesse buried the hunter deep in the woods beyond the town. Torn with anger and regret, he stood by the grave a moment. He hadn't wanted to kill the man, but he'd had no other choice. It was his life or the slayer's, and although his life wasn't worth much, he wasn't ready to give it up. Although, after what Beth had witnessed, he doubted if she'd be too keen on seeing him again. Not that he would blame her.

Heavy-hearted, he willed himself back to her house. It took him several minutes to find the nerve to ring the bell. Another few

Amanda Ashley

moments ticked into history before he heard her footsteps, slow and heavy, approach the door. And another few seconds for her to ask, "Who's there?" in a voice still shaking from the aftermath of what she'd seen.

"It's me."

"Jesse…"

He heard the faint whisper of her hand against the door, the sudden increase in her pulse. Closing his eyes, he placed his hand on the wooden panel where he sensed her palm rested. "I'm sorry you had to see that."

"Me, too." Silence fell between them. "I don't think I can do this anymore," she said, her voice so low only vampire ears could hear it. "It's not your fault. It's mine. I'm just not strong enough to handle it. I'm… I'm sorry, Jesse."

"Yeah. So am I."

The quiet sound of her tears, together with the scuff of her footsteps as she turned and walked away, made him ache deep inside. Thinking it wouldn't have hurt this much if the hunter had ripped out his heart, Jesse willed himself back home.

Without Beth, his life wasn't worth living. Going to his room, he fell back on the bed, thinking he should have just let the hunter stake him and be done with it.

* * *

Try as she might, Beth couldn't think of anything but Jesse at work on Monday. She couldn't concentrate on spreadsheets or numbers or graphs when images of Jesse kept superimposing themselves on her computer screen.

Jesse materializing from a thick gray mist. How was that even possible?

Jesse, fangs extended and eyes blazing a hellish red. She had never seen anything so terrifying in her whole life!

But… had she been right to send him away?

Time and again, she told herself she had made the only logical decision. No matter how much she cared for him, there was no changing what he was. The sight of Jesse sinking his fangs into that hunter's throat had burned itself deep into her mind and there it stayed, popping up at the most inopportune times—like during the morning meeting with her boss.

Or now, while she was having lunch with Teri.

"Beth? Hey, Beth, where are you?"

"What? Oh, sorry, I was just…" Just what? Thinking about vampires? Well, one in particular.

"You look really distracted, hon. Is everything okay at work?"

"Fine. I'm due for a raise next month."

"Parents okay?"

Beth nodded.

"Hmm." Teri frowned thoughtfully. "How's your love life? Ah, I knew it. No wonder you're looking a little preoccupied. What you need is a man."

"I don't think so. How's Bobby?" she asked, hoping to change the subject.

"Growing like the proverbial weed. My sister's watching him for me. Listen, why don't we get together Friday, just you and me? I know I could use a night out and I'm pretty sure you could, too. Who knows? Maybe we'll get lucky."

The idea didn't appeal to Beth, but neither did spending Friday night at home alone. Besides, Teri was right. It would do her good to get out of the house. "All right," she agreed reluctantly.

"Great! I'll meet you at The Rusty Nail at eight. And don't you dare wimp out on me!"

* * *

Beth didn't know how she got through the rest of the week. Sending Jesse away was like losing him the first time. She moped through the days, had no appetite for anything but chocolate, and cried herself to sleep at night as she tried to tell herself she'd done the right thing.

By Friday, she looked as bad as she felt. Even her bosses had noticed. The elder Mr. Simpson asked if she had the flu. The younger one suggested she see a doctor. Mr. Clark wondered if there had been a death in her family.

She left the office at the stroke of five. On the way home, she gave herself a vigorous pep talk in hopes of working up some enthusiasm for going out with Teri that night. But all she really wanted to do was climb into bed, pull the covers over her head, and sleep.

By seven-thirty, she had managed to pull herself together. She

Amanda Ashley

wore a pair of gray slacks, a pale blue off-the-shoulder sweater, and high-heeled sandals. Make-up helped camouflage the bags under her eyes.

After a last look in the mirror, she grabbed her coat and her purse and headed out the door.

The Rusty Nail was an upscale nightclub where singles tended to hang out on the weekends. Teri was already at the bar when Beth arrived. She had no sooner taken a seat when two men strolled toward them. They had to be brothers, Beth thought. And good-looking ones at that. Blond and blue-eyed, with killer smiles, they could have been cover models.

"Evening, ladies," the taller of the two said. "I'm Sam and this is my big bro, Darren."

"Pleased to meet you," Teri said, batting her eyelashes. "Won't you join us? I'm Teri and this is Beth."

Sam nodded. "Shall we get a table?"

Nodding, Teri picked up her drink in one hand, latched onto Sam's arm with the other and tugged him toward a table in the back corner.

"So, Beth, what can I get you?" Darren asked.

"A banana daiquiri, thank you."

They made small talk until Beth's drink arrived and then they joined Teri and Sam.

Beth sipped her drink. Coming here had been a mistake. Darren was handsome and seemed very nice, but she wasn't in the mood to flirt with a stranger, or tell him the story of her life. She missed Jesse. At the moment, even that gorgeous hunk, Chris Hemsworth, would have had a hard time holding her interest.

By nine o'clock, Beth was ready to call it a night. Pleading a head-ache, she apologized for leaving so early, assured Darren she could find her way to her car alone, and made her escape.

She was almost home when a sudden urge had her turning down Jesse's street. Slowing, she pulled up in front of his house. It was a little late to visit his mother, but there were lights on in the living room.

Parking the car at the curb, Beth turned off the engine. She sat there a moment then tucked her purse under the seat, grabbed her keys and ran up the steps to the porch. She was about to ring the bell when there was an odd tremor in the air behind her. She turned, only to let out a gasp of astonishment as a woman suddenly materialized on the porch.

"Zelina." The name whispered past Beth's lips.

"We meet again. How fortuitous. I want you to knock on the door and tell the woman inside to invite us in."

"Why?"

"Because I said so."

"And if I don't?"

"I can compel you to do it, you stupid mortal."

"What are you going to do to Mrs. Salazar?"

"Nothing. Not that it's any of your business. Now, knock on the damn door."

Beth prayed no one was home as she rang the bell, blew out a sigh of regret when Reyna called, "Who's there?"

"It's me, Mrs. Salazar. Beth Frasier."

"Beth!" There was a rattle as the security chain was removed and then the door swung open. Mrs. Salazar's smile wavered when she saw Beth wasn't alone. "Who's that with you?"

"Why, I'm an old friend of Jesse's, Mrs. Salazar," Zelina said with a toothy grin.

"Oh?" Reyna's gaze moved over the woman, her expression doubtful. Another moment passed before she took a step back. "Come in, won't you?"

When Beth hesitated, Zelina gave her a push. Beth stumbled forward across the threshold with Zelina close on her heels.

Beth followed Jesse's mother into the living room, noting that nothing had changed since the last time she had been here years ago.

Mrs. Salazar gestured at the lumpy sofa. "Please, sit down you two. What brings you here this time of night, Beth?" she asked, perching on the edge of the chair across from the sofa. "Is everything all right?" She glanced at Zelina and back to Beth. "You look worried."

"No, not at all." Beth clutched her keys in both hands to still their trembling.

"I was just wondering… I mean…"

"We were just wondering if Jesse is here," Zelina said.

Mrs. Salazar shook her head. "Not right now."

"Strange." Zelina frowned. "I would have sworn he was here."

"How dare you question my word!" Reyna exclaimed indignantly.

  Amanda Ashley

There was a shift in the air and Jesse materialized in front of the fireplace. "I'm here, Zelina. What the hell are *you* doing here?"

"I came to take you away with me for a century or two."

Jesse snorted. "Not if you were the last woman on the planet."

"No?" Zelina glared at him. "Perhaps I can change your mind." She was moving as she spoke. In the blink of an eye, she yanked Mrs. Salazar from the chair, grabbed a handful of her hair and forced her head to the side.

Beth screamed in horror as the angry vampire buried her fangs in Reyna's throat.

"Zelina!"

Still grasping a handful of Reyna's hair, Zelina lifted her head. Bright red blood dripped from her fangs. Eyes burning bright, she snarled, "I'll kill them both if you refuse!"

"The hell you will!" In a blur of movement, Jesse grabbed Zelina by the shoulders and hurled the vampire across the room.

She slammed into the wall, the force cracking the plaster and knocking a picture off the wall. With a scream of pure rage, she flung herself at Jesse.

He darted effortlessly out of her way.

Zelina sprang at Jesse, fangs bared, hands reaching for his throat, when he shouted, "Zelina, I revoke your invitation. Be gone!"

And, just like that, the vampire vanished from sight.

Jesse hurried to his mother's side and knelt beside her. She lay on the floor, unmoving. Twin streams of blood trickled from two ghastly wounds in her throat.

"Is she…?" Beth choked back her tears, unable to say the word.

"Not yet." He lifted his mother into his arms, then stood. "I'm taking her to the hospital."

"I can drive you," Beth offered.

But it was too late. He was already gone.

* * *

Beth stared at the place where Jesse had been. How was it possible for vampires to move so quickly? She had been shocked when Zelina vanished from the room. Was that all you had to do to make a vampire leave your house? Just revoke your invitation? It seemed inconceivable that something so easy would be so effective, but how could she doubt it when she had just seen it happen?

And what was she supposed to do now?

She glanced at the door. Did she dare leave the protection of the house? What if that creature, Zelina, was waiting for her out there in the shadows? The thought sent a chill down Beth's spine.

Biting down on her lower lip, she went to the front window, pulled back the curtain and peered into the darkness. Was the vampire out there? Or had she followed Jesse to the hospital?

Dropping the curtain back into place, Beth curled up on the battered couch to wait for Jesse to return. Holding a throw pillow to her chest, she found herself worrying about his mother. She'd looked so fragile, so pale. Had she survived Zelina's attack?

Beth sighed. Even more worrisome, what was she supposed to do if Jesse didn't come back home tonight?

CHAPTER 11

Jesse paced the emergency room corridor, hands clenching and un-
clenching, his whole body throbbing with hatred for the woman who
had turned him. How dare she invade his home and attack his family!
His mother was the sweetest, kindest woman he had ever known. If
she died… He swore under his breath. What was taking so long?

Dissolving into mist, he slid under the door. A nurse was taking
his mother's vitals. A transfusion was in progress. He licked his lips
as the scent of blood teased his nostrils, arousing his hunger. Returning to the hallway, he resumed his own form and stepped into the
room.

Glancing over her shoulder, the nurse smiled reassuringly.

"How is she?" he asked, moving to the bedside.

"Are you family?"

"I'm her son."

"She's going to be fine. Do you know what happened to her?"

"No."

"It looks like an animal bit her."

He nodded. That was as good an explanation as any.

The nurse hooked the chart to the foot of the bed. "We'll be moving her to a room as soon as one is available."

"Thanks."

She walked toward the door, the soles of her shoes making a soft shushing sound on the linoleum floor. She paused at the door. "If you need anything, just call."

He waited until the woman left the room, then touched his mother's cheek.

Her eyelids fluttered open. "Jesse."

"How are you feeling?"

"Kind of weak. That woman… she attacked me. She… she drank my blood."

"Don't think about it. If anyone asks, you were bitten by a dog."

Reyna blinked at him, her expression confused. "A dog? Why would I say that? Who was that horrible woman? Why did she attack me?"

"It's better you don't know."

"Jesse."

Even flat on her back, her voice weak and trembling, she had only to say his name to get the truth out of him. It had worked when he was a kid. It still did. "You can't tell anyone what I'm about to tell you," he said, his voice little more than a whisper. "She's not human."

Reyna's eyes grew wide. "What is she?"

Squeezing her hand, he said, "Think about it."

"No." Reyna shook her head. "That's impossible. They don't exist."

"I'm afraid they do. If she comes to the house again, don't invite her inside, no matter what she says. Do you understand?"

"*Mijo*, are you saying that woman is *vampiro?*"

"I'm trying not to," he muttered. "But that's what she is."

"How do you know such a creature?" Reyna stared at him a long moment.

Jesse knew she was recalling what he had told her when he moved in, that he wouldn't be around during the day. She was remembering that he was never there at mealtime and putting two and two together and getting vampire.

His mother's expression turned to horror. "No, *mijo*! Tell me it is not true."

"I wish I could."

"And Beth? Did you… is she…?"

"No! No. I wouldn't do that to her."

"Does she know what you have become?"

"Yeah."

     Amanda Ashley

His mother closed her eyes. For a moment, he thought she was thinking about what he'd told her. And then he realized she had fallen asleep.

Leaning down, he brushed a kiss across her cheek, then dropped onto the hard plastic chair beside the bed.

A hospital wasn't a home.

There was nothing to keep Zelina from coming inside to finish what she'd started.

CHAPTER 12

Zelina paced the street in front of the hospital. She couldn't believe Jesse had attacked her. And then banished her from the house. And now he was sitting up there with his mother. Rage burned within her and with it the desire to kill someone… someone like that female, Beth.

Zelina had been a vampire for almost five centuries and every year she grew stronger. Some of her kind tried to fight what they were, desperate to cling to some last shred of humanity, but Zelina had embraced her new life. As a mortal woman, she had been a warrior. Fighting and bloodshed had been a way of life. In the old days, she had feasted on the blood of her enemies. Sometimes she thought she'd been born to be a vampire.

Jesse was one of those who yearned to retain his humanity. It made him weak.

She closed her eyes as she imagined sinking her fangs into Beth's throat and draining her dry, then tossing the body aside, a dry, empty shell.

Or materializing inside the hospital and feasting on a patient or two.

Or on Jesse's mother.

Or on Jesse.

She smiled into the darkness.

So many delightful possibilities.

She weighed them, one by one, unable to decide what to do, until the tantalizing scent of hot, fresh blood teased her nostrils. Never one to ignore the chance to feed, she followed the scent. It led her to an alley two blocks away, where three men were beating a fourth to a pulp.

"Gentlemen," she purred.

The power in her voice drew the attention of the attackers away from their victim.

The lust that burned in their eyes when they saw her quickly turned to terror as she let them see her for what she was.

Terror swiftly turned to panic when they realized there was only one way out of the alley and she was blocking it. One man, braver than his companions, or perhaps more frightened, tried to dart past her.

With one hand, she broke his neck and tossed him aside.

The other two cowered against the wall.

A glance froze them in place, allowing her to dine on them one at a time, at her leisure.

She didn't touch the dead man.

In a rare act of charity, she decided to let the injured man live.

Sated, she returned to her lair.

Her decision about Jesse and the girl could wait one more day.

CHAPTER 13

Jesse stayed at his mother's bedside until his vampire senses warned him of the coming sunrise. He kissed her on the forehead, then willed himself back home.

He found Beth asleep on the sofa. Regret ate at his soul. He never should have given in to the need to see her again. Zelina was nothing if not vindictive and now the lives of both of the women he loved were in danger.

The only way he could protect them both was to insist that they hide out in Beth's house or his mother's from sundown to sunrise. And that was hardly a practical solution, or one that either would likely agree to.

Jesse cursed under his breath. The only real solution was for him to go away with Zelina. She would tire of him sooner or later. She thrived on contention. Nothing bored her quicker than a life without conflict. All he had to do was acquiesce to her every desire.

It would mean leaving Beth again. No doubt for good this time because he couldn't ask her to wait for him. Not when he didn't know how long he would be gone. She deserved better than that.

As for his mother, if Zelina tired of him while his mother was still alive, he would find her another place to live. Some place far away from here.

Far away from Beth.

Sick at heart, he feathered his knuckles over his mother's cheek before going in search of a new place to the spend the day.

* * *

Beth woke several times during the night. Once, she thought she saw Jesse standing over her, but in the morning, she was sure she had imagined it.

Rising, she went from room to room, searching for him, but he wasn't anywhere to be found. Disappointed, she walked slowly back to the living room.

What should she do now?

The sun was shining brightly. Like Jesse, Zelina should be resting somewhere, so it should be safe to go home.

At least she hoped so.

Beth locked the front door behind her, then stood on the porch, her gaze darting left and right. It was early morning. The street was quiet, the silence broken only by the distant sound of a lawnmower somewhere down the block. Her car was still parked at the curb.

Eager to get home, she ran several stop signs along the way.

Pulling into the driveway, she sprinted into the house, locked the front door and set the dead bolt and then went to check the lock on the back door. She stood in the kitchen, one hand over her rapidly beating heart.

When she'd calmed down, Beth made a couple slices of toast and washed them down with a cup of hot coffee. She told herself she was safe until nightfall, though she wasn't a hundred percent sure she believed it.

* * *

Jesse rose as soon as the sun slid beneath the horizon. Last night, he had decided not to see Beth again, but he needed a shower and change of clothes. Dissolving into mist, he went home to see if she was still there. He slipped under the front door, felt a sharp twinge of disappointment when he realized she was gone. He wasn't really surprised. She had probably bolted out the front door as soon as she woke up. Well, who could blame her? He had brought her nothing but trouble.

He took a quick shower, washed his hair, put on a pair of clean jeans and a shirt and headed for the hospital.

* * *

"How are you feeling, *madre*?" She looked much better after a transfusion and a good night's sleep.

"Better, now that you're here. But you need to leave town before that horrible creature comes looking for you again."

"Has she been here?" he asked sharply.

"No." Reyna clasped his hand in hers. "She is a monster."

"You're right about that." He took a deep breath, blew it out softly. "I'll be leaving tonight. Zelina wants me to go away with her. And she always gets what she wants."

"What?" Reyna sat up, her eyes wild with concern. "Are you crazy, *mijo*?"

"It's the only way to keep you safe. To keep Beth safe."

Reyna shook her head. "There must be something we can do."

"I don't know what it would be." He raked a hand through his hair. "I can't watch you and Beth twenty-four hours a day."

"But if she is truly *vampiro*, we should be safe enough during the day."

"Not really. She can compel mortals to do her dirty work for her at any time. The only way to ensure your safety is to destroy her."

Reyna's dark eyes glittered. "Can you do that?"

"I don't know. She's very old. And very strong. But it's really the only way to put an end to this once and for all." Jesse shook his head. The odds of defeating Zelina were slim to none. Still, if he succeeded in destroying her, even if he didn't survive the fight, his mother and Beth would be out of danger. His only hope was that if he died in the attempt and Zelina didn't, she would forget about killing the women he loved. Like his chance of defeating his maker, the odds of that were slim. He wouldn't put it past her to kill Beth and his mother just for the hell of it.

Shit! Talk about being caught between a rock and a hard place. Better to just play it safe and do what his sire wanted.

* * *

Jesse stayed with his mother until visiting hours were over, promised to keep in touch if he could, and kissed her goodbye.

Outside the hospital, he opened the link between himself and his master. His message was short and to the point.

You win. Come and get me.

CHAPTER 14

Feeling like a wildcat in a cage, Beth prowled restlessly from room to room as the sun went down. She had spent the whole day inside even though she was almost certain Zelina couldn't be out and about when the sun was up. But she didn't know for sure and after what she had seen last night, she wasn't willing to risk it.

Now, with darkness approaching, Beth turned on every light in the house, made sure every door and every window was securely locked, and then closed all the curtains. She wished suddenly that she had a dog. A great big one to keep her company. Dogs were supposed to be able to sense spirits and things that went bump in the night.

She had never been one to drink much but at the moment a stiff shot of whiskey would be just the thing to calm her nerves. She hated being so afraid, yet she had good reason. She wondered where Jesse was, and how his mother was getting along. She should have gone to visit Mrs. Salazar today. It was too late now, but she could give her a call.

She quickly looked up the number for the hospital and asked for Room 213. Relief washed through her when Reyna answered the phone.

"Beth! have you seen Jesse?"

"No. I thought maybe he was with you."

Amanda Ashley

"He was. But he's gone to kill that evil woman."

Feeling suddenly weak, Beth sank down on the sofa. "Did he tell you that?"

"*Sí*. He said it was the only way to protect us. I am so afraid for him. Where are you?"

"I'm home." *And scared out of my mind for Jesse.* "How much longer will you be in the hospital?" Beth asked.

"They said I could go home tomorrow morning."

"Do you have a ride?"

"No."

"Call me when you're ready, and I'll pick you up," Beth offered.

"Thank you, *chica*."

"Try not to worry about Jesse," she said, and wished she could take her own advice. "I'll see you tomorrow."

Assuming we both survive the night.

* * *

Jesse paced back and forth in front of *The Devil's Den,* a sleazy Goth nightclub located just inside the town limits. It was one of the few places he knew where vampires congregated because they fit right in with all the wanna-be children of the night, some of whom could hardly be distinguished from the real thing.

He couldn't remember ever being so scared except for the night he'd discovered what Zelina had done to him. Terrifying didn't begin to describe the horror of it. He'd felt cold inside, as if someone had filled him with ice water. Noise beat at his ears, light hurt his eyes. His teeth hurt, his gums ached. He had been sure he was dying of some rare disease. Only later had he learned that he was, in a manner of speaking, already dead.

Zelina had brought him his first kill. Driven by some instinct he hadn't understood, he had buried his fangs in the old man's throat. He would never forget the way his stomach had twisted when he felt his fangs pierce flesh.

Just one taste of blood and all the pain vanished. He vividly re-called the sound of Zelina's laughter, the glitter in her eyes, when she slapped him on the back and proclaimed, "Well done, vampire!"

He thrust the memory away. Where the hell was she?

"Speak of the devil and she appears," he muttered as his sire materialized beside him.

"Been waiting long?" she asked.

"Do we have to do this?"

"I thought I made that quite clear. I want you. With me."

"I'll never be 'with you' but I'm here, so let's get the hell out of this town."

Zelina walked her fingertips down his arm. "I like it here."

Jesse stared at her. He was about to ask why she wanted to stay but he suddenly understood. It would be difficult, painful, even, to be near his mother and Beth, and know he couldn't be with them. Then, too, it would be a constant reminder that their lives would be forfeit if he didn't do as Zelina demanded.

"I'm hungry," she said, locking her arm with his. "Aren't you?"

* * *

Zelina was a ruthless hunter. She didn't bother to make it pleasant or quick for her prey. She didn't mesmerize them to ease their fear. She savaged her victims and rarely left them alive. She gloried in their terror, declaring their fear made the blood all the sweeter.

She shook her head in disgust when he took only what he needed from his chosen prey, wiped the memory from the woman's mind, and sent her away. "You are the most pitiful vampire I have ever known."

"I'll take that as a compliment," Jesse retorted. "Are we through here?"

She smiled archly as she latched onto his arm. "Let's go. I want to show you our new lair."

* * *

Beth was a nervous wreck the next few days. Every time the phone rang or someone came to the door, her heart skipped a beat in hopes it would be Jesse. But it never was. As soon as the sun went down, she went through the house, making sure all the doors and windows were closed and locked, the curtains drawn. She never went out after dark. And always left on a light or two when she went to bed.

And she kept in touch with Reyna, always hoping Jesse would contact his mother. Always disappointed.

     Amanda Ashley

The days blended one into another.

She spent New Year's Day with Reyna. Neither of them mentioned Jesse but his ghost was there. Beth was careful to be home before dark, though she wondered if it was even necessary now that Jesse had gone off with Zelina.

She thrust the thought away and went to bed early, glad that tomorrow was a work day. Hopefully a busy one that would keep her mind off the man she loved and the horrible creature who had stolen him from her.

* * *

After a week with Zelina, Jesse was ready to slit her throat or his, anything that would put him out of her reach. He had long considered himself to be a monster, but he was a saint compared to his master. She had no mercy, no compassion. She didn't just prey on men, but on women and children as well, unconcerned by the bodies left in her wake—and, apparently, not the least bit bothered by the grim headlines and grisly photos that began to crop up on the front pages of the newspapers.

It didn't take long for a string of hunters to find their way into town. Old and young, male and female, expert and novice, they arrived singly and in pairs, eager to collect the hefty reward being offered by the city. They swarmed into town armed to the teeth with sharp wooden stakes, flasks of holy water, and guns loaded with silver bullets.

Zelina laughed at Jesse's concern. "What can they do against us? We're stronger, faster, smarter. Let them come! We'll take them all out and feed their hearts to the buzzards."

"We could leave town."

"You'd like that, wouldn't you? Well, forget it. I'm not stupid. I know the only reason you're still with me is because of that woman. Well chew on this, Jesse. If you leave me before I'm tired of you, I'll kill her and your mother, too."

"Why the hell do you want me around? You don't give a damn about me. And I sure as hell don't harbor any tender feelings for you."

"True, enough." She wrapped her arms around him, her face inches from his own. "But if I can't have your love, I'll take your hate. So hate me, Jesse," she purred.

He wanted to refuse, but her power trapped him like the coils of a snake. He closed his eyes and pretended it was Beth's arms around him, Beth's lips crushing his own.

* * *

Beth curled up in a corner of the sofa, a pillow snugged against her chest. Try as she might, she couldn't put Jesse out of her mind, couldn't stop thinking about him, missing him.

Was he still in town? Or had he left with Zelina?

"Oh, Jesse," she sighed. "I miss you so much."

Beth?

She jerked upright, her gaze darting around the room. "Jesse?"

Are you all right?

I'm fine. Where are you?

Sitting in a bar.

Alone?

I wish. I'm watching Zelina mesmerize some poor devil.

Oh.

It's no fun for me, either. Are you doing all right?

I guess so. What about you? There are hunters everywhere.

I know. She's killed a few of them.

Any chance she'll go away and let you come home?

I don't know.

Beth didn't say anything, but her disappointment came through loud and clear.

I love you, Bethy. Always.

Oh, Jesse. She gasped as she felt his arms steal around her, so real, so tangible, it was hard to believe he wasn't sitting beside her. She sighed when she felt his lips move in her hair and then he was kissing her.

Beth, I know I have no right to ask, I mean, I don't know how long she's going to keep me with her, but, do you think...?

I'll wait for you, Jesse. As long as it takes.

His arms crushed her close. I love you, Bethy.

"And I love you."

I... dammit, I've got to go.

A sudden emptiness told her he was gone. But it didn't matter.

Amanda Ashley

The warmth of his touch, his words of love, lingered in her heart. She only hoped she would still be a young woman when—and if— Zelina ever tired of him.

* * *

Towards dawn, Jesse followed Zelina back to her lair. Many vampires took their daytime rest inside abandoned buildings or cellars. But not Zelina. Secure in her own strength, she took her rest in the best suite the Windsor Arms Hotel had to offer. Using her preternatural powers, she hypnotized the desk clerk into believing she had paid for the room. She also requested that the maid change the linens at night rather than in the morning.

Lying in one of the king-size beds, his hands under his head, Jesse stared at the ceiling, his brow furrowing as a dangerous plan formed in his mind. If it succeeded, the world would be rid of Zelina and her insatiable thirst. If it failed, he would meet destruction with her.

Either way, he would be rid of the monster who had turned him once and for all.

* * *

Beth stood at the kitchen sink, unable to believe what she was hearing. Had Jesse lost his mind? What he was suggesting was suicide.

Beth? Are you still there?

She had been trying to decide what to have for dinner when she heard his voice in her mind. Feeling suddenly weak, she sank down on one of the kitchen chairs. *Jesse, it's insane. Crazy. There has to be another way.*

She's too strong for me. I can't destroy her on my own.

But to kill her while she's resting… it sounds so… so… so cold-blooded. It's murder.

I don't like it, either. But I'm going out of my mind worrying about you and my mom. As long as Zelina's alive, you're both in danger. Not to mention every other man, woman and child in this town. Bethy, she doesn't just feed on people. She kills them.

All of them?

All of them. She's got to be stopped, Bethy, and I don't know any other way to do it. Write this name and number down. He's a hunter.

* * *

Beth fretted over Jesse's plan long after she hung up. His idea of having her hire a hunter to slay Zelina was insane. How could he even think of putting his life in the hands of someone who was paid to destroy vampires? What made him think the hunter wouldn't take his head, too? And where was Jesse going to get the money to pay for it?

The thought made her wonder how much hunters earned for each kill. And why was she even worrying about *that*?

She stared at the name and a phone number she'd hastily scrawled across a piece of scratch paper. How had Jesse found a vampire slayer? Google? You could find everything else there.

Picking up her phone, she started to dial the number, then disconnected the call. She couldn't do what he'd asked.

She just couldn't.

Beth, I know it's a risk, but it's one I'm willing to take.

Beth took several deep breaths. Then, before she could change her mind again, she quickly called the number Jesse had given her.

Her heart was thundering like a runaway train when a raspy voice said, "Hardesty."

"I… hello… um… are you the vampire hunter?"

"Who wants to know?"

"My name is Beth and… and I know the whereabouts of… of a vampire and I… I want you to destroy her."

"Is that right?" he asked, his voice thick with suspicion. "How did you get my number?"

"A friend gave it to me. The thing is… there's another vampire with her. And I… that is, you're to leave him alone."

The man snorted. "You gotta be kiddin' me, lady! I slay 'em. I don't save 'em."

"But he's not like her! He doesn't want to be a vampire."

"Well, ain't that just too bad. The thing is, once it's done, it's done. Where are they?"

Beth's hand tightened around her cell phone. *I can't do it, Jesse. I'm sorry.*

Please, Bethy.

"Hey, you still there?"

Jesse, didn't you hear him? He's going to kill you, too.

                    Amanda Ashley

It's worth the risk.
Not to me! she declared.
And ended the call.

CHAPTER 15

Beth let out a shriek when Jesse suddenly materialized on the sofa beside her.

"I thought we'd agreed you'd make the call," he said.

"I thought so, too. But when I heard that man's voice…" She shook her head. "He sounded like a killer."

"Well, hell, that's what he is."

"You heard him. He was going to kill you, too, Jesse. You may be all right with that, but I'm not!"

"You have to trust me, Bethy. I know what I'm doing."

"Do you? Your plan has more holes in it than Swiss cheese!"

Murmuring her name, Jesse pulled Beth into his arms. "It's the only way we can ever be together."

"Where is she now?"

"She's seducing some poor guy who thinks he's gonna score big tonight. Little does he know she's like a praying mantis."

Beth frowned at him. "What does that mean?"

"She always kills her mate afterwards."

Beth's eyes widened in horror. And then she stared at Jesse. "Do you? Are you and she…? Never mind! I don't want to know."

Jesse shook his head. "We're not. She can force me to stay with her. She can force me to hunt with her. But she can't force me to do that."

          Amanda Ashley

Beth blew out a sigh of relief.

"So?"

"All right. I'll call him again tomorrow."

Jesse gave her shoulders a squeeze, then thrust a wad of cash into her hand. "He's going to want to be paid up front."

"Where did you get all this?"

"You don't want to know. It'll all work out, *mi corazón*. You'll see."

* * *

Beth spent so much time worrying about calling the vampire hunter, she could scarcely keep her mind on her work the next day. She made numerous mistakes, but she couldn't help it. For all that, she was sorry when it came time to go home. She cleaned off her desk and did a dozen other little unnecessary tasks just to stay at work a little longer. She took the stairs instead of the elevator, dragged her feet on the way to her car.

But, eventually, she reached home.

Pulling her cell phone from her purse, she stared at it and then, suddenly eager to get it over with, Beth made the call, though she added a stipulation Jesse was sure to dislike, which was why she decided not to tell him.

* * *

Her cell phone rang soon after the sun went down.

"Hey, Bethy, I've only got a minute. Did you make the call?"

"Yes. It's set for five a.m."

"Perfect. Don't worry."

Closing her mind to him as best she could, she said, "I'll try not to."

"I love you, Bethy."

"I love you, too."

"When this is over... never mind, I've gotta go."

Beth stared at the phone. By this time tomorrow, either their troubles would be over, or... She shook her head. She couldn't bear to think of the alternative.

* * *

Dressed all in black, a sharp wooden stake in one pocket, a can of pepper spray in the other, Beth drove to the hotel to meet the hunter. She knew Jesse wouldn't approve of her tagging along, but there was no way she was going to let the hunter go into that room alone. No way she was going to let him destroy Jesse, too.

Hardesty was waiting for her outside the hotel.

From the timbre of his voice on the phone, she had expected a big, burly man with shoulders as wide as a barn door and arms like tree trunks. Instead, she found a slight man clad in a black shirt and pants and a brown vest with what looked like a dozen pockets.

He looked her up and down, seeming as surprised by her appearance as she was by him. "You ready, missy?"

"Yes."

"You got the scratch?"

Nodding, she handed him the money Jesse had given her. One thousand dollars. "Just remember, you're not to touch him."

"Sure, sure. Let's get it done."

She followed him into the lobby, her nerves humming with tension.

"Excuse me," the man at the desk called. "Are you guests here?"

Hardesty held up his hand, revealing a keycard. "Room 217."

With a nod, the man waved them on.

"Do you really have a room here?" Beth asked, her voice no more than a whisper.

"No."

They rode the elevator up to the fifth floor, then walked down the hallway to Room 507.

Beth's heart pounded so hard she thought she might faint. How were they going to get inside? Hardesty turned his back to her and reached into one of his pockets. A moment later, there was a soft *click* and the door swung open on silent hinges. The room was pitch dark.

Apparently, Hardesty had a small flashlight in one of his many pockets because a faint light suddenly swept the room, revealing a large living area.

Beth followed Hardesty toward a closed door to the left, paused when she sensed someone behind her. She whirled around as a second man stepped out of the shadows. This one looked the way she had imagined a hunter would look. He carried a wooden stake in one

　　　　　　Amanda Ashley

hand and a mallet in the other.

"Stay here." His voice, a low growl, brooked no argument.

Beth nodded, though she had no intention of doing so.

She waited until both hunters went into the other room, then she tiptoed after them. Her gaze was immediately drawn to the two king-size beds. Zelina lay on her back on the one nearest the door. Wearing a see-through negligee, her hair spread out on the pillow, she looked like a queen at rest.

Jesse lay on the other bed, wearing only a pair of jeans.

Neither of them were breathing.

"Clive, you take him," Hardesty told his partner. "I'll take her."

The big man grunted, then moved toward Jesse.

Beth cried, "No!"

And all hell broke loose.

Zelina bolted upright and in a move almost too fast for Beth to follow, flew at Hardesty.

At the same time, Clive lifted the stake and lunged toward Jesse, aiming for his heart.

Beth screamed as a shower of blood spewed from Hardesty's throat, splattering the walls, the floor, and her face.

Jesse jerked the stake from Clive's hand, pushed him against a wall and sank his fangs into hunter's throat as Zelina tossed Hardesty's body aside. She glanced at Jesse, who was bent over Clive's neck.

And then, to Beth's horror, Zelina's hand shot out and wrapped around her neck.

Beth had no time to cry out, no time to react. Only a brief moment of horror as the vampire's fangs bit into the tender skin below her ear.

Beth's scream was trapped in her throat.

I'm going to die. She closed her eyes as the thought crossed her mind but before she could comprehend it, the hand around her throat was no longer there.

She opened her eyes to a nightmare.

Hardesty lay on the floor in a pool of blood, his throat a gaping hole.

Zelina was sprawled face-down. A stake protruded from her back. And then, in a flash of white light, her body was gone.

The second hunter was crumpled in a heap. Blood leaked from two puncture wounds in his throat.

Jesse stood in the center of the room, fangs bloody, eyes a hellish shade of red.

It was too much. The room began to spin, faster and faster, and then Beth's world went dark.

* * *

"Beth? Bethy?"

She moaned softly as someone shook her shoulder.

"Beth, can you hear me?"

"Jesse?" Not wanting to see the room's bloodbath—or Jesse's vampire face again—she kept her eyes squeezed shut.

"Beth, it's all right. You're home."

Hardly daring to believe, she opened one eye and looked around, though she purposefully avoided looking at Jesse. Sitting up, she lifted a tentative hand to her face, but there was no blood. When she glanced down, she saw that she was wearing one of her nightgowns. She felt her cheeks grow warm with the realization that Jesse had undressed her. All things considered, she couldn't be upset.

Jesse had also cleaned up. How long had she been unconscious?

"Bethy? Are you ever going to look at me?"

She did so reluctantly, breathed a sigh of relief when he looked like himself again. "Was that your plan?" she asked. "If so, I think it could have been better."

"I didn't expect you to show up." He raked his fingers through his hair. "I knew the threat of danger would rouse Zelina, same as it would me. But I had to be in real danger, too, so that, if the hunter failed, she wouldn't suspect me."

"Because she can read your mind?"

He nodded.

"So how come she didn't know what you were planning ahead of time?"

"I can block my thoughts from her for short periods, usually when she's feeding."

"You could have been killed."

"It was a chance I was willing to take." He slipped his arm around her shoulders. "It was the only way we could ever be together." He took a deep breath. "If that's still what you want."

She nodded uncertainly, the memory of the carnage at the hotel all too fresh.

He hugged her close for a long moment, then kissed the top of her head. "I've got to go. The sun's coming up." He kissed her, a long, slow kiss as if he had all the time in the world, and then he was gone.

Beth stared at the place where he had been.

The danger was over.

Jesse was still alive. They could be together now.

For the first time, she found herself thinking seriously of what it would mean if she stayed with Jesse, if she became his wife.

She loved him deeply, but was love enough to bridge the vast gulf between mortal and vampire?

CHAPTER 16

Beth spent Sunday morning making a list of the pros and cons of staying with Jesse, something she realized she should have done the minute she discovered what he was. She had been so happy to see him again, to know he hadn't left town because of anything she had said or done, but because he'd had no choice.

The pro side of her list was woefully short and said only *Because I love him.*

The con side was far longer. She would age and he would not. He lived by night. She would have to lie to her friends and family about why they never saw Jesse during the day, why he couldn't eat meals with them, and on and on. So many reasons and yet none of them was strong enough to change her mind, or override the fact that she loved him. Vampire or not, she wanted to spend the rest of her life with him, as long or as short as that might be.

Her decision brought a measure of peace to her heart and soul.

Excitement fluttered in the pit of her stomach as the hours slid by. She ate a quick dinner, took a shower, washed her hair, dressed in her favorite slinky black slacks and a green silk shirt.

The sun had barely set when the doorbell rang.

Beth took a deep calming breath, ran a hand over her hair, then paused to look out the peep hole before opening the door. "Hi!"

"Hi." He whistled softly as he handed her a bouquet of red roses.

     Amanda Ashley

"You look great!"

"So do you." She stepped back to let him in, then closed and locked the door. "Just let me put these a vase."

He followed her into the kitchen, stood in the doorway while she filled a container with water and arranged the flowers. "How was your day?"

"Fine."

When she turned around, he took her hand in his and led her into the living room.

He waited for her to sit down and then he sat beside her.

Beth frowned. He seemed nervous. And he looked different somehow, though she couldn't put her finger on what had changed. "Is everything all right?"

"More than all right. You know I love you. I always have."

She nodded. "And I love you."

"No matter what?"

"Jesse, you're scaring me."

"I've got something to tell you and I don't know how to say it."

Now he was really scaring her. "What's wrong?"

"Nothing," he said quickly.

"Whatever it is, just tell me."

Abruptly, he dropped down on one knee. "Will you marry me tomorrow morning, Beth?"

"I'll marry you any time you want," she exclaimed, her heart beating double time. And then she frowned. "Did you say tomorrow *morning?*"

His smile stretched from ear to ear. "I did."

"But… how?"

"I killed Zelina."

"I know. What does that have to do with anything?"

"I'd heard somewhere that if a fledgling kills his sire, the vampire curse is broken. I thought it was just a myth, but…" He shook his head. "Imagine my surprise when I woke up this morning. I couldn't believe it. Neither could my mother. But once we got over the shock, she insisted on fixing me the biggest breakfast you've ever seen." He bounded to his feet and paced the floor. "You can't imagine what it was like, being able to eat solid food, drink a cup of coffee. I'd forgotten what a good cook my mom is."

Beth stared at him. That was it, why he seemed so different. So carefree, as if the weight of the world had suddenly fallen from his shoulders.

He stood in front of her, looking down. "I thought you'd be happy about it."

"I am! Believe me, I am. It's just... Why didn't you tell me such a thing was possible?"

"I didn't want to get your hopes up, in case it *was* just a myth."

"How could you keep news like this until now? Why didn't you come over first thing this morning? Or at least call me and tell me the good news?"

"I'm sorry." He went down on his knees again. "It's just that I wanted to be here to see your face when I told you. And I had some shopping to do."

"Shopping? You waited all this time to tell me your good news because you were *shopping*?" She didn't know why she was so angry. Zelina was no longer a threat. Jesse was human again. She should have been ecstatic. And she was. Maybe it was just the shock of it all.

Reaching into his pocket, he withdrew a small black velvet box. "I don't think you'll mind when you see what I bought." He lifted the lid, revealing a heart-shaped diamond ring set in a wide, gold band.

"Oh, Jesse," she murmured. "It's the most beautiful thing I've ever seen."

Slipping the ring on her finger, he said, "I hoped you'd like it."

"I love it. And you!" she exclaimed as she threw her arms around his neck and hugged him tight.

Resuming his place on the sofa beside her, Jesse put his arm around her and held her close. They sat like that for several moments, content to be in each other's arms.

"Are you going to miss it?" she asked hesitantly. "Being a vampire, I mean?"

"Hell, no! Well, maybe a little. It was pretty cool, being able to will myself wherever I wanted to go, being powerful, never feeling sick or tired." He kissed her cheek. "Being able to read your mind."

To her surprise, she thought she would miss that, too.

One thing he wouldn't miss was hunting with Zelina, Jesse thought, watching her torment her victims, toy with her prey, before she drained them dry. That was something he had never gotten used to. Always, in the back of his mind, had been the fear that if he lived

                    Amanda Ashley

as long as she had, he would lose what was left of his humanity and become like her—a heartless, soulless monster.

"Enough about the past." he said. "Do you know what tomorrow is?"

"Our wedding day?"

"It's Valentine's Day."

"Oh!" How could she have forgotten that? "I love you, Jesse Salazar."

"And I love you, Bethany Ann Frasier. And I intend to prove it every day and every night of our lives together, beginning right now."

Beth's eyelids fluttered down as he took her in his arms and kissed her, a long, searing kiss that burned away all the heartache of the past, a kiss filled with undying love and the promise of a long and happy future for all the years and all the Valentine's days to come.

~

Summer Wishes

CHAPTER 1

Raegan York stood on the balcony of her grandmother's beach house overlooking the Pacific Ocean. He was there again, the same man she had seen every night for the last five weeks. She didn't know who he was, had never seen his face up close, knew only that he was tall and broad-shouldered and that his hair was long and dark. He always came to the beach alone, and always at the same time, just after midnight. Hands shoved deep into the pockets of his jeans, he stood there, staring at the moon-dappled water while waves lapped at his bare feet. Sometimes, he stripped down to his briefs and went swimming. The first few times he had done that, she had been worried that he was suicidal because he was gone for so long. But he always came back.

She had been tempted, on more than one occasion, to go down and ask if he was all right, but as much as she yearned to meet him, she'd never been able to summon the nerve to approach him. There was something about him, something…well, *something*. She didn't know what it was, but it warned her to stay away.

Rae was about to go to bed when he turned and stared up at the balcony. With a start, she stumbled a few steps back, then chided herself for her foolishness. There was no way he could see her clearly, any more than she could see him. And even if he could see her, he had no way of knowing she was watching him. And yet…for an instant, she would have sworn that his gaze met hers. How else to explain the shiver of awareness that had skittered down her spine, the oddly intrusive feeling that his mind had somehow brushed hers?

It was all too freaky. Hurrying inside, she closed the balcony doors. She rarely locked them, but she did so now. And even then, she felt vulnerable. Exposed, somehow.

For the first time since she had been a child, she left the lights on when she went to bed.

* * *

Tor stared up at the balcony long after the woman had disappeared into the house. He had felt her watching him every night and knew, from eavesdropping on a few of her telephone conversations with a girlfriend, that her name was Raegan and she was house- sitting for her grandmother while she was on an extended vacation visiting family in London. Of all the things he had overheard, the most intriguing was the knowledge that Raegan was intensely curious about him, and that she was afraid he was going to commit suicide. He had to laugh at that. He could swim from here to Hawaii with little effort.

It was having a price on his head that was hard.

Picking up a rock, he threw it into the ocean, watched it skip across the water until it disappeared.

If only he could do the same.

Muttering an oath, he jogged down the beach, gradually increasing his speed, as if by doing so he could outrun his thoughts, or the hunger than plagued him with every breath. As if he could turn back time and take up the life that had been stolen from him over three centuries ago.

* * *

Two nights later, sitting cross-legged at the water's edge, Tor caught the woman's scent. Looking over his shoulder, he saw her standing at the foot of the narrow rock stairway that led from her backyard down to the beach. She was a pretty thing, with curly, shoulder-length golden brown hair and tawny skin. Her eyes were dark brown under delicately arched brows, her lips pink and perfect, her nose a bit too sharp.

He shook his head when she started walking toward him. Didn't she have any sense, approaching a stranger at midnight on a deserted

            Amanda Ashley

beach? Even as he questioned her sanity, he couldn't help but notice the gentle sway of her hips, or the way the ocean breeze played in her hair. She wore a short-sleeved pink sweater over black shorts that showed off a pair of remarkably long, tanned legs.

His jaw clenched as she drew closer and he caught the scent of her skin, heard the steady beat of her heart, smelled the warm, rich coppery scent of her life's blood.

She stopped just out of his reach. Uncertain now, she folded her arms across her chest. The beat of her heart increased and he knew she was having second thoughts.

Tor didn't rise, didn't move, just sat there, trying to look harmless. "Can I help you?"

A half-smile flitted across her lips. "Actually, I came down to see if *I* could help *you*."

"Oh?"

"You've been coming here every night for the last few weeks, and I…" A rosy flush stained her neck and washed up into her cheeks. "I was afraid you might be thinking of… I mean, I thought maybe you needed someone to talk to or…or something."

He grinned in spite of himself. "Thank you, but I have no intention of destroying myself, if that's what you were thinking."

She sighed with obvious relief, then smiled at him. "I'm glad to hear that. So…" She scrubbed her hands up and down her arms. "I'm sorry I bothered you."

"I could use some company," he said, surprising them both.

She worried her lower lip for a moment while she made up her mind.

"I'll understand if you'd rather not," he said. "You don't know anything about me. It's late. We're alone. Perhaps another time."

"Oh, what the hell," she muttered, and dropped down on the sand beside him. Not too close, though.

He grinned inwardly, amused by her thoughts. She was a little skittish. She didn't want to sit too close, lest he misinterpret that to mean she wouldn't rebuff an advance, yet far enough away that she felt safe.

Foolish girl. She was in more danger than she knew.

"I'm Rae," she said.

"Tor."

"Tor? That's an odd name."

"It's short for Salvatore, actually."

"Oh." She smiled shyly. "It's nice to finally meet you."

"Same here. So, tell me about yourself."

"There's not much to tell."

"Okay." He didn't blame her for not confiding in him. Like he'd said earlier, they were strangers. "At least tell me you're not married."

She hesitated a moment, then shook her head. "No."

"Do you live here?"

"No, I'm looking after my grandmother's house while she's away. She won't be back until August. I'm on medical leave." Raegan frowned. Why had she told him that?

He looked at her sharply. She didn't look sick. "Nothing serious, I hope."

Her gaze slid away from his. "I had some minor surgery a few weeks ago."

He lifted one brow, hoping she would elaborate, but she was staring out to sea, her expression guarded. He could have read her mind, but decided against it. It was obviously something she didn't want to talk about and, for now, he would respect that.

"So, what about you?" she asked. "Are you from around here?"

"No. I guess you could say I'm on vacation."

"Do you have family here?" With her forefinger, she traced lazy eights in the sand, back and forth, over and over again.

"My family's been gone for some time." Centuries, actually, but he could hardly tell her that. "I came to California because I've always wanted to see the Pacific Ocean."

"It *is* beautiful, isn't it?"

Tor nodded. "I never get tired of watching it," he said, although it wasn't the ocean he was looking at just now.

"I know what you mean. It's, I don't know, sort of peaceful, at least on nights like this."

Silence fell between them. Tor clenched his hands. Over the smell of sand and surf, he was acutely aware of the scent of the woman. Her heartbeat vied with the rhythm of the waves lapping at the shore. He could take her, here and now, take it all and bury her body. No one would never find her, or know what had happened to her. She would just be another young woman who vanished, never to be seen or heard from again.

But he made no move toward her, content, somehow, just to sit

     Amanda Ashley

beside her, to inhale her womanly scent, listen to the quiet beat of her heart, and pretend he was just a man, like any other.

Rae glanced at her watch. "It's late," she said. "I should probably go."

Tor nodded. "Thanks for worrying about me."

"No charge." She had a ready smile, though it didn't reach her eyes.

Rising, he offered her a hand up.

This time, she took it without hesitation. Somewhat self-consciously, she brushed the sand from the back of her shorts. Murmuring, "Good night," she jogged toward the stairs.

Tor watched her until she disappeared into the house. The sound of her voice seemed to linger in the air like the whisper of a gentle caress long after she was out of sight.

When she was safely inside, he left the beach.

It was time to hunt.

Chapter 2

That night, Raegan thought about Tor long after she climbed into bed. He was incredibly handsome, with his long black hair and soul-deep, dark green eyes. His features were clearly defined, beautiful yet masculine. She didn't understand what had prompted her to go down and talk to him. Since her ordeal, she had avoided everyone – her best friend, Audrey, her parents - friends and strangers alike. Especially strangers. Especially men. And yet she had gone down to the beach in the middle of the night, inexplicably drawn toward a stranger, certain that he needed comforting. How could she have been so wrong? And so stupid? From a distance, he had looked lost and forlorn. Up close, he had been taller, broader, radiating an aura of…what? Mystery? Danger? She couldn't put a name to it, but she'd never felt anything quite like it before.

Rae frowned, suddenly recalling something he had said. When she mentioned being worried about him, he had replied that he had no intention of destroying himself. In retrospect, it seemed like an odd choice of words.

With a shake of her head, she turned onto her side. Hugging a pillow to her chest, she stared out the balcony doors. In the darkness, sea and sky merged together. Stars danced and sparkled in the heavens and were reflected on the face of the water. Moonlight frosted the waves with silver as they advanced and receded in their endless flirtation with the shore.

The song of the ocean caressing the sand lulled her to sleep.

* * *

Tor was much in Rae's mind the following day. She slept late, as had become her wont since her surgery. Sleep was a great escape, except when the nightmares came. And they came every night. But last night had been different, and what had started as another nightmare had somehow metamorphosed into something else. And Tor had been in it. He had drifted in and out of her dreams, more like a wraithlike shadow than a man of flesh and blood.

On waking, she hadn't been able to remember the details, only that her shadow man had played a prominent part. Sometimes she had run toward him, seeking protection from an unknown evil, and sometimes she had run away from him, though she could not now recall why.

Rae spent most of the day resting on the sofa, by turns reading and watching TV, rising only when hunger or thirst drove her into the kitchen.

Time and again, she glanced at her watch, willing the hours to pass by, wondering if Tor would be on the beach again tonight. She felt an unexpected ache at the thought that he might not show up. She told herself she was being foolish. She didn't even know the man, and yet watching him the last few weeks had been the highlight of each day.

As midnight approached, she showered, brushed out her hair, and dressed in a pair of cut-off jeans and a long-sleeved gray t-shirt. Pulse racing with anticipation, she hurried toward the balcony and opened the door. Moving quickly to the rail, she glanced up and down the beach, but he was nowhere in sight.

She waited a few minutes more, an overwhelming sadness stealing through her as ten minutes turned to twenty and then thirty.

She was about to turn away when she saw him jogging along the shoreline. He waved when he saw her and she waved back, warmth and excitement spreading through her when he ran up the stairs to stand under the balcony.

"Juliet!" he called, one hand outstretched dramatically. "Come down."

With happiness bubbling inside her, she hurried out of the house and down the short flight of wooden steps that led from the side of the house to the flagstone patio and ended at the top of the stone stairway.

"Romeo!" she cried exuberantly, "I'm so happy to see you."

"And I you, my fair Juliet."

His gaze moved over her, the intensity of it making her blush down to her toes.

"I was afraid you weren't coming," Rae said, then bit her tongue. She didn't want him to know she'd been waiting for him, but it was too late now.

His next words made her feel better. "I've been waiting all day to see you."

"You probably say that to all the girls."

He shook his head, then took her hands in his. "No games between us, Raegan," he said quietly. "I want you. I think you want me, and it scares you, because we've just met."

She blinked up at him, wondering how things had gotten so serious so soon.

"You're right to be afraid." A muscle throbbed in his jaw, and he released her hands. "I should go."

"Go? But…you just said…" Rae stared at him. She had always been careful of the men she went out with. No blind dates. No pickups in bars or dance clubs. No one-night stands. She'd only had two serious relationships since high school. The first one had just sort of fizzled out. The second one had been wonderful, but had ended when Vinnie was killed in an accident with a drunk driver. She folded her arms over her stomach and took a step backward. She must have been out of her mind to even consider getting involved with anyone else.

Lifting her chin, Rae met Tor's gaze, intending to tell him to go to hell. But the words wouldn't come. Blinking back unwanted tears, she murmured, "Good night," then turned and headed back toward the house.

Feeling like a heel, Tor watched her go. He had hurt her, he thought, noting the rigid set of her shoulders. But better to do it now than later. He had almost made a mistake, one that could have been fatal for both of them, in one way or another. He had no business getting involved with a woman.

                     Amanda Ashley

He swallowed hard as he watched her climb the short flight of wooden stairs, his determination to let her go fading with each step she took.

Just before she reached the top, he ran up the steps, his hand closing on her arm.

"Wait!"

Raegan let out a startled cry, lost her balance, and would have fallen if he hadn't caught her. "Tor! What are you doing? You scared me half to death."

"I'm sorry." He pulled her into his embrace. "Don't go."

"But you just said…"

"Forget what I said. I've been alone a long time." He tucked a lock of hair behind her ear. "Give me one night."

She eyed him warily. "And if I said yes, what would you do with it?"

"Take you out for drinks and dancing under the stars."

"That sounds nice."

"How about tomorrow night?"

She pretended to think about it, even though she had already made up her mind.

He ran his knuckles over her cheek. "Pick you up at nine?"

"I'll be ready." Why did she feel so safe with him when every other man made her freeze up inside?

He drew her slowly closer, closer, giving her time to pull away, and then he kissed her, ever so gently. "Good night, Raegan."

"Good night." Wondering at his abrupt change of heart, she went into the house, then hurried to the balcony and watched him make his way down to the beach.

He waved at her, then jogged down the beach until the darkness swallowed him up.

* * *

Tor arrived promptly at nine the next night. Raegan's breath caught in her throat when she opened the door and saw him standing there. Clad in black slacks, a dark gray shirt open at the throat, and a thigh-length black leather jacket, he was breathtakingly handsome.

"I clean up pretty good, don't I?" he asked with a wry grin.

Feeling suddenly tongue-tied, she nodded.

He winked at her. "So do you." She looked as fresh and bright as a summer day in a blue sun dress and a pair of white heels.

"Thank you."

"Are you ready to go?"

"Yes." Raegan grabbed a sweater from the back of the sofa, then followed him outside, pausing to lock the door behind her.

She felt a sudden rush of unease when she saw his car. Sleek and black, it was the same color and model as the one… She hesitated when Tor opened the door, remembering all too clearly what had happened the last time she had been in a car like this. Was she making a terrible mistake?

"Is something wrong?" Tor asked.

"No." She shook the memories away. This was Tor, not some monster. "No, I…no." Taking a deep breath, she settled herself in the seat.

Tor studied her a moment, perplexed by her reaction to the car. He couldn't help noticing that she flinched when he shut the door. He grunted thoughtfully, wondering if she had been in an accident recently. Or if she had changed her mind about going out with him and lacked the courage to say so.

Going around to the driver's side, he slid behind the wheel. "All set?"

Hands tightly clenched in her lap, she nodded. She stared straight ahead as he pulled out of the driveway and onto the winding road.

Hoping to help her relax, Tor turned the satellite radio to a station that played soft rock. "How long is your leave of absence?" he asked.

"As long as I need. You never told me what you do for a living," she said, anxious to change the subject.

"No, I didn't, did I?" Damn. "I guess you could say I'm sort of between jobs at the moment."

"Oh?" She turned a little in her seat. "Are you thinking of staying in California?"

"I wasn't," he said quietly. "Until I met you."

"But you said…that is, I thought…."

"I know. I said just one night." He reached for her hand and gave it a gentle squeeze. "But I don't think one night will be enough."

* * *

   Amanda Ashley

The Sea View Inn was an upscale nightclub nestled in the hills along the coast. Tor asked for a table by the front windows, which afforded a magnificent view of the Pacific. After they were seated, Raegan ordered a virgin Bloody Mary. Tor ordered a glass of chardonnay.

"Not much of a drinker, are you?" he remarked when their order arrived.

"Not anymore."

"Oh?"

Her gaze slid away from his. "Pretty view, isn't it?"

"Yes, very."

She was good at changing the subject, he mused, and wondered what she was hiding. Once again, he fought the temptation to read her mind, determined not to pry.

Staring out the window, Raegan sipped her drink, thinking how beautiful the ocean was in the moonlight. "I was afraid of the water when I was a little girl."

"Oh? Why?"

"I got caught in a rip tide. I guess I was about ten at the time. A lifeguard saved me. It took me years to go back in the ocean, but now I love it."

Tor nodded. There was something fascinating about the sea. The endless waves reminded him of his life, ebbing and flowing with the tide, ever changing yet always the same.

He swirled the wine in his glass. The rich red hue reminded him of the need to feed. He glanced across the table at Raegan, his gaze lingering on the pulse throbbing in the hollow of her throat. He could smell the salt on her skin, hear the blood flowing through her veins.

With an effort, he drew his gaze from her neck and sampled the wine. It was rich and full-bodied, well worth the price, yet it would never satisfy his thirst.

He drained the glass, then set it aside. "Shall we dance?"

When Raegan nodded, he took her hand and led her onto the dance floor. She fit into his arms as if she had been made solely for that purpose. Her perfume teased his senses, the scent of cherry bark and almonds lingered in her hair. Desire welled within him each time her body brushed against his. But it was the warm, sweet fragrance of her life's blood that called to him, promising pleasure unlike any he had ever known.

"Tor?"

He looked down at her, wondering if his eyes had gone red with the lust for blood.

"The music stopped."

He forced a smile. "I hadn't noticed. But then, with you in my arms, who could blame me?"

She blushed, pleased and embarrassed by his words.

He drew her closer when the music started again, tempted almost beyond measure to bend her will to his. It would be so easy....

He dismissed the thought with a shake of his head. Raegan wasn't some stranger to feed on and forget. She was a lovely young woman with haunted eyes. He didn't have to delve into her mind and heart to know she was hiding a soul-deep hurt. He was sorely tempted to ferret out her secrets. Even more tempting was the slow, steady beat of her heart, the sound of her life's blood whispering his name.

"Tor?"

"What?"

"You look sort of…um, I don't know. Different."

"Different?"

She blinked at him, a slight frown creasing her brow. "For a moment, your eyes looked kind of…red."

Battling down his hunger, he smiled and said, "Must be the lighting in here."

"Of course," she agreed.

When the music stopped this time, he suggested they take a walk. He needed to be alone with her, to hold her closer than was proper on a public dance floor.

A narrow flagstone path lit by colorful paper lanterns circled the restaurant. With her hand in his, they strolled along the path until they came to a wrought-iron bench set in a small alcove formed by the branches of a large pepper tree, its leaves screening them from sight of passersby.

"I thought you wanted to walk," Raegan said when Tor pulled her down beside him.

"I just wanted to be alone with you."

"Oh."

"What troubles you, Raegan?"

"I don't know what you mean."

"I think you do. There's a sadness in your eyes that you can't

 Amanda Ashley

hide."

She lifted her chin, her body tensing, her voice going cold. "I don't want to talk about it."

"I just want to help."

"You can't help. No one can. It's over and done and I just want to put it behind me."

A single tear welled in the corner of her eye. A mortal wouldn't have seen it in the darkness, but Tor saw it clearly. It hovered there a moment, then slid down her cheek. She made no move to wipe it away.

Tor squeezed her hand. "You can tell me," he said quietly. "Whatever it is, you can tell me."

She shook her head, then buried her face in her hands.

"It's all right, Raegan. I won't ask you again."

She collapsed against him, her body shaking as her tears turned to sobs.

"Ah, shit," he muttered. Gathering her into his arms, he silently berated himself for causing her pain, yet more determined than ever to find out what she was hiding.

CHAPTER 3

The next day, Raegan couldn't remember the ride home from the restaurant. But she remembered Tor's strength as he lifted her from the car and carried her into the house and up the stairs to her room. He had left her for a few minutes so she could change into her PJs, and then he had tucked her into bed as tenderly as ever her mother had done.

He had whispered, "Sweet dreams, Raegan," then kissed her cheek. When he turned to go, she had grabbed his hand and begged him to stay. And he had obliged. Sitting on the edge of the bed, he had held her hand until she fell asleep.

She glanced around the room, but of course there was no sign of him. Now, in the light of day, she felt foolish for asking him to stay with her. She was a big girl, after all, and nightmares couldn't hurt her....

Odd, she thought. For the first time since her ordeal, there had been no bad dreams.

Throwing back the covers, Raegan wondered if she could get Tor to spend every night holding her hand. Why did she trust him when other men, even men she had known for years, made her uneasy?

After brushing her hair and her teeth, she pulled on a pair of cut-off jeans and a sweatshirt and went jogging on the beach. It was a beautiful morning, one she would have liked to share with Tor.

     Amanda Ashley

Running along the shore, it occurred to her that, in all the weeks that she had been here, she had never seen him during the day. She could understand that if he lived here and had a job, but he was on vacation. Where did he spend his days? She loved the beach, but until she saw Tor, she had rarely gone down to the water at night. Like most people, she preferred to swim when the sun was up and the air was warm, a delicious contrast to the cool water.

She shook her head. It was none of her business how or where Tor spent his days, or who he spent his time with. But she was curious just the same, and, to her amazement, a little bit jealous of the time he spent away from her.

She ran for forty minutes before returning home. After taking a quick shower, she slipped into a pair of comfy sweats, and curled up on the sofa with a glass of grapefruit juice. For the next thirty minutes, she lost herself in her favorite soap opera. It was her one guilty pleasure.

Then, following her doctor's orders, she took a nap.

Later, she went to the grocery store, made a stop at the pharmacy to renew her prescription, and another stop at her favorite take-out place for an order of sweet-and-sour pork for dinner.

Later that night, as the sun set, she brushed her hair again, checked her make-up, changed into a pair of jeans and a red-and-white checked shirt, then went out to sit on the balcony, her feet propped on the rail, hoping she wouldn't have to wait until midnight to see Tor again.

But midnight came and went and there was no sign of him.

At one-thirty, she went to bed, determined not to cry.

CHAPTER 4

Tor stood on the balcony, out of sight, listening to the soft sounds of Raegan's breathing. She had cried because of him. The thought was like a dagger in his heart. He hadn't meant to hurt her. Hell, she hardly knew him and yet he couldn't deny the connection between them any more than he could explain it.

With the stealth of a jungle cat, he approached the French doors outside her bedroom. They opened at his touch. Raegan lay curled on her side, her cheeks stained with tears.

"Dammit," he murmured. "What have I done?" Without thinking he took a step forward, only to be repelled by the threshold.

He had scarcely spoken the words when she sat up, her gaze searching the darkness.

"Tor?"

At the sound of her voice, he melted into the shadows.

"Are you here?"

Shit.

"Please be here," she whispered.

He sucked in a breath, torn between his need to ease her pain and his fear of making it worse.

Her tears were his undoing.

"Raegan." He stepped into the open doorway.

"You *are* here," she murmured.

"I was down at the beach and thought you might still be awake."
The lie left a bad taste in his mouth. "I should go."

"Don't."

It wasn't an invitation, exactly, but it allowed him to enter the
room. He crossed the floor quickly, then sat on the edge of the bed.
He slid his arms around her when she snuggled against his side.

"I waited for you, and you didn't come."

And he shouldn't be here now, he thought bleakly. His presence
was only going to complicate things further. Closing his eyes, he rehearsed what he should say to make her understand why they could
never be together, why the time he had spent with her had been a
mistake.

"Raegan, listen…" But he'd waited too long. Wrapped in his arms,
her cheek resting on his chest, she was sound asleep.

He held her until the sun chased the moon from the sky; then,
tucking the covers around her, he sought sanctuary in his lair.

* * *

Raegan woke smiling, though her happiness faded when she realized she was alone. But he had been there last night. She had fallen
asleep in his arms. Surely he would come again tonight.

Flinging the covers aside, she showered, took the last of her pre-
scribed pain medication with breakfast, then went jogging on the
beach.

It was one of those days that made you realize why people moved
to California. The sky was clear and blue, the air warm but not hot,
with a faint breeze. Gulls wheeled and soared overhead. Mothers
played in the surf with their little ones…

The grief hit her without warning, doubling her over so that she
dropped to her knees, sobs rising in her throat as tears flooded her
eyes.

I'm sorry, Miss *York*…complications…lost the baby… surgery….no more children….

The sound of childish laughter sent Raegan running for home.
Blinded by her tears, she tripped on the stairs. Heedless of the blood
dripping down her leg, she scrambled up the steps, needing to be
alone to mourn the loss of the infant she had never seen.

* * *

Tor rose with the setting of the sun, his first thought for Raegan. Ignoring the need to hunt, he hurried to her house. The scent of her blood was borne to him on the breeze even before he arrived.

He hadn't known fear in centuries, but it hammered at him as he knocked on her door. He cursed long and loud when she didn't answer. "Raegan! Dammit, girl, let me in!"

He was about to beat his fist on the door when he heard her turn the lock. A moment later she stood in the doorway, her face pale, her eyes red and swollen. From the knee down, her left leg was wrapped in gauze stained red.

"Raegan! What's wrong? What happened?"

"Nothing. Everything."

He reached for her, felt the threshold's power repel him. Apparently his ability to enter her room last night hadn't been a direct invitation but some kind of aberration. "May I come in?"

"What?" She looked at him blankly for a moment. "Oh, of course."

Tor crossed the threshold, his mind brushing hers. Fear. Pain. Regret. She was drowning in it.

"Raegan?" She seemed to have forgotten he was there. Catching her hand, he gave it a squeeze. "Talk to me."

"The baby's dead."

Tor frowned. *Baby?* What the hell? He lifted his head, nostrils flaring, but there was no scent of anyone else in the house. "What baby?" he asked quietly.

She looked up at him, her eyes tormented. "My little girl…" A fresh spate of tears flooded her eyes.

Muttering, "Well, hell," he scooped her into arms and carried her to the sofa, then settled her on his lap. "Let it all out, honey. And then we'll talk."

* * *

She sucked in a deep breath. "There were complications during delivery." A single tear slid down her cheek. "The baby died."

Tor raked a hand through his hair. He was rarely at a loss for words, but *I'm sorry* seemed woefully inadequate. He had never fathered a child, could not begin to imagine what she was feeling.

In lieu of words, he brushed a lock of hair from her brow, then kissed her cheek. "Look at me, Raegan. I can make you forget it. All of it, if that's what you want."

She stared at him. "Are you a hypnotist?"

"In a manner of speaking. It's up to you."

She considered it a moment, then shook her head. "I can't do that. It would be like she never existed at all. How can I miss her so much when I never even held her in my arms?"

She sagged in his embrace, limp as a rag doll. He stroked her hair absently, thinking that if he ever found the man who had attacked her, he would rip him to shreds.

Feeling suddenly embarrassed at unburdening herself, Raegan started to rise, only to be stayed by his arm around her waist.

"Don't go, love."

With a sigh, Raegan rested her head on his shoulder. What was there about him that soothed her so? That made everything seem better when he was near? She felt closer to him than she did to people she had known her whole life.

"Can I get you anything?" he asked.

"I should be asking you that. After all, *you're* in *my* house."

"Let's not worry about that now. Would you like something to drink?"

"Water would be nice. There's beer, if you like," she said as he eased her onto the sofa. "And wine."

Nodding, he headed for the kitchen.

Raegan stared after him, thinking how nice it was to have him there. She'd avoided being around her friends and family, not wanting to see the pity in their eyes as they tried to comfort her. Being with them only reminded her of what had happened, what she had lost.

She looked up at the sound of Tor's footsteps. "Water for my lady," he said, handing her a glass. "Wine for me."

She smiled faintly as he sat beside her, his thigh brushing against hers. He was so very masculine, so self-assured, so confident. He'd probably never been afraid of anything in his life, never ill at ease.

After a time, she murmured, "I'm sorry."

"For what?"

She shrugged. "For dumping on you like that."

"No problem." He brushed a kiss across the top of her head. "What happened to your leg?"

"I tripped on the stairs this afternoon."

"Did you go to the doctor?"

"No."

Several silent moments passed. Then Tor took her glass and put it on the coffee table next to his.

Butterflies of anticipation took wing in the pit of Raegan's belly when he reached for her.

"Shh, love," he whispered. "Nothing to be afraid of. I'm just going to hold you."

She went somewhat tentatively into his arms, her eyelids fluttering down as his arm circled her waist. She felt the brush of his lips in her hair, the soft caress of his knuckles as he stroked her cheek.

Sighing, she rested her head on his chest. Lost in the nether world between wakefulness and sleep, she imagined his tongue stroking her neck, thought she heard him speaking to her in a language she didn't understand. There was an odd pressure against the side of her neck, and then she felt nothing at all.

* * *

Tor left Raegan's house after tucking her into bed. He strolled along the beach, his thoughts troubled. He had come to California to hide out from those searching for him. He hadn't intended to stay more than a few days because it was dangerous to linger in any one place too long. He grunted softly. He hadn't intended to get involved with anyone, either, least of all a fragile young woman.

Pausing, he stared at the sea, stretching endlessly in front of him. Like his life. Opening his senses, he searched for any familiar scents, but there was only the salty tang of the sea, damp sand and seaweed, and the rot of a dead seal somewhere in the distance.

And the warm, sweet scent of Raegan that clung to his clothing.

He had taken a taste of her tonight, just a few sips. The warmth of it still sustained him.

Raegan. He should get out of her life before it was too late.

He laughed but there was no humor in it. Because it was already too late.

Amanda Ashley

CHAPTER 5

Raegan woke slowly. For the first time in months, she didn't feel like pulling the covers over her head and going back to sleep. And it was all because of Tor. Somehow, talking with him last night had eased the hard knot of pain in her heart.

Swinging her legs over the edge of the bed, she pulled on her bathing suit, grabbed a towel, and headed down to the beach for an early morning swim.

It was a beautiful day, bright and clear and already warm.

She had just spread her towel on the sand when a rather plump, middle-aged woman approached her.

"Excuse me," the stranger said. "I was hoping you could tell me where Salvatore is staying."

"I'm sorry," Raegan said, "but I have no idea."

"You do know him?"

"Who are you?"

"An old friend of his family. We've been looking for him for a good long time."

Raegan shook her head. "I can't help you."

"Can't? Or won't?"

"I told you, I don't know where he is. Now, if you'll excuse me." Kicking off her sandals, Raegan ran into the surf.

When she looked back at the shore, the woman was gone.

"What did she look like?" Tor asked. He'd come to see Raegan as soon as the sun went down. Her announcement of someone looking for him hadn't come as a surprise, though he'd thought it would take them longer to find him. Dammit. He sat back on the sofa and stretched his legs. "Can you describe her?"

Beside him, Raegan frowned. "She was plump and pretty, with dark-red hair. And brown eyes, I think. A little taller than I am."

Tor nodded. "Margaret." His brother's human wife.

"You know her, then?"

"Yeah. She's my sister-in-law."

"She said they've been looking for you for a long time. Maybe you should get in touch with her."

"No." That was the last thing he wanted. He wasn't ready to go back, not now, not ever. He liked his freedom too much to give it up.

"I'm glad you're not leaving," Raegan said. "I'd… I'd miss you."

Slipping his arm around her shoulders, he said, "I'd miss you, too, love."

"Do you have a big family?"

"Hellishly big."

"You don't sound very happy about it. I always wished I had brothers and sisters. It was lonely, being an only child."

"Funny how we always want what we don't have," he remarked.

Looking up at him, Raegan asked, "What do *you* want?"

The heat in his eyes gave her the answer before he said, "Just you."

"Tor…" The second night they'd met, he'd told her he wanted her and went on to say he thought she wanted him. And it was true. For five weeks, she had fantasized about him. But she wasn't sure she ever wanted to be intimate with a man again.

"Shh. You're perfectly safe, sweet Raegan." And far too innocent to fuse her life with his.

He stayed with Raegan until the need to hunt made it dangerous to be near her. Promising to see her again tomorrow, he kissed her goodnight.

As soon as he left the house, he felt the presence of another vampire. "Nazario? I know you're there."

     Amanda Ashley

Chuckling softly, his brother stepped out of the shadows beside the house. "I never could hide from you."

"Nor I from you, apparently," Tor muttered as he embraced his brother. "What are you doing here?"

"You know damn well why I'm here. You need to come home."

Taking a step back, Tor folded his arms over his chest. "I'm tired of that life."

"We need you, *fratello*. You're the only one who can keep our coven together now that Father is gone. They won't listen to me."

Tor shook his head.

"Dammit, Tor, if you don't come home, Cesare's pack of bloodsuckers is going to try to take us out, one by one, and when we're gone, there won't be anyone left to keep Cesare in check. Do you want that on your conscience?"

"Of course not." Cesare had been trying to destroy Tor's family for years. Though they shared the same blood, Cesare and his kind hadn't waited for the change to come on them naturally. Instead, they sought the change early by attacking and drinking from human prey. It turned them into the kind of vampires portrayed in horror movies—creatures with little regard for human life or anything else. Tor's family also needed human blood, but they didn't kill those they fed on.

"He's raised the bounty on your head." Nazario glanced around. "You shouldn't be here alone, with no one to back you up. It isn't safe."

"I can take care of myself." Tor glanced past his brother to Raegan's bedroom window. Was he putting her life in danger by staying here?

Nazario followed his brother's gaze. "This woman, she means something to you?"

Tor nodded.

"Everyone at home expects you to take Gina for your mate."

"Everyone at home can go to hell."

"Shall I tell them that?"

Tor scrubbed his hands over his face. His allegiance belonged to his own kind, but his heart belonged to Raegan. "I'll think it over. For now, I need to feed. Join me? It's been awhile since we hunted together."

* * *

Raegan spent most of the next day on the beach, thinking about Tor, wondering at his strange reaction to hearing his family was looking for him. He hadn't been happy, that was for sure. And what did *hellishly big* mean?

She was making dinner that night when he arrived at her door. As always, seeing him made her heart skip a beat. How was it possible that she had come to care for him so quickly? She'd known him such a short time and yet it seemed as if she had known him, waited for him, forever.

She lifted her face for his kiss, felt the warmth of his touch flow through her. "Come on in. I'm making dinner and it's almost ready. Have you eaten?"

"No."

"Good. I hate to eat alone."

In the kitchen, she quickly set another place, filled two plates with spaghetti while he poured the wine.

"Smells good," he said, holding her chair for her.

"Thanks. I love pasta."

He nodded as he took a seat. "Me, too. My mother makes the best in the world."

"Do you miss your family?" It was a silly question, she thought, after his reaction the other night.

"I miss the people. Not the politics."

"What does that mean?"

"My family is… it's complicated." He took a bite of spaghetti and nodded. "Tastes as good as it smells. My mom would be jealous."

Raegan flushed with pleasure.

"You'd like my mother. She…" He bolted to his feet. "Oh, hell. Stay here!"

"What's wrong?"

But he was already out of the kitchen. She heard the door slam shut as he left the house. Curious and a little alarmed, she went to look out the front window.

Tor stood on the lawn, hands clenched at his sides. A second man stood across from him. It was obvious from their body language that they were arguing. About what? she wondered.

She was about to turn away when the stranger disappeared.

Amanda Ashley

Raegan blinked. How was that possible? One minute he had been there, big as life, and the next he was just gone.

She was trying to rationalize what she'd seen when Tor returned.

"Are you all right?" he asked. "You look like you've seen a ghost."

"Maybe I have. That man…" She shook her head. "He disappeared!"

"You saw that?" Damn! How was he going to explain it? "You'd better sit down. You look like you're going to faint."

"I feel that way, too."

"Sit. I'll get you some wine."

In the kitchen, he filled her glass, then stood there a moment, trying to decide what to do. He could erase the memory from her mind. That would be the easiest solution. Or he could just tell her the truth, although that might be the worst thing he could do. It might ruin whatever chance of a future they might have together. And he wanted her in his future.

Taking a deep breath, he went back into the living room. "Here, drink this." *You're going to need it.*

"Who was that man?" Raegan sipped her wine. "How did he disappear like that?" She had seen magicians on stage make things vanish—rabbits, even people. But those were illusions, smoke and mirrors. This had been done on her front lawn.

"My brother. Nazario. He wants me to go back home with him."

"Oh. You… You're not going, are you?"

"I don't want to, love, believe me. But there's trouble brewing and I've got to go."

"When?"

"Soon." Taking his courage in hand, he sat beside her on the sofa. "I need to tell you about my family."

Something in the tone of his voice made her think she didn't want to hear it.

Taking the glass from her hand, he set it aside, then took both her hands in his. "I'm falling in love with you," he said quietly. "I know it's sudden, but I knew from that first night that we were meant to be together."

Raegan nodded. Hadn't she felt it, too? She'd been drawn to him the first time she'd seen him on the beach, although it had taken her weeks to find the courage to approach him.

"My family is very old. And we live a very long time. You've heard of …" Oh, hell, this was going to be harder than he thought.

"Heard of what?"

"Vampires."

"Well, sure, who hasn't. But what has that to do with…?" She stared at him, wide-eyed. And then shook her head. "Very funny."

"It's not funny at all. It's what I am." His hold tightened on her hands when she tried to pull away. "We aren't like the vampires in movies, although they exist, too. My people, we aren't turned. We're born this way. Until I was twenty-five, I was just like any other man. I was awake days, I ate to survive, I was subject to age and death. But all that changed on my twenty-fifth birthday. I stopped aging. And even though I can be awake during the day, the sun bothers my eyes and I'm more at home in the dark. Mortal food alone can no longer sustain me—"

"Stop! I don't believe you." She jerked her hands free and darted to the other side of the room. "Why are you doing this?"

"It's all true, Raegan. I swear it on my mother's life."

She stared down at him, her eyes filled with confusion and doubt. "Prove it."

"What would you have me do?"

"Disappear like your brother."

The words were scarcely out of her mouth when he vanished from sight.

Raegan stared at the sofa. Moving slowly toward it, she reached down to touch the cushion he'd been sitting on. If he was there, he was invisible.

She jumped when the front door opened and Tor stepped inside.

"Do you believe me now?" he asked quietly.

On legs that felt wooden, Raegan dropped down on the sofa, grabbed her wine glass and drained it in one long swallow, wishing it were something stronger. Much stronger. It was true. Tor was some kind of vampire, but unlike any she had ever heard of. He'd eaten spaghetti with garlic for goodness sakes.

He hadn't moved from the entryway, just stood there, watching her.

With tears burning her eyes, she asked, "Why did you have to tell me? Why couldn't we just have gone on the way we were?"

"I need to go home and I want you to go with me."

"Are you crazy?" She lifted her hand to her throat. "I don't want

    Amanda Ashley

to live with a bunch of… of vampires!"

He watched the thoughts chase themselves across her mind.

Her next question came as no surprise. "Have you… did you ever… bite me?"

"Just once."

She stared at him, eyes filled with revulsion and accusation.

He took a step toward her, stopped when she cringed away from him. "I won't let anyone hurt you, Raegan. You'll be safe in my home."

She shook her head. "You need to go. It's too much… I have to think…" Something she couldn't do when he was so near. She massaged her temples. "Please go."

"Will I see you tomorrow night?"

"I don't think so." Raegan closed her eyes, afraid if she looked at him just then, she would change her mind.

When she opened them again, he was gone.

CHAPTER 6

A vampire. Raegan shook her head. Impossible. Obviously, he was crazy. Or she was.

She lifted her hand to her throat. He'd bitten her, she thought, frowning. When had he done it? And why didn't she remember?

Rising, she went into the bathroom. Looking in the mirror, she turned her head one way, then the other, but there were no telltale marks.

Chewing her thumbnail, she wandered through the house, trying to make sense of what he'd said. He was a vampire. He had a brother. He wanted her to go home with him. Hah! Fat chance.

Curling up in the easy chair beside the fire, she stared out the window into the darkness beyond. Since meeting Tor, she'd been almost happy. For the first time in days, there had been whole hours when she hadn't thought about the baby she'd lost, or the horrible man who had raped her. When she didn't feel dirty, violated. Unworthy. She had been certain she would never want another man to touch her, but Tor's gentle caresses hadn't repulsed her. She'd reveled in his kisses, found solace in his arms.

With him, she wasn't afraid.

Why did he have to be a vampire?

She tapped her fingertips on the arm of the chair, remembering those first nights when she'd watched him on the beach, the way he

          Amanda Ashley

had gone swimming in the dark until he was out of sight. Sometimes it had been an hour or more before he returned.

The night they'd gone dancing and she'd imagined his eyes were turning red.

The way he always treated her so gently.

The way his voice soothed her.

The way he listened when she poured her heart out to him. There was no judgement, no empty words, just the comforting feel of his arms around her.

Was she willing to give up all that because he was a vampire?

Maybe the better question would be, was she willing to leave everything familiar behind to go off and live in a strange land with a man she hardly knew?

* * *

Tor hunkered down on his heels on the sand. He never should have said anything. What had he been thinking? That she'd brush off his news and throw herself into his arms? He glanced over his shoulder. Moonlight bathed the house in a faint silver glow.

Lights burned in the windows. Dammit! Why hadn't he kept his big mouth shut? Why hadn't Nazario stayed home?

He sprang to his feet when he saw Raegan peering out one of the windows.

Was she looking for him?

He took a step toward the house. His movement caught her attention and for a moment, their gazes met.

Tor held his breath, praying she would gesture for him to come up. That hope died when she closed the curtains and turned off the lights.

A thought took him back to his lair. He wasn't surprised to find Nazario and Margaret waiting for him inside. "What do you want?"

Nazario didn't answer, just looked at him.

"All right," Tor said, resigned. "I'm ready."

* * *

One perk of being a vampire was the ability to travel long distances in a very short time.

A quarter of an hour later, Tor and his brother materialized inside the coven's compound. It was a large, covered enclosure located high in the mountains of Northern Italy. Tor's lair was in the center of the compound. It was the largest residence, with the others spreading out from the center like spokes on a wheel.

It was not yet sunrise. After agreeing to meet with Nazario and the others that night, Tor went straight to his lair. He stripped off his clothes, took a quick shower, and climbed into bed, only to lie awake, staring at the ceiling, until darkness carried him away.

* * *

Raegan woke on the sofa where she'd fallen asleep. She knew, as soon as she opened her eyes, that Tor was gone. Not just from her house, but from the country.

He'd gone home.

His absence left a gaping hole in her heart, more painful than anything she had ever known. How could she feel this bad over a man she hardly knew?

How could she have been so foolish as to let him go? And how would she ever find him again?

* * *

Tor woke with the setting of the sun. The first order of business was to meet with the seven elders of the coven to find out what had happened in his absence. Although several were older than he, the right of leadership fell to him through his father's bloodline. He had often wished that Nazario had been the first-born.

They met in the large library located at the back of the house. Four men and three women.

Tor listened patiently as they enumerated the latest atrocities committed by Cesare and his followers—people drained of blood, animals tortured and killed.

"If this doesn't stop," Alberto declared, "the whole countryside will be up in arms against us. They can't distinguish between our people and his. He has to be destroyed, the sooner the better."

Tor nodded. He'd seen this coming for quite some time. He'd left home in hopes that some distance might give him a clearer vision of how to deal with the rogue vampires. Instead, he'd fallen in love with a mortal woman.

     Amanda Ashley

"I'll take care of it," he said. "Is there anything else?"

The elders glanced at one another. It was obvious they had something on their minds and equally apparent they didn't know how to bring it up.

Finally, Dario, the oldest member of the council, stood up. "It's long past time you took a mate. You need an heir."

"Nazario can provide it."

Alberto nodded. "And if you were unable to provide an heir, he would take your place, should the need arise. But we must plan for the worst. If anything should happen to the two of you, the direct line will cease. We can't let that happen."

Tor raked a hand through his hair. One more reason why he wished Nazario was the first-born.

"Gina's family has been most patient," Angelica remarked.

"I'm aware of that," Tor said. Gina was a beautiful woman with a mane of long black hair, deep brown eyes, a winning smile, and a voluptuous figure. Many men would have given anything to marry her. Unfortunately, he wasn't one of them. There was no magic between them, no spark. His mind wandered to Raegan. Was she getting along all right? Did she think of him at all, or did she consider herself well-rid of him?

"Tor?"

"What?"

"What shall I tell Gina's family?"

"I'll speak to them after I deal with Cesare," he said curtly. "We're done here."

* * *

Rae sat on the shore, staring out at the waves. She shivered in spite of the blanket wrapped around her. Her nightmares had returned, making her reluctant to go to bed. The nights were cold and dark and as empty as her heart. Two weeks had passed since Tor had gone away. Two long, lonely weeks.

Her parents had called several times to say hello and see how she was doing. Her grandmother had sent her weekly texts to make sure everything was okay at the house. Rae smiled at the memory. She used to brag to anyone who would listen about her grandma's Internet savvy. Her best friend had called twice to ask when she was coming home. But it was Tor that Rae wanted to talk to.

A movement to her left caught her eye. Hope leapt in her heart when she saw a tall, dark-haired man striding toward her. Tor!

She leaped to her feet, heart pounding with excitement. He'd come back!

Only it wasn't Tor.

A frisson of alarm skittered down her spine as he drew closer. And then she was running for the stairs, every instinct she possessed warning her she was in danger.

She let out a scream when a hand clamped over her arm and jerked her backward.

She screamed again, praying someone would hear her, though there was no one else on the beach. As he threw her over his shoulder, the world as she knew it spun out of control, dissolving into darkness that had no end.

* * *

"So, where is he?" Tor paced the library floor. He'd been hunting for Cesare ever since he got back home, but there was no sign of him. Tor had captured three of Cesare's vampires hunkered over a lone woman. None of the men would talk. According to pack law, they had been executed.

The woman had died from what they'd done to her.

And still there was no sign of Cesare.

 Amanda Ashley

Chapter 7

Feeling as if she were suffocating, Rae fought through layers of darkness in an effort to open her eyes. And then she wished she'd kept them closed.

Five people—three women and two men—sat on the cement floor in a circle around her. She glanced past them, but there was nothing to see except four blank walls. And a man in a small cage near a set of cement stairs.

Reluctantly, her gaze returned to the people around her.

Only they weren't ordinary people. She knew that when they smiled at her, revealing fangs that gleamed even in the dim light.

They were vampires. The kind Tor had told her about. The kind that killed their prey.

And there was little doubt about who that prey would be.

With a cry of alarm, she sprang to her feet, darted through the circle and raced toward the stairs.

* * *

Tor released his hold on the woman in his arms, all thought of feeding forgotten as Rae's horrified scream echoed in his mind. A word released the woman from his thrall and then he was gone, racing with all the speed at his command toward Cesare's fortress, all thought of his own safety forgotten as Rae cried out again.

He came up short at the outer wall. Cesare's wards prevented him from entering.

Nazario! I'm at Cesare's. He's got Rae.

His brother's reply was terse and to the point. *Get the hell out of there!*

Come here. I'm going to offer myself in her place. If Cesare agrees, I'll need you to take her home and keep her safe. You are not to bargain with him for my freedom. You are not to surrender our people or our stronghold for my return. Do you understand?

Nazario materialized beside him in the space of a heartbeat. "Are you out of your mind? Dammit, this is the stupidest thing you've ever done."

"Maybe so, but I can't leave her there. She'll be dead in a few minutes."

"He'll take you and keep her!" Nazario exclaimed, his voice ragged.

"Cesare may be a killer, but he has his own code of honor. If he says he'll release her, he will."

"You hope! Dammit," Nazario muttered. "He's here."

Looking past his brother, Tor saw Cesare standing on top of the wall. Rae's blood made a bright red stain against his pale skin.

"I'm here," Tor said, his voice flat. "Give me the woman."

"The gate's open. Come in."

"Not until you send her out."

"You give me your word? You'll come willingly? And you won't resist?"

Tor nodded curtly.

Cesare disappeared from sight only to materialize a moment later on the other side of the thick iron gate. He made a gesture with his hand, and two men dragged Rae into view.

Tor's jaw clenched when he saw her. She sagged between her captors, her head hanging. Blood leaked from several wounds on both sides of her neck. Her heartbeat was thready.

"I'm waiting," Cesare said.

"Nazario, take her home and look after her."

"No, dammit! This is wrong."

"Do as I say!"

Eyes blazing with defiance, Nazario darted forward. He wrapped

 Amanda Ashley

his arms around Rae and disappeared from sight.

"I've kept my part," Cesare said. "Will you keep yours?"

Wanting nothing more than to destroy the man who had dared lay a hand on Rae, Tor approached the gate. He hesitated a moment, then stepped inside the stronghold.

Two human slaves carrying thick silver chains ran toward him. Head high, Tor allowed them to bind his hands behind his back.

Cesare's laughter, thick with victory, rang in Tor's ears as they led him away.

* * *

Margaret stood across the bed from Nazario. A woman lay there, barely breathing, her face as white as the sheet beneath her. "Who is she, again?"

"Her name's Rae and my brother's in love with her. Hold her head still."

Stepping forward, Margaret placed her hands on either side of Rae's head, watching impassively as Nazario bit into his wrist and then patiently dribbled his blood into Rae's mouth. "Is she going to be okay?"

He shrugged. "I sure as hell hope so. Tor put his life on the line for her."

"How do we get him out?"

"I don't know if we can. If you've got any ideas... Her color's coming back. I think she'll be okay."

* * *

Voices. Rae kept her eyes closed, afraid of what she might see if she opened them. She didn't think she was in the same place as before. For one thing, she was on a feather-soft bed instead of the floor. And the voices sounded... concerned.

Opening her eyes, she found herself staring at the man who had grabbed her. She didn't know how they had gotten from where they'd been to where they were. It had all happened so fast. She'd caught a glimpse of Tor and the next thing she knew, she was here. Wherever *here* was.

"Relax," the man said. "You're safe now."

"Who are you? Where's Tor? Why am I here?"

"I'm Nazario, Tor's brother. He's in Cesare's fortress. And you're here because he's there."

Rae blinked at him. Other than the part about being Tor's brother, nothing he'd said made sense. "I don't understand."

"Tor's in love with you. He gave himself up to win your freedom. And now he's Cesare's prisoner."

Rae's heart sank as she imagined Tor locked up in that terrible place. "We have to get him out of there!" she cried, bolting upright.

"Here now, take it easy." Nazario put his hands on her shoulders to steady her. "You look like you're gonna faint."

Murmuring, "I feel that way, too," she toppled onto her side.

"She's going to be a lot of trouble, isn't she?" Margaret observed as she covered Rae with a blanket.

Nazario licked the wound in his wrist, sealing it. "I'm afraid so."

     Amanda Ashley

CHAPTER 8

Cesar's stronghold was built much like Tor's compound. A large house in the center with other, smaller residences spread out around it.

Unlike Tor's people, Cesare's kept humans—as servants and prey.

Tor saw a few of them as they made their way to Cesare's lair—frightened men and women who looked at him with fear and loathing. Vampires, too, strolled the streets. One of them was openly feeding on a young woman.

Cesare was at his lair when Tor's guards shoved him through the front door.

Cesare waved the guards away, then, looking smug, he walked around Tor, then stood in front of him. He clucked softly. "I can't believe you gave yourself up for some mortal female. What makes her so important that you would die for her?"

A muscle ticked in Tor's jaw.

The vampire cocked his head to the side. "Is her blood more potent than most? Or is she just a remarkably good lay?"

When Tor refused to answer, Cesare backhanded him across the mouth. A solid blow that drew blood. It rocked Tor back on his heels. And still he said nothing.

"Don't tell me you fancy yourself in love with her!" Cesare's raucous laughed filled the air.

Tor licked the blood from his lips. Vampires like Cesare were incapable of love.

Grabbing Tor's arm, Cesare snarled, "Perhaps a few days in the pit will loosen your tongue."

Moments later, they materialized in the bowels of Cesare's lair. There were no lights here, but then they weren't needed. Vampires had great night vision. Small, iron-barred cells lined the walls on either side. The air was fetid with the stink of old blood, death, and excrement. Stronger still was the scent of fear that permeated the walls.

Cesare shoved Tor into a cell, slammed and locked the door. "I hope she's worth it," he said with a sneer, and vanished from sight.

Muttering every curse word he knew in English and Italian, Tor paced back and forth. The silver burned and blistered his skin, then healed immediately and burned and blistered again in an endless cycle.

Knowing Rae was safe made the pain bearable. Summoning his preternatural powers, he opened his senses, reaching out toward home.

Nazario?

I'm here.

How's Rae?

She's sleeping. Her color's better. Margaret gave her something to eat. What do you want us to do?

Rae will probably want to go home. You have to keep her there.

I figured that. How are you holding up?

I've been better. But for the silver that bound him, he could have transported himself home.

The Elders met earlier today. They don't like sitting around, doing nothing. Alberto wants to storm the stronghold and kill the lot of them.

Tor grinned. Alberto had been a fearsome warrior back in the day.

So, what are you going to do? Nazario asked impatiently. Just sit in that cell and rot?

I hope not.

I think Alberto is right. It's time we cleaned out that nest of vipers.

Tor nodded. He'd often thought the same thing, especially after what he'd seen today. He'd known Cesare's vampires fed on humans, often killing them, but he'd had no idea they kept humans as slaves inside the stronghold. He'd only seen a few today, but he had sensed the presence of many more.

Tor?

We'll talk about it when I get out of here.

He just wished he knew how he was going to accomplish that without putting Rae's life and the lives of his own people at risk.

CHAPTER 9

Raegan woke slowly. She kept her eyes closed but heard nothing to indicate she wasn't alone. Throwing the covers aside, she sat up and looked around, surprised to find herself in a large room. The walls were blue, as were the heavy curtains that veiled the single window. Cherrywood tables flanked the bed. A matching dresser stood on the opposite wall. Her clothes were neatly folded on a chair in the corner. Looking down, she discovered she was wearing a modest pale-pink nightgown.

Swinging her legs over the edge of the bed, she stripped off the nightgown, then hastily pulled on her own clothes before padding to the door. She had expected it to be locked, but it opened on silent hinges, revealing a long hallway. She glanced left and right. Several closed doors were visible, as well as a stairway.

Rae took a hesitant step into the corridor, then paused, listening. But the house was quiet as a tomb. She grimaced at the thought. Because that's what it was—a resting place for the undead.

She tiptoed toward the stairway, her nerves growing more and more tense as she descended. At the bottom of the stairs, she hesitated, her gaze sweeping the room. It reminded her of a castle. A huge fireplace. Large mahogany furniture covered in dark leather. Mahogany tables. A plush gray rug underfoot. The walls were white, adorned with paintings.

Amanda Ashley

Taking a deep breath, she tiptoed toward the front door. Unlike the one in her bedroom, this one was locked.

"Good morning."

Rae whirled around, her heart in her throat. Some of the fear left her when she saw that it was Margaret, Tor's sister-in-law.

"You must be hungry," Margaret said.

"Yes, a little," Rae admitted, though in truth, she was starving.

"Come along, then. Breakfast is waiting in the kitchen."

Like the other rooms Rae had seen, this one was large and well-kept. A square table had been set for two.

"Please, sit down," Margaret said. "I hope you like bacon and eggs."

At Rae's nod, the woman handed Rae a plate piled high with scrambled eggs, bacon, fried potatoes, and toast. "Thank you."

"Coffee? Tea? Orange juice? Milk?"

"Juice, please."

"Can I get you anything else? Ketchup?"

"No, this is fine."

Getting her own plate and a cup of coffee, Margaret took the other seat. "You must have a lot of questions, so, ask away."

"Are you a vampire, too?"

Margaret laughed softly. "No."

"But you're married to one? Tor's brother?"

"Yes."

"Doesn't it bother you, what he is?"

"It did at first. But once I got to know him, I realized Nazario is a wonderful man. Kind, generous. And he treats me like a queen."

"Do you have children?"

"Not yet, but I'm hoping. We've only been married a few years."

"How did you meet?"

"At a nightclub. He was there, with Tor. They were…"

"Were what?"

"I call it trolling. They were looking for prey."

"Oh."

"I know, it sounds awful, but they aren't killers. Not like Cesare and his followers. The vampires here only take a little and they never hurt anyone."

"That's what Tor said."

"Are you in love with him?"

"I'm afraid I might be."

"He's a good man."

"Nazario said Tor's a prisoner because of me."

"He very likely saved your life."

"What will they do to him?"

Margaret reached across the table to squeeze Rae's hand. "I don't know, but I'm sure he'll be all right. Tor's very strong and very powerful and—"

"He could die, couldn't he? Because of me!" Rae exclaimed, and burst into tears. Embarrassed, she grabbed a napkin and wiped her face. "I'm sorry."

"I guess you do love him."

"Yes," Rae said, sniffling. "I guess I do. Nazario's going to try and get him out of there, isn't he?"

"I don't know. Tor made him swear not to do anything to save him."

"Why on earth would he do that?"

"I'm sure it was to protect the rest of us. There's a truce of sorts between our coven and Cesare's pack. We don't kill them, they don't kill us. It lasted for centuries. And then Cesare took power. Since then, the peace between us has been tenuous at best. Not only that, but with Cesare in command, the vampires have gotten bolder. One of the reasons we've existed for so long is that we keep what we are hidden from humanity, but Cesare doesn't care if people know about us. In fact, he seems determined to make our existence known."

Rae shook her head. "That's foolish. Doesn't he see that?"

"He knows. He just doesn't care. He hates being what he is and that hatred spills over into everything. Nazario thinks Cesare has a death wish."

"But, didn't Cesare choose to be what he is? I mean, Tor told me that taking human blood too early changes you. Cesare must have known that."

"Knowing and becoming are two different things. Nazario thinks Cesare is hoping for a war between us."

"If he's so unhappy, why doesn't he just kill himself?" she asked, her voice laced with sarcasm.

"I wish he would. If only Tor's father was here. He's the only one of us who can help Tor now. The only one powerful enough to enter Cesare's compound undetected." Sighing, she said, "Come on, let me

       Amanda Ashley

show you around."

"Do you live here?"

Margaret nodded.

"Tor told me his family was 'hellishly' big. Do you all live here?"

"Nazario is his only sibling, but Tor considers everyone in the compound to be part of his family."

"Oh."

The house was enormous. The first floor held a living area, a kitchen, and a couple of bathrooms. The basement held every possible form of entertainment—computer games, a regulation-size pool table, a boxing ring, two large-screen TVs, as well as several sofas, side tables, and chairs.

There were six bedrooms upstairs.

"This one is ours," Margaret said, indicating the first door at the head of the stairs. "And that one is Tor's." She pointed to a pair of large double doors at the far end of the corridor.

"Where are Tor's parents?"

"They're gone."

"I thought vampires lived forever."

"So they say. Tor's mother was killed by a hunter. When she died, Tor's father lost the will to live. He went to ground a hundred years ago."

"Went to ground? What does that mean?"

"He buried himself in the earth."

"Alive?"

"Yes and no. It's hard to explain, but vampires have the ability to shut down and just rest for as long as they like. Apparently, some very old vampires do that from time to time. Nazario said it refreshes them."

Rae shivered, repulsed by the very idea. Buried alive. Could anything be worse?

* * *

Tor sat with his back against the wall. Living in the dark was like being buried alive, he thought. Even with his preternatural vision, there was nothing to see.

It gave him a lot of time to think. One thing was certain. Alberto was right. It was time to rid the world of Cesare and his ilk, although doing so could mean all-out war between his coven and Cesare's pack. Unless... Tor frowned. Maybe they only needed to dispose of Cesare. Until he took command, the vampires of his pack had lived in the shadows, taking care to prey only on those who would not be missed.

Dammit! He had to get out of here.

But how?

He felt it before he saw it. A tremor in the air, a faint shimmer in the darkness that grew brighter until his father stood in the corner.

"Salvatore. In trouble again, I see. What are you doing here?"

"Waiting for someone to rescue me. What are *you* doing here?"

"Did you think I would not know you were in trouble? That I would not come for you?"

Tor struggled to his feet, no easy task with his hands bound behind his back.

His father darted forward to steady him. "I leave you alone for a few years and you end up here. Are you ready to go home, Salvatore?"

"More than ready."

Nodding, his father wrapped his arm around Tor's shoulder.

In the blink of an eye, they were home.

* * *

Rae heaved a sigh. It had been a very long day. Margaret had been wonderful company, fixing her breakfast, giving her a tour of the house, trying to keep her mind off Tor's predicament.

The house was lovely. It had everything anyone could want. But it wasn't home. She was wondering how long she'd have to stay when she felt an odd tremor in the air. She sank back against the sofa as a thick mist suddenly appeared.

Rae rubbed her eyes. Was she seeing things now? She let out a gasp of surprise when the mist disappeared and Tor and another man stood in front of the hearth. Her gaze darted from one to the other. They looked enough alike to be brothers.

"Tor!" Leaping off the sofa, Rae threw her arms around him. She was so excited to see him, it took her a moment to realize he wasn't hugging her back. Feeling self-conscious, she backed away.

Tor winked at her. "I'll hug you as soon as I get rid of these

                    Amanda Ashley

shackles.”

The man standing beside Tor cleared his throat.

“Rae, this is my father, Sandro. *Padre*, this is Raegan York. My… friend.”

“Pleased to meet you, Miss York,” Tor’s father said in heavily accented English. “Welcome to my home.”

“Salvatore!”

Rae glanced over her shoulder as Margaret ran into the room, closely followed by Nazario, who carried a pair of bolt cutters, which he quickly put to use. One snip and Tor’s hands were free.

“*Grazie, fratello*,” Tor said. He rubbed his wrists a moment, then pulled Rae into his arms. Oblivious to his family, he kissed her long and hard.

Rae knew she was blushing, but she didn’t care. Tor was here and she was in his arms and that was all that mattered.

* * *

Later, after assuring everyone that he was okay, Tor took Rae’s hand and led her out a narrow door that opened onto a side yard. He paused by a wrought-iron bench located inside a grape arbor. Sitting, he drew her down beside him, his arm tight around her.

“Are you all right?” he asked. “Did my family treat you well?”

“I’m fine.” Her gaze moved over him. “How about you?”

“Never better, now that you’re with me.” He kissed her lightly, pleased when she didn’t pull away. “You have questions?”

“What did they do to you?”

“Nothing. They threw me in a cell and left me there.”

“Margaret told me your father had gone to ground.”

“That’s true. I wasn’t sure if he’d sense that I was in trouble, but I’m damn glad he did.”

“But how could he know?”

“He’s my father and the most powerful vampire alive. There’s not much he can’t do.” His gaze met and held hers. “Where do we go from here, Rae?”

“I don’t know. Nothing’s changed.”

“Hasn’t it? You seemed awfully glad to see me.”

“Well, of course I was. I mean, I was glad you were safe.”

“Is that all?”

She lowered her gaze. "No," she whispered. "I love you. But I'm not sure that's enough."

"Will you stay here for awhile and give me a chance to convince you?"

When he was looking at her like that, she thought, how could say no?

   Amanda Ashley

CHAPTER 10

Tor met with the Elders later that night after Margaret and Raegan had gone to bed. There was considerable excitement over Sandro's unexpected return.

Tor leaned back in his chair, smiling inwardly as he watched his father take over his rightful role as the leader of their coven, a role which Tor willingly surrendered.

The first order of business was Cesare. Many suggestions were put forth, most in favor of destroying him and his whole coven once and for all.

"Tor, we have not heard from you. Having been a recent guest of Cesare's, what do you think we should do?" his father asked.

"He's a mad dog and he needs to be put down," he said flatly.

Several voices rose in agreement.

Tor held up his hand to silence them. "The thing is, until he took over, the vampires were careful to avoid detection. I think if he's out of power, we might be able to talk sense to them and persuade them to be more circumspect. We might even be able to convince them to cease killing."

Alberto snorted. "You can't change a leopard's spots."

"We outnumber them," Nazario stated. "I say we attack their stronghold and put them all down."

"They have a lot of mortals inside," Tor remarked. "Are we going to kill them, too?"

Nazario shrugged. "Collateral damage."

Tor shook his head. "I'm not willing to risk their lives. I say we get rid of Cesare and then invite their next-in-command to parley with us and see if we can't work something out."

"I agree with Tor," Angelina said. "A war with Cesare's people could cause casualties on both sides."

Sandro rose to his feet. "We have much to consider. Think about the various suggestions overnight. Ponder the consequences. We will talk again tomorrow."

With the meeting over, Tor left the house.

Outside, he gazed up at the sky. They would take care of Cesare one way or another, but it wasn't the fate of the leader of the vampires that preyed on his mind. It was Raegan. He wanted her. More than that, he needed her. For years, he had felt empty inside. And then he'd met Rae and it was like finding the missing part of his soul. If she decided to stay with him, it would not be easy. Adjustments would have to be made on both sides. He could manipulate her thoughts, her emotions, make her believe she couldn't live without him, but the very idea was reprehensible.

He thought about his brother and Margaret. They were certainly happy together. He envied the love they shared, the closeness between them, as he had envied the bond of love and trust his parents had known.

He had hoped to find that same connection with Raegan. But, after what she'd been through, maybe he was expecting too much of her. The pain of her loss was still fresh. Perhaps, in time. she could get past it. And maybe not.

A thought took him to her room.

She lay on her side, her lashes like golden fans on her cheeks, her lips slightly parted, her breathing slow and even. Her scent filled his nostrils—sleep-warmed skin, the faint flowery scent of soap and shampoo.

The longing to hold her in his arms was almost irresistible, as was the yearning to taste her again. Not trusting his self-control, he turned toward the door, only to be stayed by the sound of her voice.

"Is someone there?"

He froze, suddenly embarrassed to be caught in her room in the middle of the night.

      Amanda Ashley

"Tor?"

"Yes. I just came in to make sure you were okay."

A rustle of covers as she sat up, a click and the room filled with light.

"I didn't mean to wake you."

"It's all right."

He moved back to her bedside and sat on the edge of the mattress. "Do you need anything?"

"No." She bit down on her lower lip. "Would you hold me for a minute?"

"I'd like nothing better," he murmured as he drew her gently into his arms, although that wasn't entirely true. He could think of a couple of things he'd rather do, like make love to her until the sun came up.

She relaxed against him, her head pillowed on his chest.

Tor let out a long, shuddering sigh. The sound of her heartbeat, the rush of blood through her veins, teased his hunger. The warmth of her skin, the press of her breasts, aroused his desire. Fighting down the want and the need stirring within him, he held her until she fell asleep.

And then, unwilling to let her go, he held her until he felt the familiar tingle in his blood that preceded the rising of the sun.

Whispering, "Dream of me, Raegan, my love," he tucked her under the covers and went to seek his own rest.

* * *

She sat on a red blanket on the beach, gazing out to sea. A full moon shed its light on the restless waves. She smiled as she watched Tor dive under the nearest wave and then strike out toward deeper water with strong stokes. It was good to be home again. Good to be with him.

She lost sight of Tor as a sudden chill wind blew clouds across the moon. Scrambling to her feet, she ran down to the water's edge, let out a scream when the waves washed over her ankles. Only it wasn't water. It was blood. She tried to back away, but the blood was no longer liquid but a pair of hands, dragging her deeper and deeper into the thick, crimson tide.

She kicked and splashed, trying in vain to return to shore, fear turning to terror as the waves crashed over her head. She screamed, one last desperate cry as her mouth filled with thick red ooze.

"Rae! Rae! Wake up!"

She screamed again as something reached for her.

"Rae, it's me."

"Tor?" She sagged against him, her whole body trembling. "Oh, Tor, I had the worst nightmare."

"They'll pass, in time," he said, lightly stroking her hair.

She shook her head. "It wasn't my old dream. I dreamt I was back at my grandmother's house, sitting on the beach. You were there, too. I watched you go for a swim and when I couldn't see you anymore, I ran down to the water. Only it wasn't water. It was… it was blood. And I was drowning in it."

Tor grunted softly. It didn't take a genius to interpret that one.

* * *

After tucking Rae into bed for the second time that night, Tor left the compound. A thought took him to the outskirts of Cesare's stronghold. There were no lights burning, which meant that the humans had all retired for the night. He detected several vampires inside the wall but none of them were Cesare. No doubt that madman was out preying on some helpless mortal.

Hands shoved in his pockets, he turned toward home. He hadn't gone far when he detected the presence of someone behind him. The scent of fresh blood told him it was one of Cesare's vampires.

Tor took another few steps, then whirled around and grabbed the man by the neck. "Why are you following me?"

Recognition dawned in the vampire's eyes. "You! How did you get out? There are guards everywhere."

"Yeah, well, I felt like taking a little stroll."

The vampire stared at him, confused and more than a little afraid, though he was trying hard not to show it.

"Who did you kill tonight?" Tor asked curtly.

"No one."

Tor grunted softly. The man was telling the truth. He smelled of blood, fear, and perfume, but not death. "What's your name?"

"Why do you want to know?"

"Just answer the damn question."

"Hard to talk when you're choking me."

Tor loosened his hold. "Your name."

"Frederico."

"Are you loyal to Cesare?"

"What's it to you?"

"I'm taking a survey."

The man snorted.

"There's a war brewing if Cesare doesn't clean up his act. Whose side are you going to be on?"

"Not his! I want out, but there's nowhere to go."

"What about the rest of the pack?"

"We're split about sixty-forty against him," Frederico said. "But we're all afraid of him."

Tor regarded him a moment. "If you want out, you can come home with me."

Frederico's eyes widened with suspicion, and a tiny ray of hope. "Why would you take me in? We're enemies."

"Sometimes enemies become good friends. If you go back, tell Cesare that Sandro has returned."

"Sandro? We thought he was long dead."

"That's what we wanted you to think."

The vampire's eyes widened with sudden understanding. "That's how you got out!"

Tor released his hold on the vampire. "My offer still stands."

"Thanks, but I'd better get back and warn the others." Frederico laughed softly. "If war comes, we'd have to be as crazy as Cesare to fight against you *and* your father. Can I go now?"

Tor made a dismissive gesture and the vampire darted away and vaulted over the wall.

Tor strolled back toward home. Sixty-forty, he mused as he picked up the pace. He liked those odds.

CHAPTER 11

"Margaret, can I ask you something?"

Margaret looked up from buttering her toast. "Well, sure. What do you want to know?"

"What do you do all day? I mean, don't you get lonesome, rattling around in this big old house by yourself while all the men are resting?"

"Sure, sometimes. But I keep busy, you know, shopping, cleaning the house, doing the laundry for the single men, changing the sheets and… you know, the same kinds of things I'd be doing anywhere else."

"I'd be glad to help while I'm here."

"Oh, I couldn't let you do that. You're a guest."

"I'd really like to. I don't have anything else to occupy my time."

"Well… all right, if you insist."

As it turned out, it was laundry day. With clothing, sheets and towels, there was a lot of it. But Rae didn't mind. She rather enjoyed folding things. And it helped to pass the time. She imagined being married to Tor, living in this house, spending her days with Margaret and her nights with Tor and his family.

She frowned as she folded another towel. Maybe he wouldn't want to marry her. He probably wanted children… She blinked back a sudden rush of tears. She would have loved to have his child. A

Amanda Ashley

little boy with thick, black hair and deep-green eyes.

Hearing Margaret's footsteps, she wiped her face with the edge of a towel, not wanting the other woman to see her tears.

* * *

There was no denying the way Rae's heart skipped a beat when she saw Tor that evening. She and Margaret were in the basement, watching TV, when the men came downstairs.

Tor nodded at his sister-in-law, but he had eyes only for Raegan. Taking her by the hand, he lifted her to her feet. "I hope you all don't mind, but we're going upstairs. No chaperones required."

There were nods and waves and knowing smiles from Margaret, Nazario and Sandro as Tor led her up the steps.

The lights in the living room were turned low. A fire burned in the hearth. A bottle of wine and two glasses waited on the coffee table in front of the sofa.

Tor gestured for her to sit down. "I thought we needed some time alone. Do you mind?"

"No."

"Good. Would you like some wine?"

"Not right now, thanks."

Nodding, he sat beside her. "I know we've only known each other for a short time, but I can't imagine my life without you. I love you, Raegan. I'd like to spend the rest of my life with you."

"I don't know. We're so different. We have so little in common. We don't keep the same hours. We don't see the world the same way. You probably want kids and I… I can't…"

"Rae, you're enough for me. You care for me, don't you?"

"You know I do."

"Then that's enough for now."

"Is it?"

"Once this trouble with Cesare is settled, we don't have to stay here. We can live anywhere you want. I'll show you the world if you like, or we can find our own little corner of the world to call home. Whatever you want. Will you think about it?"

She nodded, touched by his words, by the love in his eyes.

He leaned forward, his gaze searching hers. When she didn't pull away, he slid his hand around her nape and kissed her lightly.

As he deepened the kiss, Rae felt as if all her bones were melting. She leaned into him, her hands clutching his shoulders to steady herself as the world seemed to spin out of focus.

She moaned softly. Or maybe it was Tor. They were so tightly entwined, it was hard to tell. He kissed her again and again, each time more intimate, more arousing than the last.

He rained kisses on her brow, her cheeks, the length of her neck. Heaven, she thought. Being kissed by Tor was sheer heaven… Her eyes flew open when she felt his teeth brush her skin.

"No!" She wriggled out of his embrace. "No."

"One taste?"

She stared at him, suddenly curious in spite of herself. He'd admitted to biting her once before, but she had no memory of it. His people didn't kill their prey, so it should be safe enough. And she really *was* curious.

Tor watched the indecision in her eyes, knew the exact moment when curiosity overcame trepidation.

"Will it hurt?"

"No."

"You promise?"

"Yes. Cross my heart."

She giggled nervously. Huffed a sigh. And nodded. "All right. But just a little."

Slipping his arm around her shoulder, he said, "Just relax, Rae."

She stared at him through wide, brown eyes.

He stroked her neck lightly. "There's nothing to be afraid of. I won't hurt you."

She nodded again, her eyelids fluttering down as he kissed her, just below her ear. She didn't feel any pain at all, wouldn't have known he'd bitten her if not for the sudden sensual warmth that spread through her whole body. It was the most wonderful feeling she'd ever known.

She whimpered softly when he lifted his head.

"Are you all right?" he asked.

"Are you sure you had enough?"

His soft laughter washed over her, and then he pulled her into his arms and hugged her. "I love you, Rae," he murmured. "I know we'd be good together."

Drowning in a sea of euphoria, she could only agree.

     Amanda Ashley

CHAPTER 12

It was an odd life she was leading, Rae mused as she went downstairs the next day. She stayed up late to be with Tor and his family, and found herself sleeping later and later every morning.

In the kitchen, she put on the coffee, then sat at the table, elbows bent, chin resting on her hands. She wondered if Margaret ever got tired of living here, behind high stone walls. If she ever missed being able to come and go as she pleased. What would happen when she got old and Nazario didn't.

She put the question to Margaret over breakfast. "Doesn't it bother you that you'll age and Nazario won't?"

"No. I'm going to ask him to change me."

"Can he do that? I thought… I mean, if he's born that way, how can he make you a vampire?"

"I won't exactly be a vampire. I won't have his powers, but I'll stop aging."

"Oh. Do you ever get tired of living here, surrounded by walls? It's almost like being in prison."

"To tell you the truth, sometimes I just want to run away," Margaret said candidly. "I get tired of never going out after dark unless Nazario is with me. I miss having a home of my own. He keeps telling me we'll have one someday, but I don't know when that will be. It would probably be worse if I didn't love him so much." She sighed.

And then she smiled. "We're going to have a baby. I just found out last night."

Rae stared at her a moment, her heart filled with envy. "That's wonderful. I'm so happy for you," she murmured, and burst into tears.

"Rae?"

"I'm sorry." Grabbing a napkin, Rae wiped her eyes.

"Hon, what's wrong?"

"Nothing."

"Hey, I know *something* when I see it. Is it about Tor?"

"No. Do you think I'll ever be able to go home again?"

"Well, sure, as soon as this thing with Cesare is settled. But I hope you'll stay. I've loved having you here."

"I like you, too," Rae said. "But I'm supposed to be watching my grandmother's house and I've been away too long." It was only part of the truth. She missed her freedom. She missed the beach. She missed being alone.

"It's only been a few days. I'll send my cousin, Lucia, to look after the place while you're here." Margaret gave Rae's hand a squeeze. "Don't worry. I'm sure everything will work out."

Rae nodded. "I hope so."

* * *

The Elders met just after sunset. Tor related what had happened outside Cesare's stronghold the night before, which led to a discussion of their next move. Some favored a direct attack. Others suggested taking Cesare out with the hope that those opposed to his control would subdue the others.

Sandro was all for meeting Cesare in a one-on-one battle to determine the leader of both factions. Tor agreed with his father.

Nazario disagreed. "I don't trust Cesare to fight fair."

Sandro brushed off his younger son's concern with a shrug. "The odds are on my side, don't you think?"

"I hope so," Nazario muttered.

"It is decided then. I will send word to Cesare tonight and see if he will agree to meet me in battle."

* * *

 Amanda Ashley

"You're awfully quiet tonight," Tor said, taking Rae's hand in his. The rest of the household had gone downstairs, leaving the two of them alone in the living room.

"Am I?"

"Is it because of Margaret's news?"

"Among other things."

Tor nodded. "You want to go home."

"Yes."

"That may soon be possible."

"What do you mean?"

"My father wants to challenge Cesare for leadership of the covens, winner take all."

"Oh. Can he win?"

"He thinks so."

"You don't?"

"If Cesare fights fair, he hasn't got a prayer."

"Margaret thinks Cesare wants to die."

"Maybe. But enough about Cesare. I'd rather talk about you and me. Is there a chance for us?"

Rae nodded. There was no use fighting it. Vampire or not, she was falling in love with him more and more every day. "I'm willing to give it a try and see how it goes."

"Rae!" He hugged her tightly. "I swear I'll do everything in my power to make you happy."

Contentment washed over her as she rested her head on his chest. Maybe Margaret was right. Maybe everything *would* work out.

* * *

The family gathered in the living room later that night. The tension in the air was thick enough to cut with a knife as they waited for Cesare's reply.

Rae sat beside Tor, his arm around her shoulders.

Nazario paced the floor.

Margaret pretended to read a book.

Sandro stood at the window, staring into the darkness.

Rae jumped when the front door opened, admitting a blast of cool air and a tall, dark man in a long gray cloak.

All eyes swung in his direction.

SEASONS OF THE NIGHT   139

"Did you find Cesare?" Sandro asked him.

"Yes. He and his second will meet you tomorrow at midnight in the clearing behind the old church."

Sandro nodded. "Salvatore will be my second. Nazario, you will be in charge here. Keep a sharp eye out while I am gone. Have all of our people gather here at midnight. I would not put it past Cesare to have his men attack us while Tor and I are away."

"You can count on me."

"I know I can."

Rae glanced anxiously at Tor. What did a second do, exactly? Was he there simply to make sure no one broke the rules?

They lingered in the living room after everyone else left.

"You won't have to fight, will you?" she asked.

"Worried about me?"

"Of course. How do vampires fight?"

"In some ways, just like everyone else. If neither concedes victory, which is unlikely, then it's a fight to the death. It will either be swiftly over, or it might last for hours."

"Hours?"

"Minor wounds heal instantly. Only a fatal blow will end the battle."

"Do they use weapons?"

"No. Come on," he said, lifting her to her feet. "Let's take a walk around the garden."

He was worried about his father, Rae thought as they left the house. She could feel the nervous energy thrumming through him, see the worry behind his eyes.

A full moon hung low in the sky, casting silver shadows over the back yard. A gentle breeze stirred the leaves of the trees, a soft whisper in the moonlight. The air was fragrant with the scent of foliage.

They walked in silence for a moment, then Tor pulled her into his arms and held her close. "I'm glad you're here," he murmured. "I never realized how alone I was until I met you."

His words warmed her right down to her toes.

"Will you marry me when all this is over, Rae?"

When she hesitated, he said, "We don't have to stay here. We can have a home of our own anywhere you like, although I'll have to come back from to time."

"Yes. Yes, I will."

                    Amanda Ashley

Lifting her off her feet, he swung her round and round.

"Tor, put me down," she said, laughing. "You're making me dizzy."

"Anything you say, love."

Setting her on her feet, he pulled her into his embrace. "I love you, Raegan, for now and forever."

Forever, Rae thought, as he kissed her. She liked the sound of that.

Yet, even as she let herself be swept away, she couldn't help wondering what would happen if his father lost the fight.

Chapter 13

In the morning, Raegan was a nervous wreck, unable to think about anything but the upcoming fight. What if Sandro lost? What would that mean for Tor and the rest of the coven? She wasn't a vampire. What would happen to her? Why hadn't she asked him that last night? Maybe because she was afraid of the answer?

Over breakfast, it was easy to see that the fight was on Margaret's mind, too.

Neither of them had much of an appetite, making do with toast and hot chocolate.

"I just wish this silly fight was over!" Margaret exclaimed. "Nazario said everything was peaceful until Cesare took over. Since then, it's been nothing but trouble between the covens and in the town below. If Cesare isn't stopped, we'll soon have a mob of townspeople coming after us armed with swords and stakes."

The thought conjured images from old horror movies of peasants marching on some remote castle to destroy the monster.

By tacit agreement, they decided to clean the house, even though it didn't need it. Still, the physical labor helped steer their thoughts in other directions. And when they grew tired of scrubbing, they turned to baking.

"We'll both be fat as pigs if we eat all this." Rae pulled an apple pie out of the oven and set it on the counter next to a three layer

Amanda Ashley

chocolate cake and four dozen sugar cookies.

"I eat when I'm worried." Margaret snatched up her fifth cookie, then took a chair at the table. "Besides, I'm eating for…" Biting down on her lower lip, she looked away.

"Two," Raegan said. "You can talk about the baby. It's all right, really."

"I know it upsets you. What I don't know is why."

With a sigh, Rae dropped the oven mitt on the counter, then sat at the table. "It happened almost a year ago…"

* * *

When Rae finished her story, Margaret put her arms around her. "I'm so sorry, hon. I'm sure Tor would kill him for you if you asked."

"It wouldn't bring my baby back or change what happened."

"True. But a monster like that doesn't deserve to live. None of the men here would ever do such a dreadful thing." Margaret shook her head and then smiled. "If you marry Tor, you'll be part of our family and my baby will belong to you, too. You'll be Aunt Raegan."

* * *

Rae thought about her conversation with Margaret later that afternoon. She wasn't sure how she would feel about being an aunt. Would holding someone else's child be a constant reminder of the one she had lost, or would it somehow ease the pain?

* * *

If tension in the house had been thick last night, it was a palpable presence this evening.

Tor took Rae in his arms and held her close. "My father and I are going out for a while."

"Out? Where?"

"We won't be gone long." He kissed her, hard and quick, then left the house with Sandro.

Rae glanced at Margaret. "Where are they going?"

"To feed," she replied candidly. "It will strengthen them for the fight."

"Them? Is Tor going to fight, too?"

"If all goes well, no. If not… it might be necessary."

"Don't worry," Nazario said. "My father has never lost a battle."

Rae stared at him, praying he was right, that the fight would be over quickly, that Sandro and Tor would come home safely.

Or at least alive.

* * *

At five to midnight, Tor took Rae in his arms and kissed her tenderly. "Don't worry. We'll be back soon."

She nodded, afraid to speak for fear she'd beg him not to go.

Sandro embraced his youngest son and Margaret and nodded at Rae. Tor winked at her, and then he and his father vanished from sight.

Rae stared after them, thinking that was something she'd never get used to.

* * *

Cesare and his second arrived at the clearing behind the abandoned church shortly after Tor and Sandro materialized.

For a moment, no one said anything as the seriousness of what they were about to do sank in. A fight to the death, no quarter given.

Sandro and Cesare each took a few steps forward.

Tor and Cesare's second stayed where they were, on opposite sides of an invisible circle.

Though no word was given, Sandro and Cesare were suddenly moving, lunging forward, striking out, retreating as they tested each other's defenses.

Tor kept a wary eye on Cesare's man. The vampire hadn't done anything remotely suspicious, yet Tor felt something wasn't right.

Sandro and Cesare had both done damage now. Their wounds healed almost instantly but their skin and clothing were streaked with dark-red blood that looked black in the moon's pale light.

As the fight progressed, it was easy to see that Sandro was the more skilled.

Cesare knew it, too. Tor saw the fear in the vampire's eyes, the knowledge that he was out-matched. He backed up, closing the distance between himself and his second. When he was less than a yard from the vampire, Cesare suddenly dropped to the ground.

Amanda Ashley

At the same time, his second sprang forward and drove a long wooden stake into Sandro's chest.

Sandro reeled back, his hand curling around the stake.

Tor flung himself at Cesare's man, a cry of rage erupting from his throat as he ripped the vampire's heart from his chest and flung it aside.

Cesare was moving, too. A silver-bladed knife materialized in his hand as he sprang to his feet, the weapon arching toward Tor's heart.

Tor twisted sideways. The blade slid past his heart and opened a shallow gash from chest to waist.

Tor let out a roar of pain as he grabbed hold of Cesare and broke his neck, then yanked the vampire's beating heart from his chest and tossed it away.

For a moment, he stood there, head hanging. Then he ran toward his father.

Sandro lay on the ground, unmoving, eyes closed, but still breathing.

Tor knelt beside him, grasped the stake in both hands, and yanked it out of his father's chest.

Sandro groaned deep in his throat. "Dammit, boy, that hurt."

"You're lucky he missed your heart, small target that it is."

The sound of Sandro's laughter rent the silence of the night. Sitting up, he slapped Tor on the shoulder. "Come on, son, let's go home."

* * *

Rae let out a shriek when Tor and his father—both covered in blood—materialized in the living room.

Tor held up his hand. "Relax. We're both unhurt."

"Unhurt?" Rae gestured at Tor's blood-stained shirt and the ragged hole in Sandro's.

Tor flashed her a grin. "Okay, we *were* hurt, but we're fine now."

Her gaze moved over him. "Are you sure?"

He nodded.

Nazario glanced from his father to his brother. "I take it Cesare's not going to be a problem anymore."

"You take it right," Tor said, his voice laced with satisfaction. "I'm going upstairs to get cleaned up. I'll be right back."

"Sounds like a good idea," Sandro said. "Margaret, how about having a glass of wine waiting for me when I get back?"

Rae stared after the two men as they went up the stairs, then shook her head. They had obviously been in a horrendous fight, yet they'd laughed it off as though it was nothing.

Margaret went into the kitchen, returning a short time later with a bottle of wine and five glasses. She placed them on the coffee table, then sat on the sofa beside Nazario.

Rae took the chair facing the sofa, her hands clasped in her lap. She had been worried to death for Tor, yet he came home smiling, as if destroying Cesare was just business as usual. And then she frowned.

Maybe it was.

* * *

It was very late when Margaret, Nazario and Sandro went up to their rooms.

Tor took Rae's hand and tugged her onto the sofa beside him. "Are you all right?"

"Why wouldn't I be? You're the one who went off to battle."

He smiled wryly. "It wasn't all that dangerous, darlin'."

Warmth spread through Rae. He had never called her *darlin'* before. She rather liked it.

He massaged her shoulders for a few minutes, then his hand drifted up and slid into the hair at her nape. His touch sent a shiver of anticipation down her spine.

"You're still going to marry me, aren't you?" he asked. "You haven't changed your mind?"

She shook her head, her whole body tingling as he wrapped her in his arms and kissed her, gently at first, then more deeply. She pressed herself against him, her toes curling with pleasure as his tongue teased hers. His hand glided restlessly along her side, his palm brushing the edge of her breast. Heat flooded through her at his touch and then he was kissing her as if he would never stop.

Feeling suddenly trapped in his arms, she pushed him away and lurched to her feet.

"Rae?" When he reached for her, she stumbled backward.

He frowned, only then noting that she was trembling from head

 Amanda Ashley

to foot. "Rae? It's all right. I didn't mean to frighten you."

"I'm… I'm sorry. It's not you. It's me. I'm sorry."

"You've got nothing to be sorry for, love." Moving slowly, he filled her glass with wine and offered it to her. "It will calm your nerves."

Hands shaking, she took it from him, then sat on the edge of the sofa, embarrassed by her reaction as she sipped the wine. She knew Tor would never hurt her and yet, in that moment, it hadn't been Tor holding her, but the horrible creature who had stolen her virginity.

Setting the glass aside, she clasped her hands in her lap. "I can't marry you."

"Rae…"

"Don't you see? I might never be able to… to be a wife to you."

Tor knelt before her. "There's no hurry, love. Take all the time you need." He reached for her hand, relieved when she didn't pull away. "I love you, Rae," he said fervently. "I swear I'll never ask anything of you that you're not ready to give."

Rae nodded, touched by his words.

Leaning forward, he cupped her face in his palms and kissed her gently, vowing that if he ever got his hands on the man who had attacked Raegan, the cur would curse the day he drew his first breath.

CHAPTER 14

With Cesare no longer a threat, Rae saw no reason why she couldn't go back to her grandmother's house. She mentioned as much to Tor when she saw him that night.

"Is that what you want?" he asked. "I was hoping you'd stay here."

"We can come visit, after we're married, if you like. But for now, I'd like to go back to the beach house."

"Very well, love. I'll take you home when you're ready."

* * *

Saying goodbye to Margaret was harder than Rae had thought it would be. "I'll see you again soon," she promised. "I just need to have some time alone."

Margaret nodded. "I understand. Really, I do. This place can get you down. Nazario promised to take me on a trip after the baby is born." Taking Rae's hands in hers, she said, "We'll all miss you."

"I'll miss you, too."

After she bid goodbye to Sandro and Nazario, Tor took her home.

* * *

Raegan went through the house, turning on the lights. Lucia had

Amanda Ashley

taken good care of the place while she'd been gone. The plants had been watered, the mail collected, the rooms dusted, and the rugs vacuumed.

She returned to the living room, where Tor waited for her.

"Are you going home?" she asked.

"No. I'm staying nearby as long as you're here."

"Why?"

"That's a silly question," he said, taking her in his arms. "I want to be close to you."

"You could stay in the guestroom, if you want."

"I would, thanks."

She smiled up at him, thinking how much she loved him, how patient he had been with her.

"Are you ready to set a date for our wedding?" He pressed his fingertips to her lips to still the protest he saw in her eyes. "I meant what I said. We won't consummate our marriage until you're ready. But I want you to be mine, Rae. For always. Will you?"

She nodded.

"Rae!" Taking both of her hands in his, he kissed her. "Name the day."

"I always wanted to be a June bride," she murmured. "Could we have just a simple ceremony at the courthouse here in town, just the two of us?" Once, she had dreamed of a big church wedding surrounded by friends and family. But no more. She didn't want to be the center of attention.

"Are you sure that's what you want? What about your parents?"

"I'll tell them we eloped."

"It's settled then. How about June 29th?" At her nod, he said, "We'll need a witness. Would you mind if I asked my father to stand up with us?"

"No, I guess not."

"Good, I'll take care of everything." Including asking Sandro to placate Gina's family.

Friday, June 29th, she thought. Seven days from today. Just enough time to find a dress and get her hair done.

* * *

It was comforting, having Tor in the house. Rae took a long, hot shower and slipped into her nightgown and robe, acutely aware that he was in the other room, that he would be in the house while she slept.

When Rae returned to the living room, she found him engrossed in an old Avengers movie.

Looking up, he smiled at her. "It's late. You should get some sleep."

She nodded, then kissed him on the cheek. "Good night."

"Night, sweetheart. Rest well."

Tor watched her leave the room. He had never loved anyone as deeply as he loved Raegan. In ways he didn't understand, she completed him, made him whole. It was a good feeling.

Not ready to seek his rest, he went outside and stood on the front porch. Millions of twinkling stars were sprinkled across the midnight blue sky. The air was warm, with a faint breeze.

He frowned as he caught the scent of a man. It wasn't fresh and there was nothing suspicious about it except that whoever it belonged to had been on the porch recently.

And that was suspicious indeed.

* * *

Rae woke early. For a time, she lay in bed, thinking how good it was to be back at her grandmother's house. Some of her happiest memories had been spent here with her grandparents. It was here she'd caught her first fish, learned how to ride a surfboard, had her first crush.

After dressing and brushing her hair, she went into the kitchen to fix breakfast, only to discover that the milk and eggs had spoiled.

Grabbing the keys to the car, she drove into town, intending to catch breakfast at her favorite diner, stop at Missy's Bridal Shop, then pick up a few things at the grocery store.

She sang along with the radio as she pulled out of the driveway. It had been a long time since she felt so happy and so carefree, and it was all because of Tor.

She enjoyed a leisurely breakfast, then hurried to Missy's. To her surprise, she fell in love with the first dress she tried on. It was long and elegant and in her price range. After arranging for alterations, she bought a shoulder-length veil, as well as a sheer white nightgown that

     Amanda Ashley

made her blush as she imagined wearing it for Tor on their wedding night.

Rae had just left the grocery store when she felt a sudden rush of unease. She glanced around. At first, she didn't see anything to alarm her and then, out of the corner of her eye, she spied a man watching her. A man with yellow eyes. She only saw him for a moment before he darted out of sight behind a delivery truck. A chill ran through her. She pressed a hand to her heart and took a deep breath. She was just imagining things. It couldn't be him.

Nevertheless, she quickly loaded her groceries in the trunk, jumped into the car and pulled out of the parking lot.

She watched her rearview mirror all the way home.

** * **

Tor was waiting for her in the living room when she arrived. Stepping forward, he took the grocery bags from her arms and carried them into the kitchen.

"You're up," she exclaimed, trailing after him.

"What's wrong?"

Rae frowned. "What do you mean?"

"Something spooked you while you were out."

"I'm fine."

"Like hell. Your distress woke me."

She put the milk and eggs in the fridge, tucked a box of cereal and a loaf of bread into the cupboard.

"Raegan."

She stood at the counter, her back toward Tor. "I thought I saw him."

He knew immediately who she was talking about. His first thought was for the masculine scent he had detected on the porch the night before.

"I'm sure I was wrong. I mean, how would he know I was here?"

How, indeed? he thought. With cell phones and the Internet, you could track anyone anywhere.

"It can't be him, can it?" she asked, her back still turned.

Moving up behind her, Tor slipped his arms around her waist. "I don't know, love. But if he comes here, it'll be the last thing he ever does."

That night, snuggled in bed, with Tor keeping watch in the living room, Raegan told herself over and over again that the monster who had attacked her couldn't possibly have found her. She had lived in Vermont when it happened. Even if he knew where she lived, how could he find her here, three thousand miles away?

* * *

Refusing to let her unfounded fears keep her inside, Raegan went to town the following morning in hopes of finding a pair of white satin pumps to wear with her wedding gown.

In spite of her determination not to let fear get the best of her, Rae found herself constantly looking over her shoulder as she left the shoe store.

She stopped for gas on the way home, felt a surge of relief when she pulled into the driveway.

Late that afternoon, they went to the County Clerk's Office to apply for a marriage license. There was no waiting period in California. They left the office a short time later, license in hand.

There were butterflies in Raegan's stomach on the ride home. She was going to be married. To Tor. She slid a glance in his direction. She loved him so very much. She just hoped she could overcome her fear of intimacy on their wedding night. And if she couldn't, what then? He had said he wouldn't ask for more than she could give, but how long would his patience last?

Sensing her thoughts, Tor took her hand in his and gave it a squeeze. "Rae, I meant what I said. I'll wait as long as I have to."

The gentle touch of his hand, the sincerity in his voice, the love in his eyes when his gaze met hers soothed all her fears.

* * *

They took a blanket and a bottle of wine down to the beach that night.

"I talked to Sandro while you were eating dinner," Tor remarked as he spread the blanket on a smooth stretch of sand. "He'll meet us at the courthouse Friday afternoon at five."

Rae nodded.

"Is everything all right? No second thoughts?"

"I'm a little nervous."

    Amanda Ashley

"Brides are supposed to be nervous," he said, smiling.

"Then I'm doing it right." She frowned as she looked past Tor and saw a man striding toward them. She told herself there was nothing to worry about. It was just someone strolling on the beach. But there was something about him…

She felt the color drain from her face as he drew closer. Oh, Lord. It was him. She'd know those yellow eyes, that hideous scar, anywhere.

Feeling sick to her stomach, she pressed closer to Tor.

"Rae, what is it?" Sensing someone behind him, he glanced over his shoulder.

The stranger stopped at the edge of the blanket. He was of medium height, with unkempt brown hair and crazy eyes. He looked at Raegan, a smile twisting his lips when he took his hand from his pocket, revealing a blunt-nosed revolver. "I've been looking for you," he said. "This time you won't get away. Let's go."

"She's not going anywhere with you," Tor said, his voice mild. "So put the gun down."

"Who are you?"

"I'm the man who's going to break your neck."

"I don't think so," the man replied with a sneer. "I'll plug you if you make a move."

"Really?"

Rae gasped as, in a move almost too fast to see, Tor surged to his feet and wrapped his hands around her attacker's throat. The man dropped the gun, let out a yelp as he struggled to free himself.

"We should call the police," Rae said.

"You're right," Tor agreed. "We should. But we won't."

Before she could ask what he intended to do, he had dragged her attacker out of sight.

* * *

After what seemed like hours but was only a few minutes, Tor returned alone. Rae looked up at him, afraid to ask what he'd done.

He didn't sit beside her, just stood there, his face impassive. "He'll never bother you or anyone else again."

"He's… you…?"

He nodded. "Is this going to change things between us?"

She searched her heart and mind, trying to find a sense of remorse for the man's death, but all she felt was relief and the feeling that, right or wrong, justice had been done. Right or wrong, it was over.

Instead of answering Tor's question, she reached for his hand and tugged him down beside her.

CHAPTER 15

Rae's wedding day bloomed bright and clear. She took a leisurely bath, shaved her legs. After breakfast, she drove into town to have her hair and nails done.

At odd moments, she thought about the events of last night. She felt guilty for not regretting her attacker's death. She tried to imagine what would have happened if they'd taken the man to the police station. There would have been a trial, perhaps months or years from now, with no guarantee that he would ever be convicted.

It was four o'clock when she returned home.

Tor was waiting for her. He looked beyond handsome in a black suit and tie. "Best get a move on," he said with a wink. "We have to be there in an hour."

"I'm pretty sure you can get us there on time," she said with a saucy grin.

* * *

Later, Raegan remembered only snatches of the actual ceremony. The expression on Tor's face when he saw her in her wedding gown, the way his hand held hers as the judge spoke the words that made them man and wife, the sincere congratulations of her new father-in-law.

Sandro took his leave shortly after the ceremony was over, leaving her alone with her new husband.

"Would you like to go out for dinner?" Tor asked.

Rae glanced at her gown, then shook her head. "Let's just go home."

"As you wish." He wrapped his arm around her waist. Moments later, they were in the living room at her grandmother's house.

"You look incredibly lovely," Tor said.

He'd whispered that to her before the ceremony, too, but it was nice to hear it again. Feeling suddenly ill-at-ease, she murmured, "I think I'll go change."

Tor blew out a sigh as he watched her leave the room. He didn't have to use his vampire powers to sense the tension radiating from his bride. He stood there a moment, wondering what his next move should be. And then he followed her to her bedroom and opened the door.

Rae whirled around, her hands automatically crossing over her breasts.

Tor stopped just inside the door. "Listen, darlin', I know you're nervous about tonight, but put it out of your mind, okay? After dinner, we'll just take a walk or watch a movie. Does that sound all right to you?"

Rae nodded.

"Okay." He smiled at her, then closed the door behind him.

Rae let out a sigh of relief. Was it any wonder she loved him? But how long would he love her if she couldn't overcome her fear of intimacy?

* * *

Rae stared up at the sky, her hand in Tor's as they strolled along the deserted beach. It was a beautiful night. A full moon smiled down on them. The air was warm, the water against her bare feet a nice contrast. Tor carried a blanket over his shoulder. They'd been walking perhaps twenty minutes when he drew her into his arms. "I love you, Rae," he said quietly. "More than I've ever loved anyone in my life."

"I love you, too. Thank you for being so patient with me."

He stroked her hair, her cheek, then claimed her lips with his in

     Amanda Ashley

an achingly tender kiss that made her toes curl in the sand. His arms went around her as he deepened the kiss. Wanting to be closer, she pressed herself against him, her arms twining around his neck.

Somehow, they were lying on the blanket, their bodies straining toward each other as he kissed and caressed her. Needing to touch him in return, she slid her hands under his shirt, reveling in the touch of his bare skin beneath her palm.

When he moaned softly, she withdrew her hand, only to replace it when he whispered, "Don't stop."

"Someone might come," she said.

"Not to worry. No one will see us."

And suddenly they were undressing each other, hands and lips desperate to touch and explore. It never occurred to her to be afraid. This was Tor. He had slain the dragon and rescued her from the fears that had imprisoned her.

Loving Tor, being loved by him, was beyond anything she had ever imagined. He was warm and tender, careful to take things slow and easy, willing to let her decide how fast they went.

She let out a cry of exultation when his body merged with hers, carrying her away to realms of ecstasy she had never dreamed of, filling her, completing her, until she wept with the sheer joy of it.

"I love you, husband," she whispered.

And fell asleep in his arms, secure in the belief that their love would only grow deeper, stronger, with every passing day.

The Vampire in the Attic

CHAPTER 1

Analia Collins loved Halloween. As soon as the first of October rolled around, she started decorating her front yard—scary-looking, moaning ghosts that floated on wires, a blow-up goblin, a mannequin dressed like a witch bending over a cauldron. Her favorite decoration took up most of her side yard. Fake wrought-iron fencing enclosed several large foam tombstones and an old coffin she had bought at a thrift shop. Her latest purchase, an amazingly lifelike figure of a vampire she had nicknamed Drac, rested inside the casket. Ana had always thought that, if she had to be a supernatural creature, she would want to be a vampire. Well, except for the part about drinking blood, she mused as she stepped past the pumpkins carved with scary faces that adorned her front porch and opened the front door.

She paused as she stepped into the foyer and glanced around. The inside of her house also reflected her love of the holiday—porcelain black cats, witches in all shapes and sizes, a parade of zombies marching across the fireplace mantel. Spiders, large and small, inhabited a web of black netting that hung from the ceiling. She had replaced the pretty pink tablecloth on her kitchen table with one that looked like a spider web, exchanged the white candles on the entry table with black ones. A rather grotesque but cute ceramic pumpkin, flanked by more ebony candles, adorned the top of the small chest just inside the front door. A life-size skeleton stood in front of the picture window in the living room.

She had very little sales resistance and almost every day saw the addition of one or more decorations - pictures that went from people who looked ordinary until you walked by and they changed into zombies with bright red eyes that seemed to follow you. Her windows were adorned with window clings of ghosts and bats.

The books in her bookcase were the one thing she didn't have to change. She had scores of paranormal romances as well as dozens of non-fiction volumes about the legends and myths of vampires, witches, and werewolves. As a child, she had longed to have supernatural powers, dreamed of being a vampire who could change into a wolf, fly through the air, turn into a shimmering mist, cover long distances with a thought.

Her parents had worried about her when she'd been a little girl, afraid there was something terribly wrong with a child who preferred Dracula to Disney. Now, they just shook their heads and prayed she would find a nice young man, get married, and give them grandchildren.

Not likely to happen, Ana mused as she went into the kitchen in search of a snack. She hadn't had a date in over three months. Her best friend, Jade, insisted it was because Ana wasn't looking for your typical Mr. Right, but for some mythical man who didn't exist—some tall, dark handsome guy clad in a long, black cloak who would wrap her in his dark embrace and carry her into a world filled with wonder and excitement.

"Maybe Jade is right," Ana admitted with a sigh. But who could blame her? What harm was there in hoping some dreamy, supernatural hunk would come along and whisk her away? After all, there wasn't much excitement in being a bank teller.

In the meantime, Halloween was only three weeks away. She had rented a lavish costume for the company party and enough trick-or-treat candy to feed a small army. That would have to be enough excitement for now.

 Amanda Ashley

CHAPTER 2

October. It was his favorite time of the year. The nights were longer, the weather cooler. So much easier to pretend you were a part of society when every house and shop window featured your kind. No one looked at him twice when he strolled through the malls. Hunting was a breeze. It didn't take any effort at all to infiltrate the numerous costume parties that were held all month long at homes and schools and work places. Little effort was required to mesmerize some lovely miss high on bubbly, coax her into a dark corner, and satisfy his thirst.

Sadly, hunters didn't have any trouble distinguishing the genuine from the fake. Like the two who had been tracking him for the last six months. Raiden swore under his breath. He had been careless. The hunters had taken him by surprise outside his favorite lair and damn near taken his head. He had incapacitated one of them. But the other one was somewhere in the city.

The wounds they had inflicted on him had yet to heal, rendering him weak, stealing his power. Though he wasn't completely defenseless, he was a long way from home and he didn't have the strength to dissolve into mist or transport himself to another town or another lair merely by thinking about it. So, here he was, in this dreary little town with only the clothes on his back and a credit card.

At least he still had his head!

Walking as fast as he could, he turned away from the town's main drag onto the nearest residential street. Most of the houses were all decked out for Halloween—front yards, roofs and windows cluttered with scary signs and characters that ranged from cute to creepy to the downright bizarre.

But he had more important things on his mind than fake skeletons. He needed to find a place to spend the day before the sun came up. He slowed when he came to the red brick house on the corner. Whoever lived there went whole hog for the holiday - lights, music, scary witches, ghosts, goblins and even a zombie that looked like it had escaped from the set of *The Walking Dead*. There was even what looked to be a genuine casket. The top half of the lid stood open, exposing the head and shoulders of an amazingly life-like dummy, its wispy black hair blowing in the breeze.

A coffin. Just what he was looking for.

After checking to make sure that no one was watching, he climbed into the casket, slid under the fake vampire and closed the lid. It was a little crowded with the two of them, but his companion wasn't complaining and neither was he.

Closing his eyes, he sank into the beckoning arms of oblivion.

 Amanda Ashley

CHAPTER 3

It was late when Ana pulled into the driveway. For a moment, she just sat there, admiring her yard. It looked amazing during the day and even better than last year.

Opening the car door, she stepped out and stretched her back and shoulders. It had been a long day and she was looking forward to a leisurely meal, an hour or two in front of the TV and a hot bath before bed.

It wasn't until she was cutting across the grass to the front door that Ana noticed the lid of the coffin was closed. Had someone stolen Drac and closed the casket, hoping that she wouldn't notice?

Tossing the bag of candy she'd bought on the way home on the porch, she hurried toward the coffin and lifted the lid, let out a shriek when Drac came flying out, followed by a tall, dark man clad in black jeans, a white shirt, and a long, black coat. Inky-black hair fell almost to his waist. Deep brown eyes set beneath straight brows stared at her, sending a shiver of alarm down her spine.

"What are you doing in there?" she demanded with more bravado than she felt. "Get out of here before I call the police!"

"No need for that." His voice was deep, almost mesmerizing in its beauty.

"Just… just go!" A small gasp escaped her when she saw how pale he was. "Are you ill?" Her gaze swept over him, only then noticing that the front of his shirt was smeared with what looked like dried blood. Alarmed, she took a hasty step back. Good Lord, had he been shot? Stabbed? "Should I call a doctor?"

He shook his head. "I'm sorry I frightened you."

"Are you all right?" She had never seen anyone still breathing who looked as pale as this stranger.

"I'll be fine."

His gaze met hers with an intensity she had never experienced before. Unable to look away, she felt an almost irresistible urge to ask him inside. And then, to her mortification, she hurried up the porch stairs, unlocked the door, and invited him in, wondering all the while what had possessed her to welcome a complete stranger—and a blood-stained one at that—into her home.

His very presence seemed to dwarf the living room.

She folded her arms over her breasts, her heart pounding a rapid tattoo. He was inside. What should she do now? What was *he* going to do now?

He spared hardly a glance for her or his surroundings as he shrugged out of his coat, which he tossed over the back of a chair, then staggered toward the sofa and stretched out on it.

"Can I get you anything?" she asked.

"Red wine, if you have it."

In the kitchen, she shook her head as she filled a glass with Merlot. What had made her invite this man into her house? True, she had been looking for a little excitement in her life, but a bleeding stranger with mesmerizing black eyes was hardly what she'd had in mind.

She ducked into the bathroom to grab a clean towel and a wet cloth on her way back to the living room.

Her guest lay on his back, his eyes closed. He didn't seem to be breathing. Good grief, had he died? How would she explain a dead man on her couch?

With a hand that was none too steady, she dropped the towel and the wash cloth on the floor, then touched her fingertips to the side of his neck. She let out a squeak when, with a low growl, he grabbed her arm.

"It's me!" She recoiled at his touch. Wine sloshed over the lip of the glass and dribbled onto his shirt.

With a mumbled, "Forgive me," he released her.

Taking a deep breath, Ana placed the goblet on the coffee table,

	Amanda Ashley

then pressed her hand to her heart.

He sat up after a moment and reached for his drink which he downed in a single, long swallow. Setting the goblet aside, he removed his bloody shirt and dropped it on the floor.

Ana stared at him. She had seen bare chests before, but none quite as spectacular as this one. Though his skin was pale, his physique was perfect, from his broad shoulders and chest to his six-pack abs. The only imperfections were the ugly wound in his chest—only inches from his heart—and the half-healed burns across his stomach.

She was going to need more than a wash cloth. Going into the kitchen, she grabbed her first aid kit and carried it back into the living room. "What happened to you?" she asked as she wiped away the dried blood on his chest.

"I was shot."

"Shot!" That explained the hole in his chest but not the burns. She looked at him askance but he offered no further explanation. "Shouldn't you go to the hospital and have the bullet removed?"

"It went all the way through."

Thinking that was apparently a good thing, she bandaged the ragged wounds, front and back, as best she could, applied salve to the burns, then stood there, at a loss as to what to say or do next.

Gesturing at the glass, he said, "More?"

Nodding, she went into the kitchen and refilled the goblet, then stood at the counter, gazing out the window. She was thinking of running next door to call the police when something compelled her to return to the living room.

She handed him the glass, then moved to the far side of the room. If she had expected him to finish his drink, thank her and leave, she was sorely mistaken.

Settling back on the sofa, he sipped his wine. Though still pale, he seemed a little better. It was disconcerting, the way he looked at her, as if he couldn't quite decide what to make of her. Or what to do with her.

Feeling ill at ease, she picked up his shirt, the wash cloth and towel and the first aid kit and carried them all into the bathroom. His Armani shirt was beyond repair and she tossed it into the trash. The washcloth and towel went into the clothes hamper, the kit into the cupboard under the sink.

She was pondering what to do next when she heard his voice.

Analia, come to me.

Startled, she whirled around, expecting to see him standing behind her in the doorway, but there was no one there. A shiver of unease skittered down her spine when she realized she had heard his voice inside her head, and that he somehow knew her name. Who was this guy?

She was trying to fathom how he could influence her thoughts when she found herself answering the same compulsion she had felt before. She tried to resist, but it was as if someone else was controlling her mind, forcing her to obey.

Making her way into the living room, she walked toward the tall, dark, stranger reclining on her sofa.

His gaze burned into hers and she heard his voice inside her head again, commanding her to sit beside him.

Helpless to resist, she sank down on the edge of the cushion, her heart thundering in her ears. Every protective instinct she possessed screamed at her to run, but she couldn't move, couldn't do anything but sit there, shivering and helpless as his large, capable hands folded over her shoulders to draw her closer.

"Relax," he murmured. "I will not hurt you. And you will remember none of what happened this night when it is over."

She nodded, her eyelids fluttering down when he lowered his head to her neck. Pleasure flowed through her, warm and sweet, and then the world as she knew it went black.

* * *

Lifting his head, Raiden brushed a wisp of hair from the girl's cheek. Ana was a pretty thing, with a cloud of wavy, dark red hair and bright blue eyes. Her skin, tanned and smooth, was flawless, her lips pink and perfect, her figure rounded in all the right places. Slipping his arms around her, he stood and carried her down the narrow hallway to a bedroom heavy with her scent and put her to bed.

He stood there a moment, just looking at her, surprised by an unfamiliar stirring deep inside. He had intended to leave as soon as he fed, but he was suddenly reluctant to bid farewell to such a lovely creature.

Perhaps he would stay a few days and get to know her better. It had been a long time since he kept a human slave, and even longer

 Amanda Ashley

since he made love to a woman not of his own kind.

Smiling faintly, he left the house, the taste of the woman's blood still on his tongue. The little he had taken from Ana hadn't been enough to quench his prodigious thirst.

Strolling down the walkway, he decided his first priority would have to be a new shirt. With that thought in mind, he headed for the shopping mall. Fortunately, he had plenty of time to hunt before the sun came up, as well as a convenient coffin where he could spend the day.

And, best of all, a beautiful young woman to keep him company until the dawn.

CHAPTER 4

Analia awoke abruptly, the last remnants of her nightmare fresh in her mind. It had been an oddly peculiar dream. She had been donating blood—pints and pints of it—as if she had an endless supply and anyone who wished could come and take a drink. Was that why she was so thirsty? Because she had spent the night pretending to be some kind of human blood bank?

Throwing back the covers, she padded barefooted into the kitchen where she quickly downed a tall glass of orange juice and three cups of coffee.

When the caffeine cleared her head, the events of the previous night came rushing back—and with it the memory of the nameless stranger she had foolishly invited into her house. She frowned. Had that really happened, or had that been a dream, too? Well, there was one way to find out.

Putting her coffee cup aside, she hurried into the bathroom. There was no bloody shirt in the trash can. No crimson-stained washcloth in the hamper.

Relieved, she went back into the bedroom to make her bed. "Just a silly dream," she muttered, and then, glancing at the clock, she forgot all about her nightmare.

If she didn't get a move on, she was going to be late for work.

　　　　Amanda Ashley

* * *

Fridays were always busy and the day flew by. On her way home, Ana dropped off her dry cleaning, bought gas, and then stopped at her favorite Chinese take-out place to pick up a chicken bowl for dinner.

At home, she parked in the driveway, grabbed her handbag and her dinner and started toward the porch, only to pause when she glanced at the decorations in the yard. Funny, she didn't remember closing the lid on the coffin yesterday. And then she shrugged. It had been windy today. Maybe an errant breeze had caused it to close.

She stood on the edge of the grass, oddly reluctant to approach the casket. A memory surfaced in the far corner of her mind—that of a man leaping out of the coffin… the same nameless man she had dreamed about the night before. Why did she keep thinking about a guy she had never met? Or had she? Surely she would have remembered meeting someone like that.

Taking her courage in hand, she walked briskly toward the casket and lifted the lid. And let out a shriek to wake the dead when two heads appeared.

Dropping the carry-out bag, she sprinted for the front door, let out a yelp when a large hand closed over her arm.

It was him. The stranger in her dreams. She glanced at his shirt front. It had been bloody in her nightmare… the stain a red so dark it was almost black. Only it hadn't been a nightmare. The realization sparked a flood of recollections—treating his wounds, bringing him a glass of wine, sitting beside him as if she had no will of her own while he bit her. Bit her! The memories were too vivid to have been a dream.

"What do you want?" she asked, her voice little more than a squeak.

"Just a place to spend the evening."

"There are other places. Hospitals. Blood banks. Grave yards."

His mouth quirked up in one corner. "Indeed. Shall we go in?"

Resigned, she unlocked the front door and stepped into the small foyer, keenly aware of the tall, dark-haired man behind her. The click of the lock sounded like a death knell in her ears.

Totally freaked out, she made her way into the living room, kicked off her heels, tossed her handbag on the coffee table, then stood there, hands clenched at her sides, wondering what to do next.

Wondering what *he* was going to do next.

She risked a glance over her shoulder, felt some of the tension drain out of her when she saw him sitting on the couch, thumbing through one of the magazines on the coffee table. She grunted softly. He had no trouble making himself at home. "Do you have a name?"

He looked at her over the top of the magazine. "Sure."

"Well? Are you going to tell me what it is, or make me guess?"

His smile was devastating. "What do you think it might be?"

"Edward? Stefan? Damon? Angel? Spike? Vlad? Count Dracula?"

"I can't help thinking you have a bit of a fascination for vampires," he remarked with a wry grin.

"So, what *is* your name?" she asked, her voice rising in exasperation.

"It's Fred."

"Fred?" She stared at him. "*Fred* the vampire?"

The sound of his laughter filled the room. It did funny things in the pit of her stomach.

"Actually, it's Raiden."

"Raiden." It suited him perfectly. "How did you know my name?"

He shrugged. "I read your mind, of course."

Stunned, she dropped into the chair across from the sofa. He said it as if it was no big deal, as if he hadn't violated her privacy. And then she remembered hearing his voice in her head last night, telling her to come to him, recalled how she had been helpless to resist.

She pressed her fingertips to the left side of her neck, just below her ear. The skin felt warm where he had bitten her. "It wasn't a dream," she murmured.

"No, it was quite real." He frowned. He had compelled her to forget everything that had happened the night before, yet she seemed to have a clear memory of all of it. How was that possible?

Ana went cold all over. There had been no trace of his presence this morning, so he must have disposed of all the blood-stained evidence. But why? "What do you want? What are you going to do with me?"

He lifted an inquiring brow. "What would you like me to do?"

"I'd like you to go away and leave me alone."

He looked thoughtful a moment, then shook his head. "Sorry, I rather like it here."

     Amanda Ashley

Her stomach chose that moment to growl, rather loudly, reminding her that her rice bowl was lying outside in the grass. No doubt her neighbor's cocker spaniel had already torn the bag apart and wolfed down the contents.

"Don't let me keep you from your dinner," he said.

Nodding, she went into the kitchen, her mind racing. If only she had her cell phone, she could call for help, but she'd left it in her handbag in the other room. And who would she call?

Think!

In books and movies, the police were little help. People turned instead to vampire hunters to slay the monster. But that was fiction. Wasn't it? Maybe all those movies were based on reality. Maybe there really were vampire hunters like Van Helsing, but how did you find one? Google? The Yellow Pages?

With a shake of her head, she rummaged in the fridge for the makings of a sandwich, one ear cocked toward the front room. What was he doing in there? Still reading that magazine? What possible interest could a vampire have in *Today's Home and Garden?*

Ana closed the refrigerator door, then leaned her forehead against the cool surface. Maybe she was dreaming again. Maybe she was in a hospital somewhere, totally out of her mind.

She tiptoed to the door and peeked around the corner. He was still on the couch. Just sitting there.

And then he lifted his gaze to hers.

Something passed between them, the likes of which Ana had never felt before. She had no name for it, yet it touched every nerve and fiber of her being, made her keenly aware that he was a man and she was a woman.

A woman he found desirable.

The next thing she knew, she was perched on the sofa beside him with his arm around her shoulders. His nostrils flared, as if he were scenting her. As if she were prey. Ana shivered as his fingertips caressed her cheek, slid ever so slowly down her neck, and came to rest in the hollow of her throat.

Her heart thudded in her chest. What was he doing to her?

"Analia."

That voice, deep and mellifluous, washed over her like warm water on a cool day. It left her feeling tingly and achy in places no man had ever touched. A small gasp escaped her lips as his fangs brushed her skin. Her eyelids fluttered down and she leaned into him, her hands grasping his shoulders as heat flowed through her, then swept her away on a crimson tide.

* * *

For the second time in as many nights, Raiden tucked Analia into bed. He stood there a moment, the taste of her still hot on his tongue, his body quivering with desire while a little voice in the back of his head whispered, "You want her. Take her."

It was tempting. So damn tempting. But how could he? She was young, with her whole life ahead of her. He was many things—hunter, predator, killer—but he had never taken a woman against her will, nor compelled one to surrender to him.

But looking at her now, her hair spread across the pillow, her lashes like fans against her cheeks, her lips slightly parted, the temptation was almost more than he could bear.

Turning on his heel, he went out into the night in search of prey.

 Amanda Ashley

CHAPTER 5

Ana stared up at the ceiling. It was getting to be a habit, she thought, waking up in bed with no memory of how she'd gotten there. One thing she was sure of, she hadn't made it under her own power, which meant Raiden must have carried her. And undressed her down to her underwear. She told herself that her bra and panties were more modest that a lot of bathing suits. Nevertheless, she blushed from head to foot.

Throwing aside the covers, she went to the window. Her gaze darted immediately to the side yard and the casket. Was he resting in there? What did he look like when he was asleep?

She pulled on her robe and hurried outside. She slowed as she drew closer to the coffin. Took a deep breath. And lifted the lid.

Only Drac stared back at her.

Where was Raiden? And why did she care? Sure, he was tall, dark and handsome. Sure, his very presence made her tingle in new and interesting ways. But he was a vampire! Hardly dating material. And even though she had always been fascinated by the Undead, she had never believed they really existed, much less expected to meet one.

Returning to the house, she put the coffee on, assuring herself as she did so that she was glad to be rid of him.

She tried to convince herself of that while she fixed breakfast, showered and brushed her teeth, stripped the sheets from her bed and tossed them in the washer.

But she didn't believe it for a minute.

Where could he be?

* * *

In the attic, lying on an old blanket in the dark, Raiden stirred as Analia's thoughts penetrated the dark sleep. It was a survival instinct that roused him whenever danger was near, and though she was no threat, her thoughts had been strong enough to revive him.

He smiled faintly, pleased to know she was thinking of him, to know she missed him. Even though she refused to acknowledge it, there was no denying the attraction between them. Soon, he mused as he sank back into oblivion, soon she would be his.

* * *

Ana sighed as she made her bed. She paused as she smoothed the top sheet, trying not to imagine Raiden sprawled on the mattress, his long black hair spread across her pillow... Darn! What was there about that man that she couldn't stop thinking about him?

Feeling a sudden need to be outside, she changed into a pair of sweats and tied her hair up in a pony tail. She fished her keys out of her purse, locked the door behind her and headed for the park where she often went jogging. She waved to Mr. Sinclair who was mowing his yard, and to old Mrs. Allenton, who was in her rocking chair on the front porch, her overweight Siamese cat perched on her lap.

What would her neighbors think if they knew there was a vampire in the neighborhood? What if he was feeding on them?

That possibility brought her up short. Good heavens, she had to warn her friends, but what could she say? Hi, Fran, I just wanted to warn you that there's a vampire in town, so you might want to stay inside when the sun goes down. Oh, and don't open your door to strangers.

Too bad someone hadn't warned her!

Ana jogged for half an hour before she returned home. Unlocking the front door, she wondered again where Raiden spent the day.

And if she would see him that night.

* * *

     Amanda Ashley

He woke with the setting of the sun, his senses searching for Analia. She was asleep on the sofa in front of the TV.

He willed himself into the bathroom, took a quick shower and dressed. He needed a change of clothes, he thought as he tucked his shirt into his trousers. Perhaps he would go shopping tonight. Perhaps the fair Ana would go with him.

Strolling into the living room, he stood by the sofa, gazing down at her. Such a lovely creature, her skin unblemished, her lips slightly curved in a mysterious smile. Her hair fell over her shoulders, tempting his touch.

Ana woke abruptly. She let out a startled cry when she saw Raiden standing over her and realized it was his fingers threading through her hair that had awakened her.

He looked a bit sheepish as he took a step away from the sofa.

Ana bolted upright. "What were you doing?"

"Nothing."

"Nothing?"

He shrugged. "Your hair is like silk."

Ana bit down on her lip, uncertain how to respond.

"I need to go shopping," he said. "I'd very much like you to go with me."

"Why?"

"I enjoy your company."

There were probably hundreds of reasons to refuse, but none came to mind.

Twenty minutes later, they were in her car on the way to the mall.

Ana slid a glance in his direction. "Where did you spend the day?"

"Why?"

"Just curious. I looked in the coffin, but you weren't there."

"I was nearby."

"Afraid to tell me?" she asked, only half-kidding.

"My daytime lair must of necessity be kept secret. There are too many who would take my head if they could."

"You don't think I'm one of them, do you?"

"Are you?"

"Of course not. Why are we going to the mall?" It seemed ludicrous, a vampire shopping.

"I need a change of clothes."

Nodding, she said, "We're here."

Raiden glanced at the huge structure as she pulled into the parking lot. He usually avoided such places, but he was reasonably certain there were no hunters lurking inside.

The Men's Department was just inside the doors.

"What are you looking for?" Ana asked, thinking how surreal it was to be in the mall with Raiden, as if he was just an ordinary guy and not a supernatural creature.

"The usual."

"I guess that means something black," she said, suppressing a grin. "Why do vampires insist on wearing black?"

"Why do you think?"

"To blend in with the night, I suppose."

He nodded.

She held up a blue Armani shirt. "I think you'd look great in this."

He lifted one brow. "Really?"

"Really." She held it up in front of him. "Might be a nice change of pace."

He could wear it when he was with her, he thought. "Very well." He bought a pair of slacks, socks, and underwear—all black.

Ana trailed him to the register, wondering, all the while, where he'd gotten the money to pay for his purchases. Surely vampires didn't work.

Shopping bag in hand, he asked, "Are you ready to go?"

"I'm hungry. I haven't had dinner yet."

His gaze slid to the pulse in her throat.

"The food court is upstairs," she said dryly.

They took the escalator to the second floor. Raiden grimaced as a myriad of odors assaulted his nostrils - fried meat, mustard, onions, sweet-and-sour chicken, salsa, French fries, popcorn, cinnamon rolls.

Raiden waited at a table while she bought a hot dog-on-a-stick, a diet coke, and a brownie. He had no idea what this century's food tasted like, no recollection of the meals he had once eaten. He existed on a warm liquid diet. And it was all around him.

Ana smiled apologetically as she took the chair across from his. "I'd offer you a bite but I know you can't eat."

"A bite?" He winked at her, revealing a hint of fang. "I'd love one."

She stared at him. Was he serious?

"Relax," he said. "I was kidding."

     Amanda Ashley

She might have thought so, if he hadn't bitten her before. As much as she had enjoyed it, she didn't want it to become a habit, didn't want him to think of her as prey.

She ate quickly, suddenly eager to get home, then wondered why she was in such a hurry when he would be going with her. What if he hadn't been kidding about wanting a bite?

* * *

Analia's hands were shaking when they got to the car. Apparently Raiden noticed, because he plucked the keys from her hand, then opened the passenger side door for her.

She looked at him in surprise. Somehow, she'd never pictured vampires driving, but then, she'd never pictured them shopping in the mall, either.

"How long have you been a vampire?" she asked as she buckled her seatbelt.

"A few hundred years." He settled in the seat and started the car. "Why?"

She shrugged. "I guess I never imagined vampires doing ordinary things."

"How did you think we spent our time?"

"I never really thought about it. How *do* you spend your time?"

"The same ways as everyone else, I suppose. We're not all that different, you and I."

"Yeah, right. I eat food. You drink blood. I sleep at night. You sleep all day. I'll get old and gray. You'll always look the way you do now."

"True enough. But there are a lot of hours between sundown and sunrise."

"So, how do you pass the nights?"

"I read a lot. Go to the movies. Watch TV. Take long walks." He swore under his breath. "And do my best to avoid hunters, like the one that's following us."

"What?" She glanced over her shoulder. A black van was close behind them.

"Listen to me," he said. "I'm going to pull over to the curb and get out. Don't go home. Go to the police station and tell them you're being followed."

"What are you going to do?"

"Don't worry about me." Tires squealed as he hit the gas. Three blocks later, he pulled over to the curb, stopped the car, and jumped out.

He disappeared into the night so quickly, it was hard to believe he'd really been there.

CHAPTER 6

Ana scrambled over the console. Once behind the wheel, she glanced over her shoulder, then pulled back onto the road. A glance in the rear-view mirror showed the black van was still behind her. An icy trickle slid down her spine as she drove to the police station, keenly aware of the car behind her.

She pulled up in front of the entrance and ran inside.

An officer sat behind a large desk. The name plate identified him as Sergeant Williams. He looked up as she hurried toward him. "Can I help you?"

"Some men in a black van were following me."

Interest sparked in his eyes. "Do you know who they were?"

"No."

"Did you get their license plate number?"

"No, I'm sorry."

"Do you have any idea why they'd be following you?"

Ana bit down on her lower lip. Unable to tell him the truth, she shook her head.

"Would you like me to have an officer follow you home?"

"Yes, please."

* * *

Ana waved at the officer when she was safely inside her house. After closing and locking the door, she kicked off her shoes, let out a gasp when she saw Raiden stretched out on the sofa, arms folded behind his head.

"How did you get in?" She dropped her handbag on the coffee table, then sank into the chair across from the couch.

"I slipped under the front door."

"You did what?"

"You heard me."

"How?"

"Watch closely."

Ana's mouth dropped open when he dissolved into a dark-gray mist that hovered over the sofa, then drifted toward her. She pressed a hand to her heart as it enveloped her. She had expected it to be cold, but it was strangely warm, and oddly pleasurable. And intimate. A flush heated her cheeks. The mist had no hands, yet it seemed to caress her.

She felt bereft when it withdrew.

In the blink of an eye, Raiden was back on the sofa.

"That was… was…" She shook her head. "I don't know what."

"Being able to disappear comes in handy from time to time."

She nodded. "How did those hunters find you?"

"The really good ones have some kind of vampire radar. Those two have been following me for months."

"Are they the ones who shot you?"

"Yeah."

"What if they come here?"

He shrugged. "I'll deal with that when it happens." Seeing the worry in her eyes, he said, "They won't hurt you."

"How do you know?"

"Most of them are decent men. They've got no axe to grind with you. If they come here, just tell them the truth, that you don't know where I am."

"What if they insist on searching my house?"

"Let them."

"You don't seem very worried."

"I've been dealing with their kind for centuries."

"So, what do they get out of hunting vampires? Satisfaction in destroying monsters? A reward?"

     Amanda Ashley

"Depends on the hunter."

"It doesn't sound like much of a life for hunter or hunted," Ana remarked.

His gaze moved over her. "It is what it is." Out of all the women he had known through the years, she was the only one who seemed to accept him without a qualm. He couldn't help wondering what made her so accepting, so willing to have him in her home.

Curious, he put the question to her.

Brow furrowed, she said, "I don't know. I guess I was a little unsettled the first night, maybe a little afraid, but you seemed so normal… I mean, I can sense your power, but…" She shook her head. "I don't know how to explain it except to say I've always loved vampires and the reality is better than fiction."

Ana's heart skipped a beat when he rose, lifted her to her feet, and took her in his arms.

"You are the most remarkable woman I've ever known."

She stared up at him, breathless, as his fingers delved into the hair at her nape.

"Analia."

His gaze burned into hers as his voice caressed her. She shivered as his hand cupped her neck and then he was lowering his head to hers. Her eyelids fluttered down as his lips touched hers. It was only the merest touch, yet she felt it down to her toes.

"Ana." He groaned her name. "Let me taste you."

Leaning into him, she turned her head to the side, giving him access to her throat.

In most movies and TV shows, there was always lots of blood and pain when a vampire fed on his prey, but she felt only a wave of exquisite pleasure and the desire to give him everything he wanted.

She moaned in protest when he lifted his head.

"You are so tempting," he murmured.

Cupping his face in her palms, she whispered, "Kiss me."

"Ana!" His arms went around her as his mouth captured hers, sending a thrill of pleasure straight to the core of her being. Just when she thought she might faint with the wonder of it, he drew back.

Pushing a lock of hair behind her ear, he said, "I think that's enough for tonight."

"Don't stop."

"You don't know what you're asking."

She gazed up at him, only then noticing the faint tinge of red in his eyes. It cooled her desire instantly.

He dropped a kiss on her brow, then put her away from him. "I'll see you tomorrow night," he promised.

And then he was gone.

Chapter 7

As was her wont, Ana went to church Sunday morning. She loved the hymns, the quiet, the words of hope and inspiration that made whatever was troubling her seem less worrisome. At the moment, her only concern was Raiden. She liked him too much, feared she could easily fall in love with him, and that was out of the question. Sure, he was handsome and dangerous and his kisses were dynamite, but they had no future together. Besides, he had people hunting him and she didn't want to get caught in the middle of that.

When the service was over, she lingered a few minutes, chatting with her neighbors, then went home to veg out. She usually spent her Sunday afternoons at her computer, surfing the net. Today, she searched vampire sites, looking for anything new.

She clicked on several links, surprised when one of them took her to a Facebook page. She read it twice, and then a third time.

Wanted. Information regarding the vampire known as Raiden.
Please leave your email address. I will make it worth your while.

There was no name on the site.

And no replies to the query. It sounded very much like they were offering a reward for information. A substantial reward.

Ana frowned. Wasn't that illegal?

Exiting the site, she sat back in her chair. Who would be looking for Raiden? An ex-lover? A bounty hunter? The IRS? Heaven help him if he hadn't paid his taxes, she thought, and burst out laughing. She had never heard of a vampire earning a living. And surely, with the passage of hundreds of years, the government had lost track of him. So the most likely person searching for him was probably a hunter.

Going into the kitchen, Ana threw a sandwich together. After pouring a glass of milk, she went into the living room to watch the five o'clock news, but she couldn't concentrate on the stories, couldn't stop wondering who was looking for Raiden and what would happen if the mysterious Facebook person found him.

As the sun went down, she wondered if Raiden would show up, and if she should tell him what she'd found.

* * *

Ana was dozing in her chair when she felt a ripple in the air that raised the hair on her arms. Bolting upright, she let out a squeak of surprise when Raiden materialized in front of her.

"Sorry," he said, smothering a grin. "I didn't mean to startle you."

"Well, you did!" she said crossly. "Can't you make a noise or something before you just magically appear?"

She gasped when he vanished. Shoulders slumped, she leaned back in her chair. She hadn't meant for him to go.

Her lips twitched when an unseen hand rang the silver bell on the mantel. "Very funny." Her heart skipped a beat when he again appeared before her.

"Better?"

"I guess so."

"I came to take you out to dinner."

Ana lifted a hand to her throat. "Dinner for who?"

"For you," he said, chuckling. "I've already… dined. What are you in the mood for?"

"Italian would be nice. But…" She jumped when he wrapped his arm around her waist, gasped when the world spun out of focus. Fear stabbed at her as darkness swallowed her up. What was he doing? It was like being on one of those crazy carnival Tilt-a-Wheels that spun faster and faster, until her stomach was in knots.

                    Amanda Ashley

Abruptly, the world righted itself.

When her head stopped spinning, she let out another gasp. "Are we... we can't be... in New York?"

"Maybe I'll take you to Naples next time. But it wasn't feasible tonight."

She nodded. Of course, the sun was shining in Italy. "How did we get here?"

"Didn't any of those books in your library tell you vampires can travel through time and space in the blink of an eye?"

"Sure, but..." She shook her head. "I thought it was just a myth. Like vampires themselves."

"Well, it isn't and we aren't. Ready?"

When she nodded, he took her hand and led her into the restaurant. They were just in time for the last seating of the night. "It's lovely," she murmured. The chairs were cream-colored with blue seats, the tables round with white cloths. A small vase of fresh flowers decorated each table.

Raiden ordered a bottle of red wine.

Ana ordered zucchini flowers—a combination of ricotta cheese and ham fried in light batter and served with a sweet vinegar sauce, rigatoni with grilled onions and peppers, and black mousse for dessert.

Ana sipped her wine while waiting for the first course, acutely aware of the man sitting across from her. She noticed that none of the woman in the place could keep their eyes off him. Not that she could blame them. He was amazingly handsome. Even the waitress had lingered at their table, batting her lashes at him.

"You're very quiet this evening," Raiden remarked.

"I guess I just can't believe I'm here. I've always wanted to come to New York."

"Would you like to stay?"

"Are you serious?"

"Just say the word."

"I'd love to, but I have to go to work tomorrow."

"Another time, then."

Her meal arrived a short time later. She picked up her fork, then hesitated, suddenly self-conscious to be eating in front of him. "It doesn't bother you, watching me eat?"

"No. Does it bother you?"

"Well, a little." She took a bite of her pasta. "Don't you miss real food?"

"Not so much anymore. I barely remember what it tasted like."

"That's so sad. Do you like being a…" She paused. "What you are?"

Raiden shrugged. "I don't have much choice. Love it or hate it, it's what I am."

"Maybe there's a cure. I mean, medical science has come a long way."

"Not that far, I'm afraid."

"Would you be… normal again, if you could?"

"I don't know. Have you ever thought about being what I am?"

"Well, sure. I mean, who hasn't wondered what it would be like to live forever and never grow old or sick, but, well, I'm not sure reality would be as good as I imagine." She looked at him over the rim of her glass. "Is it?"

"It's like everything else, I guess. It all depends on your attitude. You can spend your life looking for the good and accepting what you can't change, or you can be miserable."

Ana thought that over while she finished her meal.

To his credit, Raiden didn't stare at her while she ate.

She breathed a contented sigh as she took the last bite of mousse. "It would be awfully hard to give up something this good forever," she decided. "Although being young forever is a great inducement."

Raiden paid the check and they left the restaurant. Outside, he reached for her hand and they strolled down the street.

All the stores were closed now, and she was surprised to see so many people still out and about. No wonder it was known as the city that never sleeps, she mused.

"Are you ready to go home?" Raiden asked.

"I guess so," she said, although she wasn't looking forward to that mind-boggling experience of traveling through time and space again.

The next thing she knew, his arm was around her and they were in her living room.

She looked up at him, wishing he would kiss her goodnight.

"Your wish is my command," he said, and claimed her lips with his. His kiss was sweeter than the mousse she'd had for dessert. She leaned into him, her heart urging her to let him make love to her even as her common sense argued that allowing herself to care for this man was dangerous. He wasn't human. Hunters were after him. What if she got caught in the crossfire? What if they thought she was a vampire, too? She had yearned for a little excitement in her life, but putting herself in danger was foolish—almost as foolish as caring for him.

Common sense told her to send him away, the sooner the better. She wanted things he could never give her—a normal life doing ordinary things with an ordinary man, security, children.

But she didn't object when he kissed her again.

Or refuse when he asked for another taste.

CHAPTER 8

Ana could hardly keep her eyes open at Jacobs & Johnson on Monday morning. It was equally difficult to concentrate on the task at hand when all she could think about was being in Raiden's arms, the heat of his kisses, the way it felt when he drank from her… why didn't she find that more repulsive? She was feeding a vampire, for goodness sakes! She should at least be afraid. Horrified. Repelled. Instead, she couldn't wait to be in his arms again. Had he worked some kind of vampire magic on her? Was that why she was so accepting?

With a shake of her head, she clicked "Print" on her computer. Mr. Jacobs wouldn't be happy if his report was late!

* * *

Later, at lunch with Jade, it was all she could do to keep from telling her friend about Raiden. Of course, Jade knew she was hiding something.

"You might as well me," Jade coaxed. "I can see you're dying to tell me something. You got a raise? You're getting a haircut? You met a new man! Oh, that's it, isn't it? Tell me everything."

It was oh, so tempting. Instead, Ana said, "Well, I did meet a new guy. He's gorgeous but I don't think we have any future together."

Amanda Ashley

"Why not?"

Ana shrugged. "We really don't have anything in common." *Except for the passion that burns so bright between us.* "And even though he doesn't look it, he's a lot older than I am." *Centuries older.*

"So, just have an affair."

"No, I don't think that's a good idea."

"When do I get to meet him? Oh! I know. Bring him to the company Halloween party Friday night."

* * *

Ana weighed the pros and cons of inviting Raiden to the party. She supposed it was the perfect place to take a vampire on a date because he could just be himself and no one would be the wiser.

She put the question to him after dinner that night.

"A costume party. Hmm. Who should I come as?"

"Gosh." Anna tapped her finger on her chin. "Let me think. Iron Man? Doctor Strange? Jack Sparrow? I know! How about a vampire?"

"Great idea! Why didn't I think of that? I know just what to wear."

"I'll bet you do," Ana muttered.

"What are you going as?"

Lips twitching in a half-smile, she said, "Can't you guess?" Her costume was black lace over black silk with a red satin insert down the front. Very Gothic in appearance. She had also bought a rather expensive black wig, a pair of thigh-high black boots, and fangs, of course.

"A vampire hunter?"

"No, silly. A lady vampire. But speaking of hunters, I saw a Facebook page today that mentioned your name."

He nodded. "I've seen it."

"Do you know who posted it?"

"No, although I'm pretty sure it's one of the hunters who were following us the other night."

"It doesn't worry you?"

He shrugged. "If they find me, they find me."

She didn't want to know what would happen if they did.

* * *

Raiden went hunting that night after Analia had gone to bed. He was, he thought, getting far too fond of the pretty little redhead. He told himself she was just a woman like any other, but it wasn't true. There was something that drew him to her night after night. It was more than the fact that she was good company and easy on the eyes. More than her ready acceptance of who and what he was. More than the taste of her blood, although it was by far the sweetest, most satisfying he had ever tasted.

So what was it?

With a rueful shake of his head, he summoned his chosen prey to him, quickly took that which he desired, and released the woman from his thrall.

He had taken as much as he needed. Yet he still thirsted for a sip of Ana's sweetness.

Before he realized what he was doing, he was standing at her bedside. Murmuring, "Forgive me," he took her in his arms and satisfied his craving.

* * *

Ana woke up feeling sluggish, listless. Was she coming down with something? Maybe she had a fever. Heaven knew her dreams last night had been hot enough to set the sheets and blankets on fire. She'd never had fantasies like that in her whole life. Even now, she could feel herself blushing at the memory.

A glance at the clock had her jumping out of bed and into the shower.

* * *

"So, did you talk to your mysterious beau?" Jade asked later, at lunch.

"Yes, he's coming with me. How are you and Jeff doing? Has he popped the question yet?"

"Girl, if he had, you'd know it. We bought our costumes last night. We going as Han Solo and Leia."

Ana nodded. Jade's father was a huge *Star Wars* fan and he'd passed his love of the movies on to his daughter. Her house was filled with posters and figures, lightsabers and dozens of Funko Pop characters. All the decorations on her Christmas tree were *Star Wars*

                    Amanda Ashley

themed. Her tree-topper was a light-up Yoda.

Ana finished her sandwich and downed the last of her soda. "Gotta go. See you tomorrow."

* * *

Sighing, Ana shut down her computer. Finally, it was time to go home. She smiled at the thought of seeing Raiden again. But seven o'clock came and went. And eight. And nine, and there was still no sign of him.

At ten, she went to shower and get ready for bed.

At eleven, she crawled under the covers and turned out the light, wondering if she should be hurt because he hadn't shown up—or worried that some hunter had found him.

* * *

Raiden cursed softly as he dissolved into mist and drifted away on the breeze. Damn hunter. He had lost track of how many times this same slayer had tracked him down.

After leaving the hunter behind, he resumed his corporeal shape and strolled toward Analia's house. He regretted not getting there before she went to bed. Funny, how important she had become in such a short time. Until he met Ana, he'd had nothing to look forward to. Now, she was his first thought on waking, his last as he slid into the dark sleep.

Materializing inside her house, he padded down the hallway to her bedroom. She slept on her left side, her cheek pillowed on her hand, her toes peeking out from under the blankets. Murmuring, "Sweet dreams, Ana love," he kissed her brow and then, as the sun chased the moon from the sky, he willed himself into the attic.

Her scent followed him into the nothingness of oblivion.

* * *

Ana was singing along with the radio when she pulled into her driveway. Every now and then, her boss closed early on Wednesdays so he could play golf with his brother and this was one of those days.

Feeling like a kid who'd only had to go to school for half a day, she skipped along the walkway to the front stairs. She was happy to be home early, though she had no idea what to do with the rest of the day. She could always go shopping, or catch up on her laundry, or stream the last few episodes of her favorite show.

Inside, Ana kicked off her shoes, tossed her handbag on the coffee table, and then glanced at her watch. Hours until sundown. One of the biggest drawbacks in dating a vampire was being unable to call him during the day. Of course, calling a guy was something she rarely did. Still, she had spent most of the morning worrying about her vampire, and how silly was that? If anyone could take care of himself, it was Raiden.

Thinking of him reminded her that she'd forgotten to put out one of her favorite Halloween decorations. It was old and a little discolored, but the crystal ball had belonged to her grandfather. He had sworn it was the genuine article and had once belonged to a famous Gypsy medium.

Ana smiled as she climbed the stairs to the attic, remembering how Grampy Collins had gathered his grandchildren around the dining room table every year, gazed intently into the crystal, and told their fortunes.

Opening the attic door, she pulled the chain to turn on the light, blinked and blinked again at the sight that met her eyes. Raiden lay on an old blanket on the floor in the far corner.

She took an instinctive step back. The floorboard creaked beneath her weight. And he was suddenly awake and standing, his fangs bared, his eyes glowing a hellish red.

Ana spun on her heels and raced down the stairs as if the devil and all the hounds of hell were snapping at her heels.

 Amanda Ashley

Chapter 9

Raiden cursed in several languages as Analia bolted from the room. Not that he could blame her. He knew how he looked—his face distorted, fangs fully extended, eyes a hellish shade of red. But it couldn't be helped. His instinct for self-preservation had wakened him from the dark sleep as soon as the door opened. He had reacted instinctively to an unexpected intrusion.

He raked a hand through his hair. Perhaps it was for the best. Her view of vampires had been skewed, based on books and movies that portrayed vampires as sympathetic, heroic victims rather than the blood-thirsty creatures they really were.

He would likely be doing her a favor if he vanished from her life completely. He considered it for several minutes, but even as he did so, he knew he wouldn't leave her. Not unless she sent him away.

* * *

Ana ran into her bedroom and locked the door behind her. She stood there a moment, one hand pressed to her heart, breathing as if she'd run a marathon. She didn't know why she'd been so frightened. She had seen his fangs before, the red glow in his eyes. Still, he had never looked quite so dangerous or so menacing.

Sitting on the edge of the bed, she took several slow, deep breaths.

Nothing to be afraid of, she thought. It was just Raiden.

The vampire.

What was he doing now? Had he gone back to sleep, or whatever it was he did when the sun was up? At least one mystery had been solved. She knew where he took his rest.

She drummed her fingertips on the mattress as a mental image of how he had looked flashed through her mind. She hated to admit it, but he'd scared the daylights out of her. She considered going back up after Grampy Collins' crystal ball, but decided against it. She'd retrieve it some other time, when Raiden wasn't here.

A knock on the door had her practically jumping out of her skin. It could only be her uninvited guest.

"Ana? I know you're in there. I can hear your heart beating."

No surprise there, she thought ruefully. "What do you want?"

"I just want to apologize for scaring you. My reaction is instinctive when someone approaches me while I'm at rest. You must know I don't mean you any harm."

She mulled that over.

"Do you want me to leave?"

"Yes. No." Blowing out a sigh, she opened the bedroom door, relieved to see that he looked like himself again.

"I really am sorry," he said quietly.

"You should have told me you were staying in my attic." She frowned at him. "How can you be awake? The sun is still up."

He shrugged. "I'm okay as long as I don't go outside."

"Then why don't you sleep at night like everyone else?"

"It isn't natural for me to be awake during the day. The sun weakens me, leaves me vulnerable."

"Oh. Where were you last night?" She clapped her hand over her mouth. She hadn't meant to ask. After all, it was none of her business.

"I ran into that hunter again. I've known some dedicated slayers in my time, but this guy…" Raiden shook his head. "He just won't quit. He must have some kind of super radar because no matter where I go, he manages to track me down."

"I'm sorry."

"It's not your fault."

Ana's gaze slid away from his. He was a vampire. He had frightened her more than she wanted to admit, but she couldn't help remembering what it was like to be in his arms. And how crazy was

     Amanda Ashley

that?

"Do you mind if I take my rest in your attic?"

She considered it a moment, then shook her head. "I guess not. But you should have told me that you were staying there."

"You're right."

"Is it safe?"

"For who? You or me?"

"Both."

"I'll know if he's nearby."

"I guess it's okay then."

"In that case, I'll see you in a couple of hours. What can I do to show you how sorry I am for frightening you?"

"Just don't do it again."

"I promise." Taking her hand in his, Raiden turned it over and kissed her palm. He would rather have taken her in his arms and kissed her until her knees were weak, but the darkness was whispering his name and he had no choice but to answer.

* * *

Ana sat on the sofa, an untouched cup of tea cradled in her hands. Was she making a mistake, letting Raiden stay here? What did she really know about him? Nothing, except that he was an old vampire and a hunter was after him. What did he really want with her? When he asked if he could stay in the attic, maybe she should have told him to leave.

Suddenly needing to be out of the house, she called Jade. They made arrangements to meet for lunch at their favorite sushi place, then take in an early movie. And perhaps dinner afterwards.

It wasn't that she needed to get out of the house, she admitted as she grabbed her handbag and a jacket. It was Raiden she needed to get away from.

At least for today.

* * *

It rained Thursday morning. Not a light mist, not a shower, but a deluge that came down in sheets. The skies were black and lowering. Lighting lit up the clouds. Thunder pounded overhead like Apache war drums.

Ana sat at the kitchen table, a cup of coffee at her elbow, wishing she didn't have to go to work. A glance at the clock warned her she'd better get a move on if she didn't want to be late.

She was about to step into the shower when the phone rang.

Her boss' voice boomed over the phone. "Analia? I'm glad I caught you at home. The power's out here on the south side. The electric company says it's likely to be out most of the day. If you don't hear from me by tonight, I'll expect you to be at work in the morning."

"All right. Thanks for letting me know."

"Stay dry," he said with a chuckle, and ended the call.

"Thank you, Lord," Ana murmured. Stepping back into her slippers, she pulled on her robe and headed downstairs, looking forward to another cup of coffee and a day off with nothing to do.

She let out a startled gasp when she stepped into the kitchen and found Raiden sitting at the table. In spite of her surprise, her first thought was that she hadn't brushed her hair or her teeth.

"So," he drawled. "No work today?"

She started to ask how he knew, then realized that, with his enhanced senses, he had probably overheard Mr. Johnson's call. Or read her mind. "Right. The office is closed because of the storm," she said, taking the seat across from his. "A whole day off with nothing to do."

"I think you were looking for this the other day." He reached for something on the floor. When he straightened up again, he had her grandfather's crystal ball in his hands.

"Thank you. I've been meaning to get it, but…" She shrugged. He was asleep up there during the day and at night, when she was with him, she didn't think about it. "My Grampy Collins said it was the real thing."

"Yeah? Was he a fortune teller?"

"Only to us kids. I remember one year he made my mom really mad because he told me and my sister what we were getting from Santa Claus." Ana laughed at the memory.

The sound, the sparkle in her eyes, touched something deep inside Raiden. He had no such happy memories. He had been born into poverty and never known anything else until he ran into a vampire late one night. The same vampire who had killed his wife, his two daughters, and his unborn child. For decades he had wished the

     Amanda Ashley

vampire had killed him, too.

Ana's laughter died at the formidable expression on Raiden's face. "What's wrong?"

"Nothing. I was somewhere else for a moment. Tell me more about your family."

"Well, there's really not much to tell. My dad works as a lab technician. My mom was a dental assistant. She quit work until Gina and I were in high school. My folks live in Washington. My sister lives in Portland with her husband, Jason. I work as a receptionist at the law firm of Jacobs & Johnson."

He nodded. A typical American family. "Where'd you get your fascination with vampires?"

"Old movies, I guess. My grandfather loved Halloween. And old horror flicks. You know, *The Wolfman, Frankenstein, The Mummy, Dracula…*" She shrugged. "I guess I never outgrew it."

"I must say I'm glad you didn't," he said with a smile. And then he sobered. "You were gone when I woke last night."

Ana's gaze slid away from his. "Yes. I went out with one of my girlfriends."

"You were avoiding me because of what happened yesterday afternoon."

She started to deny it, but what was the point when he could read her mind? "Yes."

"Are you afraid of me now?"

"No." She wasn't afraid of what he was. She was afraid of the way he made her feel, of the strong sexual attraction between them, and where that might lead.

"Do you want me to leave?" he asked quietly.

Biting down on her lower lip. Ana met his gaze. Then shook her head. Right or wrong, she wanted him to stay. "I want to know about you. Living so long, you must have seen a lot of changes in the world."

A muscle twitched in his jaw. "My life is not something I care to talk about or remember."

"Has it been so bad?"

"You have no idea."

She mulled that over for a moment. How could she get to know him if he wouldn't talk about himself or his past? She'd let it go for now, she thought, and then frowned. "I can't get used to your being awake during the day."

"Like I said, I'm okay as long as I stay inside. If it's stormy, the way it is now, I can even go outside, as long as the clouds hide the sun. Makes it seem like night."

"Ah." She glanced out the window. "I love to walk in the rain."

"I'd be happy to walk with you."

"Really?" At his nod, she said, "Just let me go get dressed. I won't be but a minute."

* * *

Ana felt a shiver of delight when Raiden reached for her hand.

"Have you always liked walking in the rain?" he asked.

She nodded. "Ever since I was a little girl. My dad used to take me. He made it seem like an adventure, bundling me up in a heavy jacket and boots and gloves. We'd walk through the puddles on our way to the park. There was a shallow depression in the middle of a grassy area that always filled with about a foot of water. He always let me run through it. It seemed kind of dangerous to me at the time. Did your dad..." She bit down on her lower lip, remembering that he didn't like to talk about his past.

They strolled in silence for a time.

Raiden glanced at Ana. She was fairly bursting with curiosity about his life before he was turned. He had never shared his past with anyone before, but perhaps Ana had a right to know. "Talking about my mortal life is painful," he said quietly. "I was born in Romania. It's a beautiful country. We lived in a small village, just a few hundred people. Marriages were arranged in those days. My parents chose the youngest girl of the family who lived on the farm next to ours."

"Were you happy together?"

"We weren't unhappy. Life was hard, but it was good. We had two daughters... and a child on the way. And then one night three vampires attacked us while we were on our way home from visiting my in-laws. It happened so fast..." Raiden clenched his hands at his sides.

"It's all right," Ana said. "You don't have to tell me anymore."

"But you'd like to know."

"Well... yes. But not if the memories make you unhappy."

"Like I was saying, it all happened so fast. They killed Crina and

　　　　　Amanda Ashley

my daughters. I tried to save them, but there was nothing I could do. When one of the monsters turned on me, I didn't fight him. I wanted to die, too. But he didn't kill me… I don't know why.

"When I woke the next night, I was a vampire, although I didn't realize it at first. Not until Crina's father came by and I attacked him. I stopped before I killed him. Horrified by what I'd done, I left the village."

Raiden fell silent. When he spoke again, his voice was flat, void of emotion. "The next few years are a blur of blood and death. I hunted the vampires who had killed my family and when I found them, I destroyed them." Killing his master hadn't been easy, though it could have been worse. Luckily, the one who turned him wasn't more than a fledgling himself. Had he been ancient, it would have been impossible. "After that, I left Romania. I don't remember where I went or how I got there.

"Gradually, I learned to control the hunger that plagued me. Countries changed. The old ways died. Hunters flourished. I left Europe and came to America, hoping to find a new life." Taking her hand again, he resumed walking. "Try as you might, you can't escape what you are."

CHAPTER 10

Ana thought about what Raiden had said off and on at work the next day. *You can't escape what you are.* But what if he could? What if there *was* a cure for vampirism?

Instead of meeting Jade on her lunch hour, she found a quiet corner and spent the time online looking for vampire cures. One site said you couldn't turn a vampire into a human again because they were already human. Another said killing the one who turned the vampire might do the trick, but Raiden had killed the one who turned him, so that didn't work. A third link said it was caused by a virus and there was no cure for it. The last one she read said there was supposedly some miracle potion, but no one knew what it was or, if it was real, where it was.

Discouraged, she went back to work. It wasn't until she was on her way home that she remembered the company party was that night.

* * *

In the attic, Raiden listened to Ana as she got dressed for the party. He grinned ruefully, thinking that whatever the season, he was always in costume. Ana was humming softly. She was unlike any woman he had ever known—a mixture of wisdom and naiveté,

　　　Amanda Ashley

sensuality and innocence. But, most amazing of all was her acceptance of what he was. He knew she was occasionally frightened of him, but then, who could blame her?

At seven o'clock, he went downstairs.

Ana grinned when he entered the living room. "I love your costume."

"And I, yours." She looked ravishing. The dress, floor-length with long sleeves and a modest V-neck, covered every inch of her yet she had never looked sexier or more desirable. "Are you ready to go?"

"Yes, just let me grab my keys and my coat." The rain had let up, but the sky was still overcast.

* * *

The party was in full swing when they arrived at the hotel. The sound of so many beating hearts, the scent of so much blood, quickly aroused Raiden's hunger. With an effort, he tamped it down, thinking he should have fed earlier.

After checking Ana's coat, they moved into the ballroom, which was appropriately decorated. No cheap costumes here, he noted. Cowboys, knights, kings, queens, clowns, wizards and witches, Star Wars and Disney characters, and of course, vampires, milled around the room. The costumes, most of which must have cost hundreds of dollars, all looked authentic.

A long buffet table held sandwiches and salads, a variety of finger foods, drinks, and a dozen kinds of dessert. Other tables of varying sizes were scattered around the edge of the floor. Most were occupied.

"Would you care for a drink?" Ana asked. "The company's paying for everything."

"A glass of red wine would just hit the spot." And hopefully help ease his hunger.

Ana ordered a strawberry daiquiri for herself.

They were looking for a table when Jade waved them over.

"Do you mind if we sit with my friend?" Ana asked. "Jade's been dying… oops, wrong choice of words! Shall we say *anxious* to meet you."

"Lead the way."

Ana grinned at the look on Jade's face when she got a look at

Raiden.

Introductions were made and Raiden and Jade's date, Brett, shook hands.

"Nice turn out," Ana remarked after she and Raiden were seated.

Jade nodded. "Even old Mr. Johnson is here. He's the head of the company," she told Raiden. "He's close to ninety and rarely attends company functions. I'm surprised he's here tonight."

"I heard he was going to retire and turn everything over to his son, who's happens to be my boss," Ana remarked. "I'm not sure I'm ready for that."

After a few minutes of conversation, Raiden asked Ana to dance. Excusing themselves, they left the table.

"Are you enjoying yourself?" Ana asked.

"Always, when you're in my arms."

She smiled up at him. "We don't have to stay if you want to leave."

He shrugged. "I'll stay as long as you want."

"Do you mind if I get something to eat?" Ana asked when the song ended.

"Of course not. I'm going to step outside for a few minutes."

She lifted one brow.

"I need a little fresh air."

"Oh? You won't be gone long, will you?"

"No." He squeezed her hand. "Enjoy your meal."

Jade got in line behind Ana at the buffet. "Girl, he is gorgeous, although he seems a little pale, don't you think?"

"He burns easily, so he tends to avoid the sun."

"Really? He doesn't look like the hot-house flower type," Jade said, grinning. "Anyway, tell me everything! Is it serious?"

Ana shook her head. "No."

"No? I don't believe you. I mean, the way he looks at you. The way *you* look at *him*?" Jade shook her head. "Girl, I saw sparks."

"I told you, we don't have anything in common. And he's older…"

"Who cares? Ana, don't let this one get away."

* * *

Raiden prowled the outskirts of the hotel, searching for prey. He didn't have to wait long. A young couple dressed as Padme and

　　　　Amanda Ashley

Anakin emerged through a side door. They paused, startled to see him waiting there.

It took only moments for Raiden to mesmerize them both, take what he needed, and release them from his thrall.

Muttering, "May the Force be with you," he returned to the ballroom.

* * *

Ana searched Raiden's face when he returned to their table. He'd fed. She wasn't sure how she knew. He didn't look any different, she thought. Or did he? Not quite so pale, perhaps.

Reaching for her hand, he said, "Let's dance."

A wave of contentment swept over Ana when he took her in his arms. They moved together as if they'd partnered for years.

Raiden tilted her chin up, his gaze intent on hers. "What is it?"

When she didn't answer, she felt the brush of his mind against hers.

"Yes, I went out for a bite," he said, answering her unspoken question. "Is that a problem?"

"No, it's just that… that I knew you'd… ah, dined, and I was wondering how I could tell. You don't look any different."

"The changes are extremely subtle. Most mortals don't detect anything. I'm surprised you did."

"Me, too," she said. And wondered what it meant, and why she was able to pick up on something so intangible in someone she hardly knew.

An hour later, Ana was ready to go home. She said goodbye to Jade and Brett while Raiden retrieved her coat.

Outside, she handed him her keys, slid into the seat when he opened her door. She felt a rush of nerves as he drove home though she wasn't sure why. It was almost as if she were standing on the edge of a precipice where one wrong step could mean redemption or destruction.

Raiden didn't have to look at Ana to sense her distress, though he had no idea what was troubling her. For once, he couldn't read her thoughts. Did she realize she was blocking him, and if so, how was she able to do it?

He pulled into the driveway and cut the engine then went around to open her door.

He trailed her up the stairs and into the house. "Analia? What's wrong?"

She gazed up at him, wishing he would kiss her. When he lowered his head to hers, she closed her eyes. It seemed incredible that he was here, this amazing man who was so much more than a mere mortal. She scarcely knew him—perhaps she would never really know him— and yet she had never been drawn to anyone the way she was to him. The thought gave her pause. Was he manipulating her thoughts? Making her feel this way because of some ulterior motive on his part?

Frowning, she pushed him away.

"Something wrong?" he asked.

"Are you making me feel this way? Using some kind of vampire compulsion?"

"Is that what you think?"

"I don't know. I've never felt this way about anyone before."

"Neither have I, not for centuries." His knuckles brushed her cheek. "Maybe you're practicing a little feminine witchcraft on me."

"Maybe I am," Ana said, grinning. "My great grandfather was rumored to be a practicing witch."

Raiden grunted softly. A witch in Ana's background might explain how she was able to block her thoughts. "You're the prettiest sorceress I've ever seen."

"Don't tell you believe in that kind of thing?"

"Why wouldn't I?"

She frowned. Why not, indeed? If there were vampires, why not warlocks and witches. Maybe she possessed a little magic. Maybe that was why she'd been able to detect the subtle changes in Raiden after he fed? "Everything's happening so fast between us. I don't even know you."

"Nor I you." His gaze caressed her. "But I'd like to change that."

Ana's heart skipped a beat. "Why?"

"Why?" He drew her into his arms again. "Because no woman I've ever known has accepted me the way you have, or made me feel like a man instead of a monster." His finger traced her lower lip, back and forth. "I love your smile, the sound of your laughter, the way your heart beats with excitement when we've together."

"Oh."

He smiled down at her. "I haven't compelled you in any way," he

Amanda Ashley

assured her. "Your feelings, whatever they are, are your own."

"So, where do we go from here?"

"I guess that's up to you." His knuckles grazed her cheek, ever so lightly, and then he kissed her until her toes curled and she stood breathless in his arms. "Whatever you decide, my sweet Amalia, be sure it's what you want."

Chapter 11

Raiden's parting words followed Ana to sleep and were waiting for her when she woke up Saturday morning.

Whatever you decide, be sure it's what you want.

What *did* she want? Did he expect her to make some sort of choice now, when they had known each other such a short time? Was he pushing her because he planned to leave the city soon?

What did *she* want? Was she falling in love with Raiden? She enjoyed spending time with him. Just being near him made her happy. His kisses filled her with desire. His voice did funny things in the pit of her stomach. And when he took her in his embrace… She blew out a sigh. She would gladly stay in his arms forever. But… did she want to spend the rest of her life with a vampire? She would age and he would not. Gazing into the future, she saw herself taking all her meals alone, going to church by herself, never having children, always waiting for the sun to go down so they could be together.

Changing her whole life so she could be with him.

Did she want to be a vampire? The longer they were together, the more likely it became that she would find herself thinking about that. Maybe asking him to turn her. As sure as she knew he was sleeping upstairs, she knew it was a decision she would one day have to make if they stayed together.

She tried to imagine what it would be like—sleeping days, existing

Amanda Ashley

on nothing but a warm, liquid diet, lying to her parents about why she couldn't open presents on Christmas morning, never again eating any of her favorite foods, not being able to see herself in a mirror… Of course, being able to turn into mist or to simply will herself wherever she wished to be might be fun. But then, if she was a vampire, where would she go?

Throwing back the covers, she padded barefoot into the kitchen and started a fresh pot of coffee.

Taking a seat at the table while she waited for the Mocha Java to brew, she glanced up. Raiden slept in her attic. When he wasn't hiding out, did he sleep in a coffin? Or a bed?

He could be awake in the daylight as long as clouds hid the sun. Could all vampires do that? Or just the old ones?

If she stayed with Raiden, would they live here, in her house? Or would he insist that they move? Did he have a place of his own? If so, how often did he have to move so people didn't notice that he never aged?

So many questions—and they all came down to one—what *did* she want?

* * *

In the attic, Raiden stirred, awakened by Ana's tumultuous thoughts. She had many questions, many doubts, not that he could blame her. Choosing to stay with him was not a choice to be made lightly. Hoping he could accept whatever she decided, he slid back into oblivion.

* * *

Ana weighed the pros and cons of staying with Raiden all that day. Whether she was dusting, vacuuming, changing the sheets on her bed, or taking time out to watch the latest Tom Cruise movie on Netflix, Raiden preoccupied her thoughts.

By dinner time, she was no closer to a decision than she had been when she woke up that morning.

Ana was putting her plate in the dishwasher when she sensed a tremor in the air and knew Raiden was standing behind her. She took a deep breath, then turned to face him. "Hi."

"Evening." For the first time since she'd met him, he looked uncertain. "How was your day?"

Ana shrugged. She had the feeling he knew exactly how her day had been and that he was aware of every single thought that had flitted through her mind. "Pretty much like every other Saturday."

"Mine, too," he said with a lopsided grin.

She cocked her head to the side. "You didn't really need to ask, did you?"

"No. Your concerns came through loud and clear."

Feeling uncomfortable, Ana pulled out a chair and sat down. "Do you have any advice?"

Taking the chair across from hers, he said, "Sadly, no. This is a decision only you can make. But there's no hurry, unless you want me to leave."

"I don't. After all, I've known you less than two weeks. Even if you were just a normal guy, I'd need a little more time."

"Time is something I have plenty of."

She nodded, wishing she had centuries instead of years.

"I can make it possible," he said quietly. "Just say the word."

"How is it done, exactly? Is it like in the books and movies?"

"Depends on the movie or the book."

Of course, she thought. In some instances, the vampire had to bite the mortal three times. But it always involved an exchange of blood. His next words confirmed it.

"I would drink from you until you were at the point of death and then give you my blood. You would remain unconscious until you woke the next night, a fledgling vampire."

"Does it hurt?"

The one who turned him hadn't been concerned about Raiden's feelings. He had gorged himself and then, for some unknown reason, he had decided to spare his prey's life. "It depends on the vampire," he said, pushing old memories aside. "I would make it pleasant for you."

"Have you ever turned anyone else?"

"No."

"Have you ever wanted to?"

"You mean another woman?"

She hesitated a moment before saying, "Yes."

His gaze burned into hers. "I never met a woman I wanted to spend eternity with. Until you."

          Amanda Ashley

Raiden's words warmed Ana to the very depths of her being. Somehow she was on his lap, her arms twined around his neck, his mouth hot on hers, his hands sliding restlessly up and down her back as his tongue stroked hers. She pressed against him, her whole body on fire for his touch, her heart racing as if she'd run a 5K as fast as she could. Where had he learned to kiss like that?

Her moan of pleasure was muffled as he groaned his need. It cut through the hazy fog of passion that had engulfed her. Breathless, she pulled away from him. "Raiden… we have to… to stop."

He groaned again, longer, deeper, his desire evident.

Ana eased off his lap, took a deep breath, and poured herself a glass of cold water. If she wasn't careful, she was going to give herself to him body and soul. She could feel his gaze—as hot as his kisses—burning into her back.

"Ana, are you all right?"

Blowing out a breath, she turned to face him. Her voice was somewhat shaky when she said, "Why wouldn't I be?"

"I can hear your heart pounding," he answered with a wicked grin. "I can smell your…"

"Never mind!" She turned away, her cheeks flaming.

She stiffened when his arms crept around her waist, then relaxed against him. There was no use pretending that she didn't want him or that his kisses had no effect on her senses. She was mad for him.

But was that enough?

She flinched when someone knocked at the door. Of all the times for a visitor, she thought irritably. Or maybe it was the best time.

Slipping out of Raiden's arms, she smoothed her skirt, combed her fingers through her hair and went to see who had come calling.

* * *

Leaving the safety chain in place, Ana peered outside. A man of medium height with shaggy blond hair and a crooked nose stood on the porch, his eyes hidden behind dark glasses. "Can I help you?" she asked.

"Yes, ma'am," he said, "I'm looking for a… a man. Raiden. Have you seen him?"

"I'm sorry, no."

"I'm sorry, but you're lying," he said, and kicked in the door.

Before Ana could react, he shoved past her, his head snapping back and forth as he perused the room. She was about to ask what the hell he thought he was doing when Raiden stepped out of the kitchen.

The stranger stopped in his tracks, his right hand delving into his jacket pocket. It came out holding a pistol, which he fired point-blank at Raiden's chest.

Ana screamed as blood splattered across the wall behind Raiden. One minute he was standing there, the next his hand was around the stranger's throat and he was lifting him off the floor.

The man dropped the gun, his fingers clawing helplessly at the hand slowly choking off his breath.

Ana pressed her hand to her mouth as the intruder's face turned blue and then purple. When he stopped kicking, Raiden let him go.

Like a puppet with the strings cut, the man crumpled to the floor and lay still.

"Did you… is he…?" She had never seen a dead body before, but this one definitely looked dead.

Jaw set, Raiden nodded.

"Who… who was he?"

"I don't know his name, but he's been tracking me for almost a year."

"He was a hunter?"

"Yeah."

"Did you have to…" Fighting the urge to vomit, she made a vague gesture toward the body.

Raiden didn't answer. Instead, he headed for the attic stairs. Only then did she remember that he'd been shot. Was this hunter the same one who had wounded him before?

She filled a bowl with warm water, found a couple of old towels and then, filled with trepidation, she followed Raiden up the stairs.

He was stretched out on the floor, not moving, his eyes closed.

Kneeling beside him, she peeled off his shirt. The bullet hole—small and round—had barely missed his heart. "Raiden? It's me. I'm just going to wash away the blood."

He grunted.

With hands none too steady, she soaked a cloth in the water and wiped away the blood, noting, as she did so, that the wound was already closing, though it remained red and angry-looking. Silver, she

     Amanda Ashley

thought. Had it pierced his heart, it would have killed him.

She dried his chest with a clean towel, then, remembering that the bullet had gone through him, she nudged him onto his back. The exit wound was larger, ugly and ragged. She wiped away the blood, then sat there, just watching him. It took her a few moments to realize he had probably slipped into the dark, healing sleep of his kind. Leaning forward, she brushed a kiss across his brow, then gathered up the towels and bowl and tiptoed toward the stairs.

"Ana." His voice was heavy, tinged with pain.

Pausing in the doorway, she glanced over her shoulder.

"I'll take care of the body later. And repair the door."

Nodding, she left the attic. Downstairs, she gathered the bloody towels and the bowl and carried them outside. She tossed the soiled cloths into the trash can, dumped the water on the grass.

He could have been killed. Even though she had known Raiden only a short time, he had burrowed his way deep into her heart. She tried to imagine her life without him and couldn't. And that, she mused, gazing up at the sky, was the answer to her dilemma.

Or maybe not. He had killed a man in her house, in front of her very eyes. Self-defense or not, he had killed a man. Surely, with his amazing powers, he could have spared the hunter's life. Then again, Raiden had told her the man had been hunting him for almost a year. Had Raiden let the hunter live, it was unlikely the man would have given up.

Returning to the house, Ana found an old blanket, suppressed a shudder as she covered the body. Though it was still early, she took a quick shower, slipped into her nightgown and climbed into bed.

She didn't turn off the light.

Closing her eyes, Ana took several, deep calming breaths, but sleep wouldn't come. Sitting up, she reached for the paperback on the bedside table, but she couldn't concentrate on the story. Try as she might, all she could think about was the vampire in the attic and the body on the living room floor.

She couldn't live like this. Although she loved having Raiden here in spite of everything, she couldn't face the thought of another night like this one. From now on, she would always wonder if some other hunter would burst into her house one night and end up dead on the floor. Or, worse, have some hunter show up and drive a stake into Raiden's heart.

Better to end it now, before he burrowed any deeper into her life. Before telling him goodbye became impossible.

Chapter 12

It was nearing three a.m. when Raiden padded down the stairs and into the living room. He grinned wryly when he saw the blanket covering the corpse. Very tidy, his Ana, he mused as he lifted the body, blanket and all, and willed himself to a vacant lot in the next town.

With preternatural speed and strength, he dug a hole six-feet deep and lowered the shrouded hunter into the grave. After filling it in, he dusted off his hands and went in search of prey. There were vampires who fed off the dead, but he had never done so.

He walked for several blocks. The streets were deserted and quiet. Only two kinds of people tended to be awake at this time of the morning—bad guys and the men and women who arrested them.

He was about to give up the hunt when he saw a police officer checking the door of a drug store. The cop looked up at the sound of Raiden's footsteps. Raiden mesmerized him with a glance. After quickly satisfying his thirst, he released the man from his thrall, and dissolved into mist.

Raiden resumed his own form inside Ana's house. He paused on his way back to the attic, turned, and made his way into her bedroom.

He wasn't surprised to find her sleeping with the light on. Truth be told, he was surprised she hadn't thrown him out of the house. She lay curled on her side beneath a pale pink blanket. He lifted a lock of her silky hair, letting it sift through his fingers as his mind brushed hers.

She was dreaming… of him. A thought took him inside her mind, into her dreams, his real self replacing her dream image…

They were sitting on the edge of a long, wooden pier. A bright moon shone down on them. She was staring out at the ocean, at the moonlight reflected on the face of the water. Unable to resist, he took her in his arms and kissed her. She kissed him back and then she stood. Puzzled, he stood beside her. She smiled up at him, then she took his hand and they jumped off the edge of the pier. She let out a shriek as the water turned to blood…

He withdrew from her mind and the room when she bolted upright, a second scream issuing from her throat.

Breathing hard, Ana pressed a hand to her chest as she glanced wildly around the room. She looked down at her nightgown, expecting it to be covered in blood, but it was still pale pink.

Not real. Not real. Just a nightmare.

And yet… She frowned as she slid back under the covers and closed her eyes. Was it her imagination or was that Raiden's scent on her hair?

* * *

When her alarm went off, Analia got up, dressed, and walked to church. She needed inspiration. She needed peace. She needed to decide what to do about Raiden.

As always, Ana lost herself in the quiet beauty of the chapel, the comforting words of the hymns. The sermon that morning was on love, hope, and forgiveness.

Ana sighed. Did she love Raiden? Could they possibly have a life together? Could she forgive him for all the lives he had taken? How could she reconcile sharing her life with a man who had taken innocent lives?

Her gaze wandered to the beautiful painting of the Savior that hung on the wall behind the altar. She looked at Him for several moments and then smiled faintly. Raiden's sins weren't hers, nor were they hers to forgive.

She wondered if the minister had somehow read her thoughts when he intoned, "We are required to pardon all those who offend us. But only the good Lord can forgive men—and women—of their iniquities."

Ana frowned. Did Divine clemency include vampires?

It was raining outside when the service was over. Ana took shelter in the small coffee shop around the corner from the church. She ordered a cup of hot chocolate and carried it to an empty table.

A moment later, Raiden ducked inside. He looked remarkably dry. How was that possible?

Her heart skipped a beat as he walked toward her.

He gestured at the empty chair. "May I?"

"Of course."

Pulling the chair out, he asked, "Whose soul were you praying for, Ana? Yours? Or mine?"

His question hit a little too close to home and brought a flush to Analia's cheeks.

He opened his senses, letting his mind brush hers. Ana's thoughts were conflicted. She wanted him but was afraid to commit to a relationship with a vampire. With good reason, he thought. She feared the differences between them were too great to overcome, that once the initial attraction wore off, she would regret giving herself to him. She didn't want to hurt his feelings…

Raiden grunted softly, not knowing whether to laugh or cry. No one had considered his feelings in hundreds of years, certainly not the vampire who turned him.

Well, he would make it easy for her.

"Do you want to walk me home?" she asked after she finished her hot chocolate.

"It would be my pleasure."

When they stepped outside, Raiden produced a long, black, hooded cloak—seemingly from out of nowhere—and draped it around her shoulders.

Holding it close, she murmured her thanks. It kept her remarkably warm and dry.

They walked in silence for a while, then Ana said, "Aren't you cold?"

"No. The weather has little effect on me. Neither does the rain."

Only then did she notice that the rain fell *around* him, not *on* him. Why hadn't she noticed that before?

At home, she shook out his cloak, then hung it from the hall tree. When she turned around, he was standing close behind her.

"Ana."

Nodding, she closed her eyes. As always, Raiden's kisses filled her with indescribable pleasure. She pressed herself against him, wanting to be closer. When he lifted her in his arms, she locked her hands behind his neck and rested her head on his shoulder. He carried her into the living room where he sat on the sofa with her cradled in his arms.

She hadn't made out with anyone for a long time, but for the next hour, they kissed and caressed each other like randy teenagers, touching and tasting, and indulging in some innocent exploring.

"Ana, let me."

To most men, that would have meant sex. But Raiden wanted something even more intimate. She tilted her head to the side, felt a familiar thrill of sensual pleasure as he bit her, ever so gently.

He took only a little, ran his tongue over the tiny, twin wounds and kissed her lightly.

"Where are you going?" she asked when he rose from the sofa.

"The sun's coming out."

"Oh." Try as she might, she couldn't hide her disappointment.

He kissed her again, a slow, sweet kiss that made her heart ache and her toes curl.

And then he vanished from the room.

She spent part of the afternoon reading. Later, she did her nails while watching TV. After dinner, she found herself repeatedly checking the time. She had expected Raiden to come downstairs when the sun set, but it was almost nine and there was still no sign of him.

Maybe he'd overslept, she thought. And maybe he was out searching for prey. If they were going to be together, she would have to get used to that, gross as it seemed. But as the hours went by, she began to realize he wasn't coming that night. Fighting back her tears, she showered, pulled on her nightgown, and slipped into bed.

Lying there, unable to sleep, she realized that his last kiss had really been goodbye.

It was then that the tears came.

* * *

Ana dragged herself to work Monday morning and when the day was over, she had no memory of anything she'd done.

     Amanda Ashley

By Tuesday, sorrow had turned to anger. How dare he leave her without so much as a farewell!

By Wednesday, anger had turned to acceptance. She was better off without him. Had he stayed longer, they would probably have ended up making love and that would have been a catastrophe. He was a vampire, for Heaven's sake! What girl in her right mind would even think about making love to someone who wasn't even human? Yes, she was better off without him. After all, there was no point in spending time with a guy you had no possible future with, no matter how handsome and sexy he seemed to be.

By Thursday, she had convinced herself that in spite of what he'd told her, Raiden had worked some kind of spooky vampire magic to make her think she cared for him.

Friday was Halloween. That night, she slid into her costume, filled a huge black bowl with candy and turned on the outside lights. It was her favorite night of the year and she wasn't going to let Raiden or anything else spoil it for her.

She smiled a welcome as the first trick-or-treaters hurried up to the porch.

But deep inside her heart, where she refused to look, lurked a yearning to see one tall, dark vampire.

* * *

Raiden stood in the shadows behind a tree in the small, open field across from Analia's house. He had told himself leaving her was for the best—for him and for her. By the next night, he knew he'd made a mistake, at least where he was concerned. She was the best thing that had happened to him since he'd been turned all those centuries ago and even though he wasn't good for Ana, he couldn't bring himself to leave. He had lingered outside her house each night, careful to stay out of sight, content to be close enough to hear the sound of her heartbeat, smell the warm womanly scent that was Analia's alone. Long after she'd gone to bed, he slipped into her room for an hour or two, just to be near her. He never touched her, though the temptation was almost overpowering. It was wrong of him to spy on her while she slept, but he needed to be close to her.

Now, hidden from sight, he watched Ana hand out candy to the neighborhood trick-or-treaters. The sound of her laughter soothed him, even as it caused an ache deep in his heart, an ache her affection had once filled.

Suddenly unable to watch any longer, he willed himself to another city. He was a vampire. He had no place in the mortal world, no business pining over a woman he could never have like some love-sick mortal. He was a vampire and he needed to feed.

Opening his senses, he stalked the dark alleys of the city in search of prey.

* * *

Ana sighed as she closed the door on the last of the trick-or-treaters. She put the empty bowl in the kitchen sink, took a can of soda from the fridge and wandered into the living room.

Sinking down on the sofa, she stared blankly at the opposite wall. She had been kidding herself, pretending she was over Raiden, that she was better off without him, that she didn't need him. What did she care if he was a vampire? Hadn't she always wanted one of her own? There had even been a time, when she was very young, when she thought it would be fun to be one of the Undead. But she had outgrown that particular fantasy. Hadn't she? Or had she just buried it along with all her other childhood dreams?

If she was going to be honest, she had to admit that she missed Raiden desperately, that she would have given anything to have him back in her life for a day or a lifetime.

Hope flared in her heart when the doorbell rang. Was it him?

Setting the coke can on the coffee table, she ran to answer the door.

   Amanda Ashley

Chapter 13

Analia stared at the man on the front porch. He was over six feet tall with a face that looked like it had been through a meat grinder. Tufts of gray hair sprouted from his head. He wore a shiny black patch over one eye. Unable to mask her horror, she took a step back, intending the slam the door in his face, but he blocked it with his foot.

"Where is he?" the man growled. "I know he's staying here."

"I… I… you're mistaken. I live alone." She bit down on her lower lip. She shouldn't have said that.

"You're lying and wasting my time." Strong-arming her out of the way, the man stormed into the house.

Ana stared after him, momentarily stunned. What should she do? Call the police? Run like hell?

She was leaning toward the latter when the man grabbed a handful of her hair and threw her across the room.

"Tell me where he is or I'll break your neck!"

"I don't know!" She screamed the words at him when he strode toward her, his eye filled with malice. "He's not here anymore!"

Grabbing her by the arm, the man dragged her through the house. When they reached the attic stairs, he paused. "What's up there?"

"A storeroom."

He grunted softly. "No windows in that room. Perfect place for a bloodsucker." He nodded to himself. "I'll wait."

"Wait?"

"For sunrise."

Blinking back tears of fright, she stammered, "But he's... not... staying here... anymore!"

The man sneered at her. "So you say. I'll just wait and see. And if you're lying to me, I'll kill you after I destroy him."

Ana couldn't stop trembling as he hauled her back into the living room and shoved her down on the sofa.

"Stay there! Don't move a muscle!"

Hands tightly clasped in her lap, her head aching from when he'd thrown her across the room, she watched him prowl back and forth, pausing now and then to look out the windows.

When he stepped into the kitchen, she jumped to her feet and ran toward the front door, screamed when his hand clamped over her shoulder.

"I told you not to move!" He slapped her once, twice, the sounds like gunshots in the quiet house. And then he gave her a push toward the sofa.

Ana staggered as she tried, and failed, to regain her balance. She let out a cry as she fell, her head striking the corner of the coffee table. The world spun out of focus and then went black.

The hunter cursed as he knelt beside her. Stupid woman. Should have done what he'd said.

It was his last thought in mortality as a strong hand circled his throat and slowly squeezed the life out of him.

Tossing the man aside, Raiden knelt beside Analia. Blood poured from a wicked looking gash in the back of her head. Her breathing was shallow, her heartbeat growing fainter by the second.

"Ana? Ana! Can you hear me?"

Her eyelids flickered, then opened. "You... came... back."

"I was a fool to leave you. Listen to me. We don't have much time."

"I can't see you."

"Listen! I can save you. Is it what you want?"

Her eyelids fluttered down and her head lolled back.

"Ana!" Damn! He was losing her. With a murmured, "Forgive me, love," he gently sank his fangs into her throat.

CHAPTER 14

She was dreaming. A horrible man burst into the house demanding to see Raiden. He scared her with his rough appearance and his dire threats. She told him the truth—Raiden wasn't staying in her house any more. The thought brought the sting of tears to her eyes. She missed him, missed him more than she would have thought possible.

From out of nowhere came dozens of little ghosts and goblins. They ran through the house, shouting, "Trick or treat, smell my feet! Give me something good to eat!"

Suddenly, there was an excruciating pain in the back of her head. She felt herself falling, falling, into infinity, slipping into a yawning abyss from which there was no escape.

Raiden… where was Raiden? She hadn't said goodbye. It took all her waning strength to whisper his name. "Raiden…"

And he was there. Her vampire, gazing down at her through dark, mesmerizing eyes. Leaning over her. Begging her to "Drink, Ana! Drink!" His voice grew harsh, frantic. "Analia! You must drink!"

She gagged as thick, warm liquid trickled over her tongue and down her throat and then she was clinging to him, suckling at his arm like a hungry baby at its mother's breast as warmth flooded her entire being.

She drank and drank, afraid she would never get enough.

Moaned in protest when he wrested his arm away.

And then she floated down, down, down, into a deep, velvety

 Amanda Ashley

black void.

Raiden sat back on his haunches, watching the gash in Ana's head knit together. He smiled as the color returned to her cheeks. Her heartbeat gradually grew stronger, though it beat less frequently than before. Subtle changes crept over her, although only another vampire would notice that her skin was a little more pale, her hair a little darker, thicker.

Lifting her into his arms, he carried Ana to her room, removed her shoes and costume, and put her to bed. Wetting a cloth, he washed the blood from her hair as best he could, then drew the covers up to her chin. She would sleep through the night and when she rose tomorrow evening, she would be a new vampire. He briefly considered taking her up to the attic but decided she would feel better waking in her own bed.

He glanced out the window, his brow furrowed. Would Ana hate him for what he had done? Searching his heart, he knew he would do it again. She was alive and that was all that mattered. She might hate him for a century or two but be that as it may, he would cling to the hope that she would eventually forgive him and let him back into her world.

Returning to the living room, Raiden slung the hunter's body over his shoulder and willed himself to the same vacant lot where he had buried the other slayer. The two could keep each other company, he mused as he dug the grave. Hopefully, they would share the same hell.

Returning to Ana's house, Raiden made sure all the doors and windows were locked, turned out the lights. He took a moment to look in on his new fledgling, then made his way up to the attic.

Stretching out on the floor with his hands locked behind his head, he wondered what the morrow would bring.

* * *

Analia woke slowly. Lying there, eyes still closed, she tried to figure out what was wrong. There had been no dreams last night and that was passing strange. Her dreams were always vivid and in color and she always remembered them. She frowned as myriad scents tickled her nose. There were no plants in the house, yet she could smell grass and trees. Funny, she had never noticed that before.

She rolled onto her side, her frown deepening as she heard Mr. and Mrs. Cruz, who lived next door, talking about whether or not they should buy a new refrigerator. From the other side of the house, she heard Miles Parker and his nine-year old son calling back and forth as they took out the trash.

Maybe this was another dream.

Opening her eyes, Ana sat up and glanced around the room. The colors of the walls, the curtains and the carpet seemed to leap out at her. Why did they look so vibrant? Why did she feel so light, as if she could just get up and float away?

Why was it still dark outside?

She glanced at the old-fashioned clock on the wall. It had belonged to Grandma Carolyn. Seven o'clock. Had it stopped? Surely it wasn't seven at night!

Standing, she went to the window and drew back the curtains. The lights were on in the house next to the vacant lot. Evan Turner was coming home from work.

Ana shook her head. She had slept the whole day away. She groaned softly. And she'd missed work.

What was going on?

Deciding there was no point in getting dressed, she pulled on her robe and padded into the kitchen. There were two messages on her phone—one from Jade and one from her boss, both wanting to know where she was.

Suddenly hungry, Ana opened the refrigerator. Nothing inside looked good, but she was starving, her stomach cramping with pain. She had never felt such agony. Maybe she was coming down with the flu.

Another pain struck and she doubled over. A doctor. She needed a doctor.

Moaning softly, she reached for the phone. Then, aware that she was no longer alone, she whirled around. "Raiden!" she gasped. "I'm so glad to see you. I need help."

"And I'm here to give you what you need."

"What do you mean?"

"Do you remember nothing of last night?"

"No, but it doesn't matter now." Groaning, she clutched her stomach. "I'm sick."

He shook his head. "No doctor can fix what's ailing you."

          Amanda Ashley

Ana stared at him, her brow furrowed in confusion. "I don't understand." Her eyes widened when he bit into his wrist, opening a shallow gash. Dark red blood oozed from the wound.

Before she realized what she was doing, Ana sprang toward him, her hands grabbing his arm, her mouth latching onto the stream of dark crimson.

She drank and drank and then, horrified by what she was doing, she pushed him away. "What's happening to me? What have you done?"

"A hunter came looking for me last night. He broke into your house. He didn't mean to hurt you…"

"I remember now!" She lifted a hand to the back of her head. "He pushed me and I fell against the coffee table."

Raiden nodded. "You were dying when I found you."

"Dying?" Ana stared at him. Her inexplicable craving for blood suddenly made sense. "You turned me into a vampire," she murmured, and wondered why she wasn't more upset. Even though she had been fascinated with vampires most of her life, she had never seriously wanted to be one, not when it meant living only by night, giving up all her favorite foods, her job, forever hiding what she was from her parents, her friends.

She frowned as a little voice in the back of her mind asked if she would rather be dead. And the answer was no. What was done was done and she was glad to still be alive.

"I hope you can find it in your heart to someday forgive me," Raiden said quietly.

"Forgive you? For what? For saving my life?"

"You're not angry?"

"No. I feel like I should be, but I'm not." She shook her head. "I can't explain how I'm feeling." She shook her head again. "Strangely light, as if I could just float away."

He smiled. "Your connection to the earth has shifted. It no longer has the same hold on you it once did."

"I guess I have a lot to learn." Which surprised her, since she had spent most of her life studying books and movies about the undead creatures of the night. Of course, reality was bound to be different. "Will I be able to turn into mist and move faster than human eyes can follow and do all the crazy, wonderful things you can do?"

He nodded. "I would be happy to teach you everything you need to know, if you'll let me."

"What other choice do I have?" she asked with a saucy grin. "You *are* the only vampire I know."

"Lucky me."

"Are you?" she asked, all humor gone from her voice.

"Analia, I consider myself the luckiest creature on the face of the earth to have met you. And even luckier that you didn't drive a stake through my heart the first night we met."

"That never even occurred to me," she admitted sheepishly. "All I saw was a tall, dark, handsome man who was bleeding."

"Like I said," Raiden murmured, drawing her into his arms. "Lucky me."

Her eyelids fluttered down as he kissed her, long and slow and deep.

Who's the lucky one now? she thought. Her arms twined around his neck as he drew her even closer.

After several moments, Raiden drew back. "Will you be mine forever, Analia?" he asked, gazing into her eyes. "I swear I'll do my best to make you happy all the days of your life."

"Are you asking me to marry you? Seriously? I mean, we just met!"

"We can have a long engagement," he said, grinning. "As long as you like. After all, we have a lot of time to get to know each other better."

She tilted her head to the side, thinking it over, and then nodded. "I'd like that," she decided. "As long as we don't take *too* long."

"Ana!" He kissed her again, longer, deeper. What a remarkable creature she was! She had accepted him as he was, as if it was the most natural thing in the world to find a vampire in your front yard. Even more amazing, she had accepted becoming a fledgling without a trace of anger or regret. Truly a most remarkable woman.

Analia leaned into him, certain in that moment that she had found the man she had been looking for all her life. Of course, she hadn't expected him to be a vampire, but she wasn't complaining. Instead of forty or fifty years together, they could have centuries.

She sighed with pleasure as Raiden crushed her close. Yes, indeed, she thought. Halloween would always be her favorite holiday.

     Amanda Ashley

A Thankful Heart

PROLOGUE

There is a legend among vampires that every three hundred years a mortal female will be born who would be sympathetic to the Undead. No vampire will be able to kill her but would, instead, be drawn to protect her. If he drinks from her, her blood will nourish him as no other. If he drinks from her three times, the third bite will produce a rare exchange of power that will also strengthen her.

Not only that, but if this unique female is turned, she will possess all of a vampire's preternatural powers but none of their weaknesses. She will have the ability to continue to partake of mortal food, though she will need to drink blood from her sire once a year. She will not be subject to the dark sleep.

But, most amazing of all, she will be able to bear the child of the vampire who turns her.

Of course, it's only a legend.

CHAPTER 1

Rylee North stared at the dozens of decorations in the window of the Hallmark store. Halloween wasn't even over yet and already witches and black cats had been replaced with cute little pilgrims, fat ceramic turkeys, Indian salt-and-pepper shakers, and colorful cornucopias.

Thanksgiving. Bah! Humbug! What did she have to be thankful for? She'd lost a job she loved. She was behind in her rent. Her landlord was threatening to have her evicted if she didn't pay up. She hadn't had a date in eight months. Her parents had called a week ago to let her know they were getting a divorce. And her best friend had just gone off to Iceland to study the mating habits of puffins.

Oh, yeah, she had a lot to be grateful for.

Lost in a bog of self-pity, she turned away from the window. It was Friday night and everywhere she looked, she saw happy people strolling down the street. Couples, hand-in-hand. Carefree teenagers laughing as they hurried along. Young lovers gazing soulfully into each other's eyes, oblivious to the world around them.

Unable to endure another minute, she turned down the alley behind the drug store. She usually avoided taking this shortcut to her apartment building at night because the alley was pitch black and had been the scene of a rather grisly murder a month ago, but tonight she just didn't care. She had no one to turn to for help, no one to care if she lived or died. If she couldn't

     Amanda Ashley

come up with her long over-due rent, she might be living in this very alley next week.

At the halfway point, she came to a sudden stop, her gaze searching the darkness.

There was something or someone lurking there, in the shadows just ahead.

With her heart thundering in her ears, she turned on her heel and ran back the way she'd come only to let out a shriek when she slammed into something hard and unyielding.

A second scream lodged in her throat when a hand covered her mouth. She fought against her attacker, her nails raking her assailants' arm as she kicked and twisted in a vain effort to escape.

But it was impossible.

He let her struggle until she was breathless, her legs weak, and then he gently brushed the hair away from her neck.

Rylee froze as his tongue laved the tender skin beneath her ear and then… oh, Lord, was he biting her?

It was her last thought before she pitched headlong into oblivion.

* * *

Reluctant to open her eyes, Rylee let out a long slow sigh. She'd been having the most wonderfully erotic dream, she hated to let it go. Stretching her arms over her head, she sat up, then frowned. This wasn't her bedroom. Or her house. Where the heck was she? The room was large and square, dominated by an old-fashioned, canopied bed and little else save a carved rosewood wardrobe. No windows. No mirrors. No pictures.

Swinging her legs over the edge of the very large bed, she was about to stand up when the door opened and a tall, dark man clad in black sweat pants and a black tee shirt stepped into the room.

Rylee blinked at him. He stood over six feet tall. Long black hair. Incredibly beautiful black eyes beneath thick lashes. A slash of a nose. A sensuous mouth. Broad shoulders, slim hips. Bare feet. She was so shocked by his appearance it took her a moment to remember to be afraid.

With a squeak, she scrambled to the far side of the bed and drew the covers up to her chin, as if that would protect her.

The man lifted one dark brow in amusement. "I brought you something to drink."

His voice was as deep as ten feet down. He held out his hand.

Only then did she notice he held a small bottle of orange juice.

"Drink it." His voice was compelling.

As if she had no will of her own, she took the bottle from his hand and drained it, surprised by how thirsty she was.

Her heart jumped into her throat when he took a step toward the bed. "Don't come any closer!" She broke the mouth of the bottle against the wall behind her, then waved the jagged edge in front of him. "I'll... I'll hurt you if you come any closer!"

He glanced at her weapon and then he laughed. It was a remarkably robust sound, filled with wry amusement. "You're dripping orange juice all over my clean sheets," he said, his voice still tinged with laughter. "Calm yourself, child. I mean you no harm."

"Then why did you bring me here?"

"I found you in the alley. Would you rather I had left you there, prey to muggers and rats?"

Rylee shivered, then frowned. What had she been doing in an alley?

"You're obviously feeling better," her benefactor mused. "If you tell me where you live, I'll drive you home."

She shook her head. "That won't be necessary."

"As you wish."

"So... I can go?"

He made a long, sweeping gesture toward the door. "A word to the wise: stay out of dark alleys."

With a curt nod, Rylee jumped off the bed and ran out the door, only to pause when she found herself in a long hallway. She glanced right and left, then headed for the staircase. It led to a large living room decorated with what looked like antique furniture. If she hadn't been in such a hurry to get out of there, she would have loved to take a closer look. But she was all too aware of the man standing at the top of the stairs, watching her every move as if she were a rabbit and he a hungry hawk.

With a last glance at him, she opened the heavy front door and bolted outside, then skidded to a stop when she found herself in the dark, sur-rounded by a high stone wall with no apparent way out. Dark clouds lowered overhead, shutting out both moon and stars.

She didn't know where she was, but it sure wasn't anywhere near her

     Amanda Ashley

apartment on Ninth Avenue.

Maybe she should have accepted the man's offer to take her home. After all, if he'd meant her harm, he'd plenty of time to do it.

She jumped when he suddenly appeared before her.

"My offer to take you home still stands."

Rylee bit down on her lower lip, still reluctant to accept, until a distant drum roll of thunder reminded her that a storm was on the way. "Thank you. That would be nice."

"Just let me get my car."

Rylee nodded. She watched as he disappeared into the darkness. There was no other word for it. One minute he'd been there and the next he was gone, though she hadn't seen him move.

She glanced over her shoulder when lights pierced the night followed by the deep purr of a powerful engine. The next thing she knew, he was helping her into the passenger seat of a sleek automobile that was as black as the clouds overhead.

Rylee gave him her address, fervently praying that home was where he would take her even as she wondered why she wasn't more afraid of him. He was, after all, a stranger.

Once they left the house behind, she realized they were on the outskirts of the city. Funny, she had never noticed that big old house before.

She breathed a sigh of relief when her apartment building came into view.

Reaching for the door handle, she said, "Thank you for bringing me home, Mr....?"

"Call me Andreas. And it was my pleasure. May I know your name?"

After a moment's hesitation, she said, "Rylee. Rylee North."

He smiled, displaying remarkably even, white teeth. "Good evening, Miss North."

Rylee stepped onto the sidewalk, murmured, "Good bye," and shut the car door firmly behind her, certain she would never see him again.

* * *

Andreas watched the lovely Miss North cross the sidewalk and enter the lobby of her apartment building. She was a comely young woman, her hair the dark red of autumn leaves, her eyes an unremarkable shade of brown that he nevertheless found enchanting. She was nicely rounded in all the right places, not too short, not too tall. And terribly unhappy. Her loneliness, her frustration with her life, had touched something deep within him, a compassion he hadn't felt in centuries. It intrigued him. Why had this female affected him this way? He had not taken a mortal life in centuries, but one sip of her blood and he had wanted it all. Never in all his four hundred years had he tasted anything so sweet, so addicting. Never had he felt such warmth, such power, flowing through him. He might have taken it all but some intangible force he had never before experienced stopped him before he inadvertently took too much.

He had preyed on many women. But this one's blood was uniquely different from all the others, almost as if she had a built-in protection against vampires. And why his overwhelming urge to help her when he'd never had any interest in looking after any of the others? But then, most of them hadn't been as unhappy or as troubled as this one.

He considered her problems one by one as he drove away.

She needed money in a hurry. He had more than he could ever spend.

She hadn't had a date in months. He would be all too happy to take her anywhere she wished to go.

She needed a job. He had no doubt he could find her suitable employment. He hadn't had a mistress in a good long while, he mused. And she would do nicely, though she didn't seem the type to settle for anything less than marriage.

Her parents had divorced. He wasn't a matchmaker but if she wished, he could compel them to reconcile.

Her best friend had gone off to Iceland. He could always summon her back.

He grinned into the darkness. Perhaps he would start at the top of the list and work his way down.

     Amanda Ashley

CHAPTER 2

Smothering a yawn, Rylee stepped into her slippers and headed for the kitchen, only to pause when she noticed someone had pushed a small, square, white envelope under her door.

Curious, she picked it up and turned it over in her hands. There was no writing on it save her name in a bold masculine scrawl. Looking at it sent a shiver down her spine.

It was from him. Andreas. Although how she knew, she had no idea.

She didn't know whether to open it or flush it down the toilet.

In the end, her curiosity got the better of her.

The envelope wasn't sealed. She lifted the flap and pulled out a single sheet of parchment paper.

> *My dear Miss North ~*
> *I would be honored if you would accompany*
> *me to the theater. If you are agreeable,*
> *I shall pick you up at 7:30 this evening.*
> *Ever your servant,*
> *Andreas*

How very formal, she thought as she folded the invitation and tucked it back in the envelope.

After dropping the invite onto the coffee table, she went into the kitchen to fix breakfast. She hadn't been on a date in months and the idea of dressing up and going to the theater was tempting. But did she want to go out with a guy she hardly knew? One who was a little mysterious? Even a little scary? But very, very handsome?

She pondered his invitation while she lingered over a second cup of coffee. And then a third.

She thought it over while she did her hair and nails—just in case she decided to accept. And later, while going through her closet looking for something suitable to wear.

That was when she made her decision. She didn't have a single thing that was nice enough, dressy enough, to wear to the theater.

Discouraged, she went into the living room and sank down on the edge of the sofa. It was just as well. In this day and age, a girl would have to be insane to go out with a complete stranger. Still, she had let him drive her home.

She had just decided not to tempt fate a second time when there was a knock at the door. Wondering who it could be, since everyone she knew was either home with their kids or at work, she opened it just a crack.

A delivery man stood there, a large, gift-wrapped parcel in his hands. "Miss North?"

"Yes."

"This is for you."

"I'm sorry, I think you have the wrong address. I haven't ordered anything."

He checked the label and shrugged. "Right name, right address," he muttered, and trust it toward her. "Have a nice day."

Nodding, she closed the door, then stared at the package. The return label read Saks Fifth Avenue, Beverly Hills. With a shake of her head, she sat down on the sofa and opened the box. Inside, she found a black silk dress nestled in a bed of white tissue paper.

When she lifted the dress from the box, a small envelope fell on the floor. A note inside, written in a familiar hand, said,

> ***Miss North, please forgive my impertinence,***
> ***but I saw this is the window and thought of you.***
> ***I hope you will wear it tonight***

   Amanda Ashley

with my compliments.
Your servant,
Andreas.

Rylee stared at the dress. She had seen it in a Saks catalog just the other day. She had never dreamed of owning such a dress, not with a price tag of eight hundred dollars.

She ran her fingertips over the silk, loving the smooth, cool feel of it.

How could she accept such a gift?

How could she refuse?

And how had he known she didn't have a thing to wear?

* * *

Andreas arrived at her door at exactly 7:30. For a moment, she could only stare at him. Who was this gorgeous stranger and why did he want to go out with her? Wearing a black thigh-length coat over a black suit and a crisp white shirt, he looked like he had just stepped out of the pages of GQ.

He lifted one brow under her open-mouthed stare, making her feel like a total idiot.

"Are you ready?"

She'd forgotten the way his voice made her insides turn to mush. "Yes. No. I just need to put on my shoes." She hesitated a moment, then said, "Please, come in." She frowned as a strange sort of ripple stirred the air as he stepped inside. "Sit down. I'll just be a minute."

Andreas watched her hurry out of the room. He made her extremely nervous, but that was to be expected. After all, he was a stranger. He had been somewhat surprised when she invited him inside.

He glanced around the room. It was small, but tidy, furnished with a flowered loveseat, an overstuffed chair and a coffee table. The kitchen was off to the left. He assumed the bedroom and bath were behind the closed door on the right.

She smiled uncertainly when she returned, blushed to her hairline as his gaze moved over her. "Thank you for the dress. It's lovely."

He inclined his head. "As are you, Miss North. Shall we go?"

Rylee followed him out the door and locked it behind her. She gaped at the sleek black car waiting at the curb. She had seen a Maserati Gran Turismo advertised in magazines, but she had never seen one on the road. And never in a million years expected to know someone rich enough to own such an expensive automobile, let alone ride in one.

He opened the door for her and she slid into a leather seat that was softer and more comfortable than her bed. Wondering what Andreas did for a living, she watched him walk around the front of the car, felt a shiver of excitement as he took his place at the wheel.

The engine purred to life with a low growl.

Rylee searched her mind for something to say but drew a blank. Had she made a mistake, going out with him? How did she know he was actually taking her to the theater? How could she have been so stupid? She sent an anxious glance out the window, felt an overpowering wave of relief when the Pantages Theater loomed ahead. A large banner across the front proclaimed *Jekyll and Hyde* was playing.

He pulled up in front of the valet parking area.

Excitement thrummed through Rylee as they walked hand-in-hand into the theater and took their seats, front row center.

She opened her program, acutely aware of the man beside her. He radiated sex appeal and she was far from immune. Certainly any female who had reached the age of puberty would be as smitten as she was.

"Have you seen this play before?" he asked.

"No. Have you?"

"Several times. I think you'll enjoy it. The music is quite good. You know the story, of course?"

She nodded. Dr. Jekyll was the good guy, Hyde his evil alter-ego. As she recalled, the story didn't have a happy-ever-after ending.

But it was fascinating and the music was wonderful, especially *This is the Moment*. Listening to it always gave her goose bumps.

Andreas spent most of the play watching Rylee. Judging by her expressions, she was completely lost in the story. Wide-eyed at the soaring hope in the song, *This is the Moment*, near tears with the heartbreaking *In His Eyes*, captivated by the dark sensuality of *A Dangerous Game*. There were tears in her eyes when the curtain closed.

"So," he asked as they left the theater. "Did you enjoy it?"

"Very much. I've never been to a play before. It was… magical."

"Indeed."

　　　　Amanda Ashley

He sensed her apprehension as the valet brought his car around. "Would you care to go out for a drink? Or something to eat, perhaps?"

She bit down on her lower lip. "Could we go out for ice cream?"

He stifled the urge to laugh as he assured her that would be fine. He had never been inside a modern ice cream parlor. For one with few surprises in his life, he was always open to a new experience.

Rylee glanced at her dress and then at Andreas as they entered Nell's Ice Cream Shoppe. Most of the other customers were wearing jeans and tee shirts. "I guess we're a little overdressed."

Andreas chuckled. "Perhaps. But, no matter. Order whatever you wish."

She asked for a banana split with double hot fudge and whipped cream, looked at him askance when he didn't order anything.

Shrugging, he said, "I don't care for sweets."

"Why didn't you say something? We could have gone somewhere else."

"I'm fine." He followed her to a small table and took the seat across from hers.

"Would you like a bite?"

He lifted one brow, then he nodded. A bite was all he could handle. "It's quite good." And was, in fact, better than he remembered.

"You sound surprised. Don't tell me you've never had ice cream before."

"Not for a very long time." Ice cream had been around for centuries. Alexander the Great had eaten snow and ice flavored with honey and nectar. The treat had gradually made its way to the New World.

"Why? You can't be dieting. You're in great shape," she remarked, and then, feeling her cheeks grow hot, she focused her attention on scooping up the last bit of hot fudge.

She couldn't resist stealing glances at him on the ride home. His presence was almost overpowering. Everything feminine within her quivered at his nearness.

Andreas pulled up in front of her apartment and cut the engine, then sat back, his arm resting along the back of her seat. "Did you have a good time?"

"Yes, thank you for everything. The play was wonderful."

"May I see you again?"

Feeling like Cinderella being asked out by the Prince, she bit down on her lower lip. As attractive as he was, there was something about him, something that hinted at danger, that made her wary. Yet he had been a perfect gentleman.

"Miss North?"

"I wish you would call me Rylee."

"My pleasure. I would love to see you again."

His voice touched a chord deep within her. After a moment, she nodded slowly. "I'd like that."

"I'll call you tomorrow evening, if that's all right."

"Fine."

He walked her up to her apartment, waited while she unlocked the door.

Rylee stepped inside, then stood there, debating whether to invite him in. It was late. If she asked him inside, would be misinterpret it for a different kind of invitation?

"Rylee?"

When she looked up, he cupped her face in his hands, lowered his head, and kissed her lightly. "Until tomorrow," he said quietly, and closed the door.

She lifted her fingertips to her lips. She had been kissed before but never like that. It had been feather-light, yet she could still feel of press of his lips against hers.

"Tomorrow," she murmured.

She could hardly wait.

Amanda Ashley

CHAPTER 3

Rylee was still thinking about his kiss when she woke in the morning. And then she frowned. It was November first. Her overdue rent was supposed to paid today. Her landlord had threatened to evict her on the spot if she didn't come up with the money.

What was she going to do? Where would she go?

She glanced at the black dress Andreas had bought her. Maybe she could take it back. Probably not. It had been worn. She didn't have a receipt, or an account at the store. And deep down, she was glad she couldn't return it.

After a quick breakfast and two cups of coffee, she put on her favorite jeans and her most flattering sweater, applied her make-up, and went downstairs to see if by some miracle she could convince Mr. Marley to give her one more month.

Heart pounding with trepidation, she knocked on the door, forced a smile when it opened.

"Miss North," her landlord said jovially. "What can I do for you this fine morning?"

Rylee frowned, confused by his demeanor. She had expected anger and a demand to pay up or get out. "I… um… you see, it's like this…"

"I was told you might stop by to collect a copy of your new lease. I have it right here, signed and dated." He reached behind him and plucked an envelope off a side table. "Marked paid in full for the entire year."

Speechless, Rylee blinked at him. Paid in full? For a year?

"Did you win the lottery?" he asked, a twinkle in his eyes.

"I wish."

"Well, no matter." He smiled broadly as he handed her the envelope. "If you need anything fixed, just let me know! I'm here to help."

"Yes. Of course. Thank you." Stunned, she turned and made her way upstairs, the envelope tightly clutched in her hand. Someone had paid her rent. For a year. But who? And why? She hadn't told anyone about her depleted financial situation and even if any of her friends knew, none of them could afford to pay a year's rent in advance, not for themselves and certainly not for her.

Back in her apartment, she went into her bedroom to change her sweater for a sweatshirt. She dropped the envelope on the dresser, then glanced at the black dress hanging from the closet door. Andreas had enough money to blow eight hundred dollars on a dress for a stranger.

Had he paid her rent? She shook her head. Why would he? And how could he possibly have known that she couldn't afford it?

* * *

He called her as soon as the sun went down. "Rylee, it's a lovely night. Would you like to go for a drive?"

"Where to?"

"Wherever you like."

She debated a moment, thinking that if he meant to hurt her, he'd already had several chances to do so. Feeling suddenly bold, she said, "That would be nice. Thank you."

"Pick you up in half an hour?"

"I'll be ready." She put on her favorite sweater for the second time that day, grabbed a lightweight jacket from her closet, pulled on a pair of boots.

He arrived right on time.

As he'd said, it was a lovely night for a drive. He had a different car tonight, a silver Audi convertible with the top down.

The weather was warm but not hot, the sky clear. As they left the town behind, the stars seemed to multiply from hundreds to millions. Maybe

     Amanda Ashley

billions. How long had it been since she'd taken time to notice the beauty of the night sky?

They drove in silence for a while and then he pulled the car off the road and killed the engine. "You're very quiet."

Nodding, Rylee met his gaze. His eyes were so deep, so dark, and yet kind as they looked back at her. "You paid my rent, didn't you?"

"Yes."

"How did you know I needed help?"

"I read your mind."

She stared at him, then shook her head. "Right."

"You're unhappy with your life. You made a rather unfortunate investment and lost what little savings you had. You've lost your job and your best friend."

"And how can you possibly know all that?"

"I told you. I read your mind."

"That's impossible."

"Is it?"

Something in his eyes changed. It sent shivers down Rylee's spine. Was this it? Was going out with him going to be her last and biggest mistake?

He laughed softly. "I mean you no harm, Rylee North." That hadn't been true the night they met. The fact that he'd let her live still puzzled him. He was an old vampire. He didn't need to feed as often as he had when he was a fledgling. Usually a few sips satisfied his hunger. But every now and then he needed to take it all. And that had been his intention the night he met Rylee, but some force inside had prevented him from taking her life. He still didn't know why.

Rylee frowned as images suddenly appeared in her mind. She saw herself ducking into the alley, being attacked by a tall stranger dressed in black, trying to fight him off… "It was you!" she exclaimed. "You're the man who attacked me in the alley!" She made a frantic grab for the door handle, but it was locked. Overcome with panic, she climbed over the door and bolted into the darkness, only to come to an abrupt halt when she slammed into a solid mass.

"Rylee, where do you think you're going?"

She stared up at him. How had he gotten in front of her so fast?

"Come back to the car. We need to talk."

"No. Leave me alone."

"I'm not going to hurt you," he said, reaching for her hand. "Come along now."

Helpless, she let him lead her back to the car, balked when he opened the door for her. She looked up at him, mute. How could she be afraid of him and yet yearn for him to hold her at the same time?

"You wanted to die that night in the alley, didn't you?" he asked, his voice quiet. Soothing.

Rylee stared at him. How could he possibly know that?

"I know you're hurting and unhappy and I'd like to help, if you'll let me." He shook his head, remembering how her blood had affected him, how'd he'd been tempted to take it all, but had been prevented from doing so. Instead, he had found himself wanting to protect her. He still didn't understand why.

"How did you know I was unhappy?"

He lifted one shoulder in a negligent shrug. "I read your thoughts. As I'm reading them now."

His knuckles stroked her cheek. "I can offer you another way of life, Rylee North, something different and occasionally exciting, if you're brave enough to embrace it."

"What kind of life?" Good grief, was he some kind of con man?

He laughed. "A con man? Hardly that, although I'd be very good at it."

His heated gaze moved over her, unleashing butterflies of anticipation in her stomach as she imagined his arms tight around her, his lips moving over hers.

"So, what are you, then?" she asked breathlessly. "A mind reader?" Heaven help her, what if he really *was* psychic? What if he was reading her thoughts even now? The very idea brought a flush of embarrassment to her cheeks.

Andreas went silent as the scent of her desire filled the air. He inhaled deeply and all thought of telling her the truth fled his mind. "A mind reader," he murmured, reaching for her. "That's exactly what I am."

She gasped in surprise when his arms went around her. "What are you doing?"

"Just what you hoped I would do."

She stared at him. Maybe he really was psychic! As he lowered his head to hers and claimed her lips, all her doubts faded away. Being in his arms, drowning in his kisses, was exactly what she'd been hoping for.

 Amanda Ashley

His kiss was more intoxicating than the finest wine. Shivers of delight danced up and down her spine as his tongue teased hers. Where had he learned to kiss like that? No other man had ever made her whole being tingle with such exquisite pleasure.

Feeling bereft, Rylee uttered a low sound of disappointment when he lifted his head. Cupping his face in her hands, she whispered, "Don't stop."

More than willing to please, he kissed her again and yet again, until she was writhing in his arms, desperate to be closer, willing to surrender all that she had to offer if only he would never let her go.

With some regret, Andreas put some space between them as his hunger roared to life. His yearning for her blood was all tangled up with his desire to make slow, sweet love to her until the sun came up. A little devil in the back of his mind urged him to take her, to force the dark gift on her and keep her with him forever.

Closing his eyes, he fought a silent, hard-won battle for control.

"Andreas?" Was he in pain? His whole body radiated with tension. Concerned, she laid her hand on his shoulder, jerked it away when, for a brief moment, she felt as if she was lost in a dark abyss. Brushing it aside, she asked, "Are you all right?"

A long shuddering sigh wracked his body. "I'm fine."

He didn't sound fine. His voice was rough, like sand over stone.

"Get in the car."

There was no refusing that tone of voice. She slid into the seat, jumped when he slammed the door. His hand trembled when he started the engine and put the car in gear.

Rylee stared at him as he pulled onto the road and turned the car toward home. Had she imagined that feeling of being lost in darkness? What did it mean?

It was a long, silent drive back to town. Rylee glanced at Andreas from time to time, wondering why he was so silent, so withdrawn. Had she done something, said something, to make him angry?

He still hadn't spoken a word by the time he pulled up in front of her apartment building. He hurried around to her side to open the door, but didn't help her out.

"Good night, Rylee," he said in that same rough tone.

Her gaze searched his, but she couldn't read anything in the depths of his eyes. "Good night."

He didn't walk her to her door. Standing on the building's front stairs, she watched him drive away. What had she done? One minute he had been kissing her so deeply, she thought she might go up in the flames and then, for no reason she could see, he had turned to ice.

More confused than ever, she opened the door and went inside.

* * *

Back in his lair, Andreas paced the floor from one end to the other. He had almost made a dreadful mistake. Two, actually. He had almost told Rylee the truth. Even worse, he had been on the brink of turning her just to keep her with him. Better for both of them if he never saw Rylee North again, he thought. Better for her, at any rate. He might be the worst kind of monster, but even he couldn't turn sweet Rylee against her will, no matter how desperately he wanted her.

Amanda Ashley

Chapter 4

Rylee woke to the insistent ringing of the doorbell. Grabbing her robe, she went to see who had come calling so early in the day.

"Good morning, miss," a cheerful young man said. "I was told to deliver these to your home."

Rylee glanced at the two large cardboard boxes sitting in the hallway. "What is it?"

"A delivery from Finster's."

"I didn't order anything." The market was on the other side of town. She never shopped there.

"It's a gift. Should I bring it in for you?"

Rylee hesitated, then shook her head. "No, thank you. I can manage."

"Are you sure? It's no trouble."

"I'm sure."

"Well, okay. Have a great day."

She watched him leave, then pulled the boxes inside and closed and locked the door. She stared at the cartons a moment, wondering if she should have refused delivery. There could be anything in there. Some maniac had been leaving bombs in packages all over town. She had only the young man's word that it was from the market.

Curiosity overcame caution. Shrugging, she carefully lifted a corner of the lid on the first box and peeked inside. It was indeed filled with food—milk and meat and ice cream. The second box contained bread and fruit and vegetables, condiments and salad, eggs and cereal, and a bag of candy.

She couldn't stop smiling as she carried the boxes into the kitchen and put the groceries away. Her fridge and cupboards had never been so full, not even when she had a job.

She had no doubt Andreas had sent it, though, considering how their date had ended last night, she had no idea why. As she put the last of the groceries away, she wondered if she would ever get a chance to thank him. After last night, it seemed unlikely.

She devoured an enormous breakfast, then set about cleaning her apartment. Lately, she'd given it little more than a lick and a promise but this morning, with her rent paid and her stomach full and happy, she dusted and vacuumed with a vengeance.

And all the while, she wondered where Andreas was, what he was doing, and if she would ever see him again.

* * *

He prowled the confines of his lair, impatiently waiting for the sun to set. Although he could be awake during the day, as long as he stayed out of the sun, he far preferred the night. He had made a vow never to see Rylee again, but in his heart he knew it was a promise he could never keep. His need to see her had awakened him long before sunset. He had been restlessly pacing the floor ever since.

* * *

Rylee put the book she'd been reading aside as, once again, she found herself wondering about the "other kind of life" Andreas had referred to. He read minds, of that she had no doubt. Was he some kind of stage performer? One of those people who worked nightclubs? She shook her head. She couldn't imagine him as an entertainer. She could, however, picture him as a card shark, reading minds and winning thousands of dollars from gullible millionaires in places like Las Vegas and Atlantic City. It would explain how he could afford those amazing cars. Although what part she could play in such a life was beyond her, she thought. And then she

     Amanda Ashley

frowned. Was he thinking of using her as some kind of shill? A diversion, maybe?

Lost in thought, she jumped when the doorbell rang. She knew it was Andreas even before she opened the door.

A thrill of excitement raced through her when she saw him standing in the hall. "What are you doing here?"

"I came to apologize."

"Oh?"

"You're angry."

"No, just confused. I don't understand you at all."

"Be grateful that you don't."

"What's that supposed to mean? One minute we're locked in each other's arms and the next you completely shut me out with no explanation."

"You're right."

Rylee scowled at him. "Do you want to come in?"

"If you don't mind."

With a huff of annoyance, she turned her back on him and went into the living room. If he came in, fine. If not… She tried to squelch the little burst of anticipation she felt when she sensed his presence behind her.

She sat on the sofa, her feet tucked beneath her, her hands folded in her lap.

He took the chair.

"Thank you for the food you sent."

"You're welcome."

Silence settled between them.

After an uncomfortable few moments, Rylee cocked her head to the side. "So, are you going to tell me more about this "other" kind of life you mentioned?"

"I'm not sure you're ready to hear it."

"Is it that horrible?"

"I don't think so."

"What happened last night? One minute we were… you know. And the next you were taking me home."

"I decided things were moving a little too fast."

"Really? Usually it's the girl who thinks that."

"Is it?" he asked, a smile in his voice.

"You are the most frustrating man I've ever met!"

"And you are the most intriguing woman I've ever known. Would you like to go out this evening?"

"I don't think so."

"Still angry with me?"

"Maybe."

"Change your mind, Rylee, sweet."

"What did you have in mind?"

"Nothing in particular."

"I'd like to go dancing. Do you dance?"

"Like Fred Astaire."

"Give me ten minutes to change?"

"Wear the black dress."

* * *

He took her to an upscale night club in the next town. It was one she'd never been to, and it was lovely. The dance floor was large, made of polished wood that gleamed in the lamplight. The music was live, the lights low.

They found a table in a dark corner. A waiter took their order—a dark red wine for Andreas, a strawberry daiquiri for her.

"Shall we?" Andreas asked, cocking his head in the direction of the dance floor.

Rylee nodded, her heart pounding with anticipation as he took her hand. She was so nervous, she was afraid she might trip over her own feet, but once he took her in his arms, all her fears vanished. He held her close, so close she had no trouble following him at all. It was the strangest thing, but it was almost as if they were the only two people in the room. She was only aware of Andreas, his hand at her waist holding her close, the desire in his eyes when he looked at her, the way she fit in his arms. She closed her eyes as the first song ended and another began.

Andreas felt her relax against him. He had never held a woman who felt so right in his arms, or one who tempted him so much. With his preternatural senses, he was keenly aware of the scent of her hair, her skin. Her blood. The way her heart skipped a beat whenever his body brushed hers.

Unable to resist, he captured her will with his, then lowered his head to

Amanda Ashley

her neck for a taste. Warmth spread through him, chasing away his perpetual chill, easing his hunger. He took as much as he dared, forced himself to stop before he took too much.

Before he took it all.

When the music ended, he released her from his thrall. Leading her back to their table, he ordered her a screwdriver, heavy on the orange juice.

"But I don't like those," Rylee protested. "I never have."

Holding her gaze with his, he said, "You'll like this one. It'll be good for you."

She blinked at him, then nodded.

They stayed until the club closed, dancing to all the slow numbers, making idle conversation the rest of the time.

At home, he walked her to her door, then took her in his arms. "Did you have a good time, lovely Rylee?" he asked.

"Wonderful. Thank you." She gazed up at him, waiting, hoping he would read her mind and kiss her goodnight.

And he did.

He drew her closer, his fingers delving into the hair at her nape as his mouth covered hers in a long, slow kiss that was achingly sweet and erotic at the same time.

She leaned into him, every fiber of her body yearning to be closer, closer.

"Rylee," he groaned. "Do you know what you're doing to me?"

Somewhat breathless, she murmured, "The same thing you're doing to me, I hope."

He smiled down at her, knowing, in that moment, that he couldn't let her go out of his life. "Tomorrow night?" he asked, his voice husky.

She nodded.

One more kiss and he reached past her to open the door. "Pleasant dreams, Rylee," he whispered. And she would have them. Dreams hot enough to set the sheets on fire.

He would see to that.

Chapter 5

Rylee woke tangled in her sheets, her whole body still warm and tingling from the dream that lingered in her mind. It was the first time she had ever been embarrassed by a dream, but, oh, my, it had been amazing. Andreas had carried her away to a deserted island surrounded by a crystal blue ocean. The sand had been blindingly white. He had carried her into a small round hut located beneath a blood-red sky and there, on a bed of soft white furs, he had made her every yearning for him come true as he made love to her all night long.

Throwing the covers aside, she went into the bathroom and took a long, cool shower. Then, filled with a sudden restlessness, she decided to walk to the corner diner for breakfast.

It was early and customers were few. She took a table near the window, ordered pancakes, bacon and eggs, and sat back in her chair. The day stretched before her. She missed going to work. Missed having a purpose to her day, a reason to get up in the morning. Perhaps she'd go job hunting after breakfast.

She had finished eating and was sipping a second cup of coffee when a man approached her table. He was tall, in his early thirties, with wavy blond hair and warm blue eyes. He looked vaguely familiar though she couldn't place him.

"Miss North?"

"Who wants to know?"

"My name is Alan Williamson. I own Williamson Realty. I'm looking for someone to answer the phones, read the mail, do a little filing. I was told you might be interested."

"Oh? Who told you that?"

"Mr. Andreas. I believe you know him."

Rylee nodded. "Sit down, won't you?" She recognized him now. She'd seen him in town from time to time though they had never met.

He slid into the chair across from hers. "Are you interested?"

"Yes, very much."

After discussing pay, hours and days off, he said, "If you're agreeable, I'd like you to start on Monday, say nine a.m.?"

"I'll be there."

"Fantastic. I'll see you then. Oh, dress is casual but not too casual, if you know what I mean."

Rylee nodded again. God bless Andreas, she thought as she watched Williamson leave the diner. Once again, he had come to her rescue.

And then she frowned. How had Williamson known where she was?

* * *

"Well, well, if it isn't my fairy godfather come to call."

Andreas lifted one brow, amused by her greeting. "Is that what I am?" he asked, following her into the living room.

"Definitely. You've bought me clothes, taken me to the theater, loaded my cupboards with food. And now you've found me employment. Cinderella's godmother couldn't have done better," she said, grinning. "Actually, I guess you're even better than she was, because my dress didn't disappear at midnight."

A wicked smile curved his lips. "Certainly a mistake on my part."

She stared at Andreas a moment, and then, taking his meaning, she blushed. The second time she had worn the dress, she'd been in his arms at midnight, in the middle of a dance floor.

"How did Mr. Williamson know I'd be at the diner this morning?"

"I called and told him where you were."

"Oh." And Andreas would know, she thought, since he could read her mind.

"What shall we do tonight?" he asked. "Your wish is your fairy godfather's command."

* * *

When Rylee couldn't decide what she wanted to do, Andreas suggested going to the beach. It was California, after all. The weather was cool but not terribly cold. The sky was clear, the moon full and bright.

Clad in jeans and a t-shirt, her bathing suit underneath, Rylee sat cross-legged on a blanket gazing out at the water. Andreas sat beside her, his thigh against hers. That touch alone was enough to keep her warm. What was there about him that made her whole body come alive whenever he was near? Her heart skipped a beat when he draped his arm around her shoulders. She wanted him to hold her, kiss her, pull her down on the blanket and make love to her beneath the moon and the stars. She had known him less than a week and she was already wondering what it would be like to let him make love to her. She knew somehow that it would be amazing. The intensity of her feelings, her sudden urge to crawl into his arms, frightened her. Sometimes *he* frightened her.

Leaping to her feet, she kicked off her shoes, tugged off her jeans, and ran down to the water. It was a lot colder than the air, but it was just what she needed to cool her raging hormones.

She swam out just past the waves.

And realized she had made a dreadful mistake in going out so far when something large glided past her, so close it brushed against her leg. It moved past her, a large fin knifing sharply though the water.

Shark!

Fear and panic churned in the pit of her stomach as images from *Jaws* flashed through her mind—the girl being dragged through the water, Quinn being swallowed whole.

She was going to die. There was no way anyone could save her. Andreas was the only one on the beach. Too far away to help. And what could he do, anyway? But the creature was swimming away, toward deeper water.

Relief was short-lived. She screamed as it turned and arrowed straight toward her.

The echo of her cry still hung in the air when, suddenly, Andreas was

Amanda Ashley

beside her, holding her body close to his.

The air rippled with a current of power unlike anything she had ever experienced. She couldn't see it, but she felt it spreading around them like an invisible barrier.

Apparently, the shark felt it, too, because it turned and swam out to sea.

"Ready to go ashore?" Andreas asked.

Shivering, teeth chattering and not from the cold, she nodded.

He held her close to his side as they made their way to the shore. Once on land, he grabbed the blanket and wrapped it around her, then held her in his arms. In an impossibly short time, she was dry and warm.

* * *

Later, lying side by side, still in his arms, she wondered how he had gotten to her so fast. Then she wondered about that odd sensation she had felt while he was in the water beside her. And how it happened that her hair and clothing and skin had all dried so fast.

Sitting up, she wrapped her arms around her bent knees. "What happened out there?"

Propped on his elbow, he looked up at her. "What do you mean?"

"How did you get to me so fast? What was that funny, scary surge of energy? I've never felt anything like it. Why did the shark go away? How did I get dry so fast? I should still be wet." She frowned at him. "And so should you."

Andreas sat up. "Remember that other kind of life I mentioned? Maybe now's the time to tell you about it."

Overcome by a sudden uneasiness, Rylee nodded. She was alone on the beach with a man she had known less than a week. What if that "other" lifestyle was some kind of perversion? Or worse? What if he was a serial killer? Suddenly chilled to the bone, she clutched the blanket tighter. Had she escaped one monster only to be at the mercy of another?

Andreas shook his head, amused by her tumultuous thoughts. Pervert? Serial killer? Seriously?

She recoiled when he reached for her hand.

"Rylee?"

"Who are you? *What* are you?"

It was definitely time to have that talk. He scooted over a few feet, putting plenty of space between them. "I'm not a pervert or a serial killer," he said quietly. "But I am a predator."

Eyes wide, she stared at him, her first instinct to run, but she couldn't move.

"I'm…" He paused. He hadn't realized it would be so hard to tell her the truth. But then, it wasn't something he shared with many people. "I'm a vampire."

Rylee blinked at him, certain she had misunderstood what he said. *Vampire?* Impossible. They didn't exist. He wasn't a killer or a pervert. He was just insane. Why wasn't she more afraid? Why did she have the feeling that he wouldn't hurt her? It made no sense.

"It's true."

She shook her head. "There's no such thing."

"Yes, there is. And you're looking at one."

"And that's your idea of a *different* kind of life?"

"Believe me, darlin', it *is* different."

Rylee shook her head again. "It's impossible."

He shrugged. "I'm living proof."

"Vampires aren't alive."

"Not in the normal sense, no."

"So, why haven't you bitten me?"

"How do you know I haven't?"

She lifted a hand to her neck.

"Only a couple of times," he said. "Once on the dance floor."

What if it was true? She was tempted to ask him to prove it, but if he really *was* a vampire, that seemed inordinately foolish. "Why haven't you turned me?"

He lifted one brow. "Why would I?"

"Isn't that what vampires do?"

"Are you suggesting I make you what I am to prove I'm telling the truth?"

"No!"

Andreas laughed softly as he pulled her into his arms. Noting her tension and the wariness in her eyes, he murmured, "Relax, Rylee, my sweet innocent, I would never hurt you. Believe that if you believe nothing else."

"I think I'd like to go home."

"As you wish." Rising, he wrapped his arm around her, blanket and all,

     Amanda Ashley

then summoned a little vampire magic, and transported them back to her apartment. Taking her hand in his, he kissed her palm. "Good night, fair lady."

Rylee shivered as his lips brushed her skin.

And then, to her amazement, he vanished from her sight.

* * *

Rylee stared at the place where Andreas had stood only moments before, then glanced around her apartment, her head reeling. How had they gotten here?

Vampire.

She didn't believe in such things, yet how else to explain everything that had happened tonight? He had disappeared in front of her very eyes. She had seen magicians make things disappear, but those were illusions – like David Copperfield making the Statue of Liberty disappear.

She searched her mind for a logical explanation. *Witchcraft?* She considered it a moment and then rejected the idea. She didn't believe in witches and warlocks, either.

Curling up in her favorite chair, she stared out the window. He could read her mind. He could make it look as if he had vanished into thin air. Somehow, they had traveled from the beach to her apartment with no apparent means of transportation.

Maybe he really was an incredibly skillful magician. That had to be it. It made far more sense than believing in vampires. Well, her hat was off to him. He was right up there with Copperfield, Penn and Teller, Siegfried and Roy, Criss Angel.

And then she frowned. If Andreas was a magician, why on earth would he want her to believe he was a vampire? For laughs? Some kind of weird joke? If so, he definitely had a bizarre sense of humor, that was for sure.

So, he read minds and did illusions, but she had never heard of a magician who could influence a shark. And what about that weird sensation she'd felt in the water? She never saw him eat. She never saw him during the day...

"Oh, for goodness sakes, Rylee Jean North, stop letting your imagination get the best of you. There are no such things as vampires or witches or goblins or... or zombies."

With a shake of her head, she took a quick shower, washed her hair, and went to bed.

Only to dream of vampires and witches and things that went bump in the night.

CHAPTER 6

Lost in thought, Andreas prowled the dark streets. Rylee's reaction to his confession hadn't been what he'd expected. He had anticipated shock, revulsion, fear, but not total disbelief. Perhaps it was just as well.

He had been a vampire for almost four hundred years and in all that time, he had only told one other woman the truth of what he was. It had been a fatal mistake. On hearing the truth, she had run out of his lair and into the night where a carriage had run her down. She had died instantly from a broken neck. Recalling that now, he wondered what insanity had possessed him to tell Rylee. Perhaps it was a blessing in disguise that she hadn't believed him.

Taking a seat on a bench near the entrance to the park, he closed his eyes and opened his senses. Mankind missed so much. Sights and sounds and smells that were hidden from mortal perception. The ability to transport himself wherever he wished to be, to dissolve into mist, to change shape at his whim, to run faster, jump higher, move quicker than any man ever dreamed of.

To read Rylee's mind. To insinuate himself into her dreams and make love to her all night long.

Rylee. A thought took him to her side. She looked like a fairy-tale princess, her hair spread like a dark nimbus across her pillow, her lips slightly parted.

His mind brushed hers. She was dreaming about witches, running from a coven in fear for her life. With the ease of long practice, he slid inside her mind and chased the witches away. She was ever so grateful, something he quickly turned to his advantage as his thoughts influenced her dreams.

When he left her bedroom an hour later, she was smiling.

And so was he.

* * *

Rylee woke slowly, her thoughts conflicted. She'd had a wonderfully sexy dream about Andreas last night. He had kissed and caressed her and in some way she didn't fathom, it had convinced her that he was, indeed, a vampire. Maybe it was because she had known, even in her sleep, that he was there, in the room with her. She took a deep breath and his scent filled her nostrils, confirming her suspicions.

It had been no phantom lover who had caressed her but a man with substance.

A man who wasn't even a man, but a vampire. Funny, it didn't seem so far-fetched now.

Vampire. She was falling in love with a creature of the night, a man who was no longer human. She lifted a hand to her neck. He had confessed that he had bitten her twice but she had no memory of it, no telltale marks on her skin. Why couldn't she remember? What else had he done to her?

Rising, she pulled on a robe, then padded into the kitchen to make a pot of coffee.

When it was ready, she poured herself a cup and carried it to her computer. She had never believed in the supernatural. She had never had any kind of paranormal experiences. She wasn't psychic, she didn't have visions, she didn't see ghosts.

Yet she knew without doubt that Andreas was a vampire. A very old vampire. How?

When her computer booted up, she clicked on Google and typed in *vampires.*

There were over 95,000 possible results. Vampires: The Real Story; The Bloody Truth About Vampires; The Great New England Vampire Panic; A Natural History of Vampires; The Real Dracula: Vlad the Impaler, and

Amanda Ashley

on and on and on.

Vampires were virtually immortal. They could move faster than the human eye could follow. They healed almost immediately. They didn't age. They didn't get sick. They couldn't reproduce. Sunlight was fatal to all except the oldest of them. Fire, beheading, or a wooden stake through the heart would destroy them. Pure silver burned their flesh. They could change shape and turn into mist. Some said they couldn't cross running water. They couldn't enter a home without an invitation; when it was revoked, they had to leave instantly. She paused when she read that, wondering if it was true.

A link on one of the vampire pages led to links about other paranormal creatures—witches and warlocks, trolls and ogres, shape-shifters and fairies. Rylee frowned as a distant memory surfaced and she heard her great-grandmother's voice calling her "my little fairy child" and telling her that someday her true self would emerge, whatever that meant.

Returning her attention to the topic at hand, Rylee clicked on another vampire link.

An hour later, she sat back and rubbed her eyes. It would take days to read every web page devoted to the undead. And even if she did, there was no way to know which information was true and which was fabrication.

And none of them could help her decide what to do about Andreas, not in the long run. And not if he should come calling tonight. Should she tell him she believed him? Should she rescind his invitation? If she rebuffed him, would she be putting her life in danger?

With a shake of her head, she realized her life had been in jeopardy since the night she met him. She just hadn't known it until now. She closed her eyes, trying to sort her thoughts, and heard a quiet voice—one that sounded very much like her great-grandmother's—assuring her she had nothing to fear from Andreas or any other vampire. Rylee frowned as that same voice assured her that he wouldn't be able to kill her even if he tried.

And then a horrible thought crossed her mind. If Andreas was a vampire, and she had no doubt that he was, then someone had to turn him, which meant there was more than one. How many more? Dozens? Hundreds? Thousands? Now that was a scary thought. She wondered if there were other vampires here in town, and if Andreas had ever turned anyone, and if so, what had happened to them?

When her stomach growled, she scuffed into the kitchen where she made an egg sandwich for breakfast and washed it down with another cup of coffee.

It was eleven a.m. She had about seven hours until sunset.

Seven hours to decide what to do if Andreas knocked at her door.

$* * *$

Andreas woke with the setting of the sun. One minute he was trapped in oblivion. The next he was awake and aware of the day, the time, and his surroundings.

Opening his senses, he sought for a connection to Rylee and knew immediately that she no longer had any doubts that vampires existed.

Frowning, he showered and changed his clothes, wondering, all the while, what had happened to convince her that his kind existed. Surely reading a few pages on the web hadn't persuaded her of the truth when nothing he had said convinced her. His frown deepened with the realization that even in her sleep, she had somehow known that not only was he in her dreams, but in her bedroom, as well. That his kisses and caresses had been real.

He shook his head in disbelief. He had walked in a multitude of other dreams through the years, but no mortal female had ever realized that those dreams were real.

How had Rylee discerned the difference? And what did it mean? Was it possible she possessed some innate paranormal power? She wasn't a witch, he knew that. Witch blood was cold and bitter and Rylee's was warmer and sweeter than any he had ever tasted. She wasn't a werewolf; they were compelled to change when the moon was full. Too pretty to be a troll or a goblin. Fae, perhaps? Was that why he was so drawn to her? It was said that vampires got on well with the fae folk.

Had taking her blood more than once somehow aroused a power lying dormant within her? Or was she one of those rare people who seemed born to become vampires?

He turned the puzzle over in his mind while he dressed. The first night he'd met her, he had intended to prey on her, but something—some indefinable force—had prevented him from doing so. Why? And why wasn't Rylee more afraid of him? Even now, when she knew the truth, she had no real fear of him.

Amanda Ashley

He was still trying to unravel the mystery when he took to the streets in search of prey.

* * *

Rylee stood at the kitchen sink, drying her hands while she watched the sun set behind the distant mountains. Was Andreas awake yet? What was it like for him, during the day? Was he literally dead to the world? How often did he have to drink blood? What happened if he went too long without it? How old was he? Had he ever been married, either before or after he'd been turned? Did he have children and if so, were any of them still living?

So many questions. Did she dare ask them? Would he give her the answers? Did she really want to know?

"Curiosity, thy name is woman."

Startled by the sound of his voice, she whirled around. "You really need to stop sneaking up on me like that!"

"Sorry. You can blame my lack of manners on all those questions running through your mind. You may ask me anything you wish, my sweet Rylee. Should I answer your questions in order, or do you want to ask them yourself, one by one?"

She shook her head. "You don't have to answer any of them. Your private life is really none of my business."

"Quite the contrary. I've given it a lot of thought, and we are connected, you and I, though I'm not sure how. You've felt it, too, haven't you?"

Nodding, Rylee tossed the towel aside and went into the living room. Moving to the sofa, she curled up in one corner. Following her, Andreas took a place at the other end of the couch.

He regarded her a moment, then said quietly, "When I succumb to the dark sleep, it is truly like death. Some few of us ancient ones can be awake during the day, though we must avoid direct sunlight. As for blood..." He shrugged. "Fledgling vampires need more than older ones but we never lose the craving for it. Going without for an extended period of time is painful. Lack of blood has been known to drive vampires insane. As for my age, I was twenty-nine when I was turned."

He paused when she leaned forward, eyes wide as she waited for him to go on. "I've been a vampire for a very long time. Almost four hundred years."

"Four hundred years," she murmured.

He nodded. "Longer than others, not as long as some. I was married, briefly. It was an arranged marriage, as was the custom at the time. She was a pretty thing. Given time, I might have grown to love her. Sadly, she died in childbirth a year after we wed, and the infant with her. I never married again."

"I'm sorry."

"It was centuries ago. I barely remember her."

Rylee sat back, her arms folded, as she contemplated what he'd told her. "Do you like being a vampire?" she asked, after a moment.

"Honestly? Yes."

"Did you ask someone to turn you?"

He laughed softly. "I've never known anyone in their right mind who *asked* to be a vampire. I was turned by one of the ancient ones who was looking for someone to keep him company."

"I never imagined vampires getting lonely," Rylee murmured. But then, she'd never really thought about it. Head cocked to the side, she asked, "So, did you stay with him?"

"For a quarter of a century. Until he walked out into the sun."

Rylee looked at him in horror. "Why would he do that?"

"Caius had been turned back when Rome ruled the world. I think he was just tired of living."

She shook her head, unable to believe anyone would willingly choose such a terrible death. Surely there was nothing more painful than being burned alive. "Do you ever get lonely?"

His gaze held hers. "Not since I met you."

Rylee's heart skipped a beat as a palpable warmth passed between them. "Why do we seem so connected?" she asked, somewhat breathlessly. "Why aren't I afraid of you, of what you are? I should be scared out of my mind, but I'm not. Why?"

Moving to sit beside her, Andreas ran his knuckles over her cheek and down the side of her neck. "I can't explain it, either, Rylee, my sweet. But there it is." His gaze moved to her throat. She must have noticed, because she lifted her hand to her neck. As if that would protect her.

"Rylee?"

　　　Amanda Ashley

She heard the question in his voice, the yearning. Saw the hunger rise in his eyes. He had tasted her before. He'd told her so even though she had no memory of it happening.

"It was only a little both times," he assured her. As if that made a difference.

Her first instinct was to refuse. Surely no one would willingly allow a vampire to bite them. But the more she considered it, the more curious she became.

"I can make you forget, once it's done, if you like."

"No." She stiffened a little as he brushed her hair behind her ear, gasped when she felt his tongue slide over her neck. "Will it hurt?" she asked tremulously.

"Not at all. You might even like it."

She didn't believe him, but there was no pain at all when he bit her. It felt strange, knowing Andreas was biting her—feeding on her—and yet it was also strangely arousing. Surely nothing, not even letting him make love to her, could be more intimate than letting him drink from her. He was part of her now, she thought, and she was part of him. Two halves of the same whole. A gradual warmth spread through her, filling her with an odd sense of power and euphoria, making her feel as though she could take on the world and win.

A soft cry of protest emerged from her lips when he lifted his head, breaking the fragile link between them, sending her spiraling down into oblivion.

Andreas swore under his breath as Rylee went limp. What the hell? Had he killed her? But that was impossible. He hadn't taken that much. Dammit! What had he done?

He placed his hand on her brow, then stilled as he let his mind connect with hers. In some indefinable way, he could sense changes taking place inside her, though he had no idea what that meant or how it was possible. He could understand it if she had taken his blood, but he had taken hers.

"Rylee?" He patted her hands, her cheek. "Rylee."

Her eyelids fluttered open and she stared at him blankly. "What happened?"

"Beats the hell out of me. I guess you fainted."

"I've never fainted in my life."

"First time for everything, I guess," he said, helping her sit up. "How do you feel?"

"I don't know."

"Stay there." Hurrying into the kitchen, he opened the refrigerator and pulled out a bottle of orange juice. He filled a large glass and carried it to her. "Drink it," he said. "All of it."

She didn't argue.

When she drained the glass, he put it aside. "Are you're sure you feel all right?"

"Never better." She smiled at him. "Stop worrying, I'm fine. Maybe you just took too much."

He nodded, even though he knew it wasn't true.

Something bizarre had happened between the two of them.

Something that had never happened with any other woman.

* * *

Andreas pondered the evening's events long after he bid Rylee goodnight. He had taken her blood, and in some way he didn't understand, it had strengthened *her*. How was that even possible? He thought back to the first night they had met. He hadn't fed in a while and had intended to drain her dry. Instead, he had been compelled to protect her, even from himself. To help her. Why? That was the question that haunted him. Why?

Why did she have this effect on him?

What made her different from the hundreds of other women he had known? He frowned as bits and pieces of an ancient legend surfaced in his mind, some myth about a mortal woman that vampires were unable to harm. A woman who, if turned, would become some kind of super-human with all the powers of a vampire and none of the weaknesses.

He shook his head. It was only a fable, he mused, and then he grunted softly. Mortals thought stories of vampires were only make believe, too. But they existed. And maybe the woman of myth and legend did, too.

The thought that Rylee might be that woman followed him into oblivion.

Amanda Ashley

CHAPTER 7

Rylee slept late. On waking, she was surprised that she hadn't dreamed or, if she had, she didn't remember it. What she did remember was Andreas biting her and how amazing it had been, and how she had fainted dead away afterwards. He had been surprised, too.

She had fed a vampire. The thought brought a smile to her lips. And then she frowned, overcome by an unexpected wave of jealousy as she realized that she didn't want him to drink from anyone but her. And how weird was that, not to mention unlikely? Surely no one person could ever satisfy a vampire's insatiable thirst and survive. Was it possible every woman who fed him felt the same possessive bond she did? And if so, how did they bear it when he left them?

How would she feel if he left her? Best not to think about that now.

Shuffling into the kitchen, she glanced at the calendar, her eyes widening when she saw the big red X on Monday. She had completely forgotten about her new job. After breakfast, she'd go through her closet and see what was ready to wear and what needed to be sent to the cleaners. Although she didn't know how she was going to think about going to work with all that was going on with Andreas!

Andreas. Just thinking about that sexy vampire made her smile. Who'd have thought that letting him drink her blood would have such a profound effect? She felt close to him in a way she didn't understand. Did he feel the same about her? Or was she just another source of food, a willing woman among so many others?

Fighting down a rush of jealousy, she wondered how many others? As old as he was, he'd probably lost count!

Pushing the thought out of her mind, she ate a quick breakfast, then went to her bedroom to assess her wardrobe.

* * *

Andreas woke abruptly. For a moment, he felt disoriented, which was highly unusual on waking. His first thought was for Rylee. Fearing she might be in some kind of trouble he opened the link between them, but she was in no danger.

And as far as he could tell, neither was he. So, what had roused him from the dark sleep in the middle of the day?

Rising, he padded naked up the stairs to the living room, his preternatural senses expanding with each step. His lair, deep underground, sometimes hindered his finer powers.

Eyes closed, he stood in the middle of the room. At first he felt nothing. And then, on the very edges of perception, he caught the scent of another vampire. And then another. All told, three vampires had invaded his territory sometime in the night without his noticing. Two were young, no more than a hundred. The third was older, stronger.

And they were all here for Rylee. She *was* the woman the ancient ones had spoken of, he thought. If he'd had any doubts, they'd been shattered by the sudden arrival of the other vampires. Somehow, his drinking from her last night had alerted others of her existence.

But they had come too late. Rylee was already his.

There would be no doubt of that once his blood ran in her veins. And he intended to make that happen at the first opportune moment. All he had to do was convince her it was necessary.

With a shake of his head, he returned to his lair. Resting strengthened him and he had a feeling he would need all the power at his command to persuade her.

* * *

　　　　　Amanda Ashley

Rylee expected to see Andreas at her door when she opened it after dinner. Instead, she found a rather handsome young man with pale blond hair and the lightest blue eyes she had ever seen. "May I help you?"

"I hope so." He had a winning smile.

Rylee frowned at him. "I'm sorry, I don't understand."

"May I come in?"

No! Andreas shouted the word in her mind. *Don't!*

Rylee glanced behind her, expecting to see him there. But the room was empty. "I'm busy now," she said, intending to shut the door. "Sorry."

His hand shot forward to prevent its closing. "You will let me in." His gaze captured hers, his voice suddenly soft and compelling. "You have something I need."

"Something you need," she repeated.

"My name is Leon," he said in that same mesmerizing voice. "Invite me in."

"Of course. Come in, Leon."

As he stepped across the threshold, Andreas materialized in front of Rylee, shoving her aside with one hand while his other hand locked around Leon's neck.

Startled out of her trance, Rylee watched in horror as Andreas ripped the other man's heart from his chest. Sickened by the sight, she ran into the bathroom and vomited up her dinner.

She was still on her knees in front of the toilet when Andreas handed her a damp washrag.

"I'm sorry you had to see that," he said quietly.

After wiping her mouth, she said, "How did you know…?"

"I sensed his presence. Just in time, as it turns out."

"Was he a…?"

Andreas nodded. "A young one. Not only young, but foolish to come into my territory without my permission." He debated whether to tell her about the other two, then decided to wait until the horror of what she had just seen had waned.

"Why did he come here? Was he looking for you?"

"No. He was looking for you."

"Me?" She looked up at him, her eyes wide. "Why?"

There would never be a better time to tell her what he suspected than now. Taking her by the hand, he helped her to her feet.

Rylee wiped her face with a dry towel, but hesitated to follow him when he headed toward the living room. "I don't want to go back in there," she said.

"It's all right. I took care of it." He had wrapped the body in the throw rug beneath it while Rylee was in the bathroom. Fortunately, vampires didn't bleed profusely. He had then transported the body to a vacant lot where the sun's light would disintegrate it.

Rylee followed Andreas into the living room. She didn't know how he'd gotten rid of the dead vampire so quickly, but there was no sign of the body, thank goodness. She huddled on the sofa. "Why?" she asked again. "Why did he come here?"

Andreas took the chair opposite the sofa. "I'm going to tell you what I think. I doubt if you'll believe me, but I'm pretty sure it's true." He took a deep breath. "There's a legend among vampires that every three hundred years a girl child is born who will be sympathetic to my kind. No vampire will be able to hurt her."

Rylee's eyes widened. "You think it's me, don't you?"

Nodding, he said, "That first night in the alley, one taste of your blood and I wanted to take it all." He blew out a sigh. "I haven't taken a life in centuries but that one taste filled me with warmth and a sense of power unlike anything I'd ever known. Heaven help me, I might have drained you dry but *something* prevented me from taking too much. Some mystical force I'd never felt before."

"And that makes you think *I'm* this woman of legend?"

"Yes. You felt different after I took your blood the other night, didn't you?" Words from the legend rose in his mind: *The third bite will produce a rare exchange of power that will also strengthen her.*

Rylee nodded, her brow furrowed. "I felt as if you were part of me and I was part of you. And I felt…"

"Go on."

"I felt, I don't know, powerful, invincible."

"Interesting."

"Is that normal? Is there something wrong with me?"

"No, it's not normal. And no, there's nothing wrong with you."

"So, what does it mean, exactly?"

"The legend says that if this woman is turned into a vampire, she will inherit all of a vampire's powers but none of their weaknesses."

     Amanda Ashley

Rylee stared at him, speechless. Become a vampire? No way!

Seeing the horror in her eyes, he said, "Think about it, sweet Rylee. You'd never age, never be sick. You'd be like Wonder Woman," he said, a smile in his voice.

"Would I have to drink blood?"

"Once a year. From me."

That might not be so bad, she thought, especially if it made her feel as wonderful as she'd felt after letting him drink from her. "Would I have to sleep during the day? Give up eating?"

"No."

"There has to be a downside. What about children?"

"You will be able to bear a child. My child," he said, hope evident in his tone. "Perhaps for you that would be the downside."

"Only your child?"

"Only the child of the vampire who turns you."

"I thought vampires couldn't reproduce."

"Mating with you makes it possible."

Mating. The thought sent a shiver down her spine. "What if I marry a human male?"

"I don't know. The legend doesn't say anything about that."

Rylee cocked her head to the side, her gaze moving over him. Was he telling her the truth? If so, it was the most outlandish story she had ever heard. "You said women like I'm supposed to be are born every three hundred years. What happened to the others?"

"I only know of one. She lives in Germany with her vampire husband."

"What if I don't let you turn me?"

"Other vampires might come here looking for you. Not to kill you, but to drink from you. Your blood is unique. I've only taken a little, but it has already enhanced my powers. Some will want to turn you so you can give them a child." Once turned, she would be forever bound to the vampire who sired her. He debated whether to tell her that, then decided against it, at least for the time being.

"Is that what you want from me? A child?"

"I just want you, my sweet Rylee. Mortal or vampire or both, I want you." And that, at least, was the whole truth. "Once you are turned, the other vampires will leave you alone. But, for now, my blood will prevent any other vampire from bringing you across. Think of it as insurance."

"I need time to think about all this," she murmured. "I'm still not sure I believe any of it."

"Well, if Leon didn't convince you, I don't know what will."

"Did you have to kill him?"

"He came into my territory uninvited."

"*Your* territory?"

"I've—you should pardon the pun—staked it out for over a century. It's mine. Any vampire who comes here without my permission is risking destruction."

"That seems so… so medieval. Are you going to hunt down the others and kill them, too?"

"If they're smart, they will have taken the hint and left town. If not…?" He shrugged then reached for her hand. "Enough about them. You can't deny the attraction between us, Rylee, my love. Even before you drank my blood, we were connected somehow. I think I was meant to find you. I know you were meant to be mine. But the choice is yours. I won't force it on you."

She nodded, overwhelmed by the sudden turn her life had taken. Was she really the embodiment of some ancient vampire legend? It sounded so far-fetched and yet, the more she thought about it, the more convinced she was that it was true.

"Like you said, you need time to think, so I'll leave you to it. You won't see me again unless you call me."

"But…"

"If you need me, I'll know. If you want me, you have only to call my name." Rising, he squeezed her hand, then kissed her palm. "Sweet dreams, Rylee."

She blinked and he was gone. If she let Andreas turn her, she mused with a faint smile, she would be able to do that, too. And so much more. What would it be like, to have all of a vampire's amazing powers? To live forever and never get old or sick? To always be as she was now? To marry Andreas and have his child?

She frowned. Would their child be a vampire? Or mortal? Or both?

She did, indeed, have a lot to think about.

     Amanda Ashley

CHAPTER 8

Rylee tossed and turned all night long, her thoughts chaotic. Did she want to be a vampire? Did she want to remain human and spend the rest of her life with Andreas, watching herself grow old while he stayed the same?

What would it be like to be part vampire and part human? That question was uppermost in her mind when she finally fell asleep. In her dreams, she let Andreas turn her. She drank his blood and felt her whole body undergo a miraculous change. When she cut herself, she healed instantly. She needed only a few hours' sleep each night. She ate whatever she wanted and never gained an ounce. They married and she had a baby girl born with a full set of teeth and tiny white fangs. When Rylee nursed the baby, she was horrified to see that, instead of milk, she produced blood.

She woke in the morning with her own horrified cries still ringing in her ears.

Muttering, "Just a dream," she ducked into the shower.

* * *

She spent the rest of the day doing busy-work. She went through her closets and dresser drawers, sorted through all her clothes, throwing away things she hadn't worn in years. She rearranged the kitchen cupboards, cleaned out the refrigerator. And all the while she weighed the pros and cons of becoming what Andreas insisted she was destined to become.

But he'd also said the choice was hers. And that was the problem. She couldn't decide which path to follow: stay human or become some sort of legendary half-vampire, half-human. And what if she wasn't really the woman he thought? What if meeting Andreas was all just some kind of cosmic coincidence?

Andreas… She hardly knew him, yet she felt closer to him than anyone she had ever met. Knowing she wouldn't see him again unless she called him made her feel empty inside, as if she'd lost half of her soul.

By sundown, she had the mother of all headaches. She ate a grilled cheese sandwich for dinner, took a long soak in a hot bubble bath, and went to bed early.

Andreas came to her in her dreams, his dark eyes filled with love as he took her in his arms and flooded every fiber of her being with joy. He whispered her name, his voice husky with love and desire. His power slid over her skin. His hands caressed her, every touch filled with an aching tenderness, a need that went beyond the physical. He was a preternatural being and yet she knew that, in some way she didn't quite understand, she held his future in her hands.

Rylee, beloved. I've waited centuries for you.

His voice, soft and low. Was it real? Or merely a part of her dream?

When she woke Sunday morning, her cheeks were damp with tears.

* * *

An hour later, Rylee went to church. She hadn't been to a worship service in years but she felt a sudden need for inspiration beyond her own. She was in love with a vampire. No doubt he had killed people to survive. Yet she felt that he was a good man.

The prayers, the hymns, the minister's words of hope and help, soothed her troubled spirit. It wasn't for her to judge him. It wasn't his fault he was a vampire.

There was a second service half an hour later and she sat through that one, too.

She walked out of the church feeling at peace for the first time in days.

     Amanda Ashley

*   *   *

The vampire rose with the setting of the sun. Aware that he was in another vampire's territory and not wishing to be discovered, Lycon went hunting in the next town. His prey was a middle-aged woman and when taking her blood didn't satisfy him, he sought a second victim before returning to the town where the woman of legend lived.

In addition to the master vampire, Andreas, there was another vampire seeking the female. Using his preternatural powers, Lycon went in search of the other, younger vampire. Dawson was barely a hundred, and still had much to learn. Unfortunately, he would not get the chance.

Tracking Dawson was all too easy. Lycon found him sitting in a high-backed booth in a dimly-lit club, a woman at his side. He staked the young vampire before he realized what had happened.

The woman stared at Lycon, eyes wide with fright.

"Lucky for you, I'm not hungry anymore," he murmured, and vanished from the saloon.

Outside, he went in search of the master of the city, but the wily vampire was not to be found.

Lycon grunted softly. Sooner or later, Andreas would lower his guard. And when the master vampire had been destroyed, the woman and the town would be his.

*   *   *

Andreas smelled vampires and death as soon as he stepped out of his lair. The second young vampire was dead, destroyed by Andreas' old nemesis, Lycon, who had dared to come into his territory. As Andreas had told Rylee, such a breach of etiquette was not to be tolerated.

Opening his senses, Andreas made sure Rylee was safely at home before he went in search of prey. He fed quickly, every instinct alert. It would be foolish indeed to let his guard down now, when there was another master vampire in the city. Only one thing could have tempted Lycon to invade another master's territory, and that was Rylee. Being an old vampire, Lycon would know the only way to obtain his goal was to destroy Andreas first.

Andreas smiled into the darkness. He had not lived this long by being careless. And he had one advantage the other vampire did not—he had taken Rylee's blood.

In the end, that would make all the difference.

CHAPTER 9

Filled with excitement, Rylee squared her shoulders as she opened the door to the Williamson Real Estate Office. It was a rather grand place. The reception area was carpeted in dark green. The walls were a lighter shade, hung with photographs of beautiful homes. A desk stood opposite the door. Several chairs were grouped in front of it. A flowered sofa stood against one wall.

She smiled as Alan Williamson stepped out of his office.

"Miss North, right on time! Welcome to our team."

"Thank you."

"Let me show you around."

She spent the next few minutes being introduced to the three realtors who worked at the office. Two were men—Dave Ogden, who was young and single, and Bob Klein, who was middle-aged and married. The third was a woman. Clair Duval appeared to be in her late forties. They all welcomed her warmly, especially Dave.

After the introductions were made, Mr. Williamson showed her the lunch room, then explained her duties and left her to it.

Rylee took her place behind the desk. She spent a few minutes looking in the drawers, familiarizing herself with the contents, and hoping she could do a good job. The people were friendly, the pay was good, and she was glad to have something productive to do with her days.

The hours passed quickly, with many phone calls to be answered, mail to be opened, and appointments to be made.

All in all, Rylee was sure she would be happy working there. Until she stepped out of the office to go home and she remembered that Andreas was no longer the only vampire in town and it was dark outside.

She blew out a sigh. Andreas had assured her they couldn't kill her. But having a strange vampire drink from her, or worse, turn her so she could bear his child, was, in some ways, an even more horrible fate. Andreas had assured her that his blood would prevent that, but what if he was wrong?

* * *

A week later, Andreas stood in the shadows across from the real estate office. He had waited there every night to make sure Rylee reached home safely. He had hoped she would call for him but the link between them remained silent. Still, whether she chose to stay with him or not, he felt responsible for her well-being, especially now, with Lycon in the neighborhood.

Jealously reared its ugly head when he saw a tall, young man walk Rylee to her car. They talked for several minutes, then Rylee slid behind the wheel and drove away.

Andreas imprinted the man's face and scent in his mind before following Rylee to make sure she arrived safely home.

Rylee paused when she got out of the car. She glanced around, her gaze probing the shadows, certain that Andreas was nearby, but when she didn't see him, she shrugged it off and went into the house. She locked the door and shot the dead bolt home, then kicked off her shoes.

She had been too busy learning her new duties to have much time to think about Andreas but now she couldn't think of anything else. She had missed him dreadfully the last week. More than once, she had been tempted to call him, but she had to be sure of her decision. Once made, there would be no going back.

Rylee, beloved. I've waited centuries for you.

How many times had those words, spoken with such yearning, such tenderness, played in her mind in the last week?

And what was she going to do about Dave Ogden? It had taken her completely by surprise when he asked her out when he walked her to her

Amanda Ashley

car. She'd thanked him and said she would let him know.

One more decision she didn't want to make.

She glanced out the front window on her way to the kitchen, froze when she saw a man standing on the sidewalk, staring at the house. She felt chilled to the bone when his gaze met hers.

Darting forward, she pulled the drapes, then stood there, panting as if she had just run five miles.

* * *

Lycon smiled as he strolled down the street. The woman of legend was young and remarkably pretty. When he sired her, she would be bound to him forever. And when that was accomplished, she would bear him a son.

* * *

Veiled in shadow, Andreas watched Lycon walk past him, then pause at the end of the block, head lifted to scent the wind.

He stood there several moments, then strode back toward the place where Andreas waited. "I know you're there."

Andreas materialized in front of him. For a time, they regarded each other in silence, two powerful beings who generally made an effort to keep out of each other's way.

Andreas spoke first. "You're trespassing."

Lycon shrugged. "Just passing through."

"Cut the crap. We both know why you're here. And you're too late. She's mine."

"Not yet."

"Her blood runs in my veins."

Nostrils flaring, Lycon looked at him sharply. Something that might have been jealousy flashed behind his eyes. And then he spread his hands in a placating gesture. "We were friends once. We could share her, for old time's sake."

"As I recall, the last time we tried that, it didn't work out so well."

"That was centuries ago."

Andreas nodded. "I heard you tired of her, and killed her."

"She was nothing," Lycon said with a shrug. "A peasant girl, easily replaced."

"I will not have Rylee meet the same fate."

"Surely you don't think I would treat the mother of my child in such a way."

"We'll never know."

The low purr of an engine caused Lycon to glance over his shoulder. He frowned when a police car came around the corner. "To the victor belong the spoils," he said confidently. And with that, he turned and jogged down the sidewalk.

Andreas waited for the police car to drive past, then crossed the street to Rylee's porch and rang the bell.

* * *

Rylee stared at the door, fear and hope brewing like a storm inside her. Fear because she knew there were other vampires in town, hope because it might be Andreas. And then she frowned, remembering that he'd said he wouldn't bother her unless she called him.

Taking a deep breath, she peered through the peep hole, felt her heart leap when she saw Andreas on the porch.

She quickly unfastened the chain and unlocked the door. "Hi."

"Mind if I come in?"

"Of course not." She stood back, then closed the door after him. "I'm surprised to see you." Happy, she thought, but surprised. "Shall we sit down?"

Nodding, he followed her into the living room.

Rylee sat on the sofa, hands clasped in her lap, suddenly afraid that the only reason he'd come was because he had bad news. His first words confirmed that fear.

"There's a master vampire in town. He's almost as old as I am. And…"

"And he's coming for me?"

Andreas nodded. "Vampires are capable of hypnotizing humans to do their bidding. I came to warn you not to talk to strangers, and to be wary of everyone, even people you know. Lycon can't force himself into your house, but he can compel someone else to break in and force you out."

Rylee felt the blood drain from her face. If she wasn't safe in her own home, what was she to do? How could she go to work if everyone she met

Amanda Ashley

could be a potential threat? It wasn't her life that was in danger, but her freedom.

Andreas nodded. "If Lycon turns you, he will be your master. The only way you can be free of him is to destroy him, something few fledglings can accomplish."

"You said your blood would protect me."

"It will. But if something should happen to me...."

Rylee stared at him, too stunned to speak, as she imagined herself at the mercy of some strange vampire, forced to bear his child. "What am I going to do?"

"You can come and stay with me. Lycon cannot enter my home. No mortal will be able to pass the wards around it. You will be safe there."

"But only at night. What am I going to do in the day time? I need to go to work."

"I'm afraid that's out of the question."

"But..."

"I will talk to Williamson."

Rylee arched one brow. "Talk?"

Andreas smiled faintly. "I will convince him you need some time off. Your job will be waiting for you when this is over."

"When will that be?" she asked, although she was sure she knew the answer.

"When Lycon's dead. Or I am."

Just as she thought. She drew in a long breath and released it before asking, "What if he wins?"

"Then I would advise you to stay in my house and hire a vampire hunter to destroy him. And hope no other vampires find you."

"That's not much comfort."

His gaze moved over her, his eyes dark with an emotion she couldn't decipher.

She didn't pull away when he reached for her, but went willingly into his arms. She wasn't afraid when he was near. With Andreas beside her, she felt like she could slay vampires or dragons or anything else that threatened her.

"Come home with me, Rylee," he said, his voice husky. "I've missed you more than you can imagine."

She knew exactly how he felt. The nights they had been apart seemed like years. And staying at his house did seem like the wisest course of action. Still, she didn't want to have to depend on him to protect her. It made her feel weak, helpless. And yet, against a master vampire, that was exactly what she was. Lycon might not be able to kill her, but he could still overpower her, make her his captive. Why risk her freedom when she didn't have to?

Her decision made, she declared, "We'll fight him together."

And hoped that, when the time came, she'd find the courage to back up her words.

CHAPTER 10

Rylee packed a bag and Andreas transported her to his house on the hill. Once there, they got in his car and he drove her to an appliance store where she picked out a small refrigerator and a stove. Andreas insisted on paying for them. The clerk promised they would be delivered the following afternoon.

From there, they drove to the market where Rylee bought an ice chest, as well as a couple of pots and pans, a coffeemaker, a set of dishes, and silverware. She also bought an assortment of easy-to-fix meals, fruit, sandwich stuff, and a large bag of ice to keep cold things cold until the refrigerator arrived. This time, she insisted on paying, even though it maxed out her last remaining credit card.

On the way home, she didn't miss the fact that Andreas seemed even more alert than usual, which was a blatant reminder of why she was moving in with him in the first place.

* * *

Andreas stood in the kitchen doorway, arms folded across his chest as he watched Rylee put away the groceries and cook wear. He had lived in this house for a century and in all that time, no one had ever used the kitchen.

It felt right, having Rylee in the house again. In four hundred years, he had rarely missed anyone or anything. As a fledgling, he had regretted the loss of his humanity. He had pined for his family, missed being human. But that had only lasted a year or so. It hadn't taken long for his vampire nature to take over. Since then, he had lived a mostly solitary life. Vampires were not social creatures, nor were they given to sharing territory or prey.

But Rylee was different. He liked looking after her, being near her, listening to the beat of her heart, hearing her voice. Just her presence made him feel almost human again.

As if sensing his thoughts, she turned to face him. For a moment, her gaze searched his. And then her eyes widened. "I make you feel human?"

He frowned at her. "Are you reading *my* thoughts now?" That could be dangerous, indeed.

"So it seems," she said. And then she smiled. "Turnabout is fair play, don't you think?"

"Not in the least."

"Why? What are you hiding?"

Andreas shook his head. He would have to take care to block his thoughts from now on. He didn't want her prying into his past. She wouldn't like what she saw there.

After putting away the last of the pots, she reached into the ice chest for a soda, which she carried into the living room.

Andreas followed her, then stood by the fireplace.

Keenly aware of his presence, she looked around the room. The last time she'd been here, she'd had other things on her mind than the furnishings. The tables and the cabinet in the corner were all made of heavy wood. Mahogany, perhaps. She was certain they were all antiques. As was he, she thought, grinning. The paintings looked expensive, as did the massive tapestry on the wall to the right of the sofa. The glass-fronted cabinet was filled with vases and figures made of jade and crystal. A pair of bookcases, both stuffed to overflowing, flanked the fireplace. Oriental carpets covered the floor.

"Your home is lovely," she murmured.

"Thanks. Would you like to see your room?" he asked, picking up her suitcase.

"Sure." She followed him up the stairs and down a carpeted hallway to

Amanda Ashley

the last door on the right.

"I hope you like it," he said, and opened the door.

Rylee stepped inside, her eyes widening as she glanced around. It was a beautiful room. The walls and bedspread were a pale blue, the ceiling white, the floor polished oak. A four-drawer dresser stood against one wall, a carved wardrobe took up most of another.

Unlike the rest of the house, this room wasn't done in antiques. Setting her suitcase on the edge of the bed, she had the feeling that he had decorated this room recently. And just for her.

"Is it all right?" he asked, dropping her suitcase at the foot of the bed. "If not, we can change it."

"I love it. Thank you."

She felt her cheeks grow warm as his gaze moved from her to the bed and back again.

"There's a bathtub through that door," he said. "Clean towels. Soap." His lips twitched in a roguish grin. "I'd be happy to stay and wash your back."

"Maybe some other time," she said.

"Good night, Rylee."

"Good night."

She blew out a sigh when he left the room, quietly closing the door behind him.

She was in danger here, too, she thought, as she kicked off her shoes and began to undress. Maybe even more danger than Lycon represented.

* * *

Fighting the urge to seduce the woman reclining in the tub upstairs, Andreas went out on the balcony off the living room. From here, he could see the lights of the city. If he chose to, he could open his preternatural senses and hear the voices coming from the houses below.

He stood there for several minutes, wondering if it had been a good idea to bring Rylee here. The scent of her hair, her skin, the sound of her voice, was enough to arouse not only his hunger for her blood but his desire for her sweet flesh. The fact that she wanted him, as well, only made her harder to resist.

An errant breeze carried the scent of vampire. *Lycon.* He was lurking in the shadows somewhere nearby. It reminded Andreas that he needed to persuade Rylee to drink from him. A small taste wouldn't turn her, but it would strengthen the bond between them.

Tomorrow night, he thought. He would talk to her about it tomorrow night.

* * *

After breakfast, boredom set in. Feeling like a caged tiger, Rylee paced from the living room to the kitchen and back again. She had only spent a few days at the realty office, but she had enjoyed it. Working had given her a sense of purpose and accomplishment, a way to fill her time. Now, because of some stupid legend, she was trapped in this prison with nothing to do. Although she had to admit, it was very nice, as prisons went.

As the morning wore on, she decided to explore the rest of the house. On the main floor, in addition to the living room, there was a good-sized area which she suspected was meant to be a dining room, though it was hard to be sure, since it was empty. There was also a den which looked unused. In the kitchen, she found a large pantry behind a door she hadn't opened last night.

Upstairs, there were six bedrooms, all unfurnished except for the one she had slept in. It wasn't the same one she had awakened in that first night, she thought. Or was it? Had he removed his own furniture and redecorated it just for her?

She wondered where Andreas took his rest. Did he even stay in the house? Or was his lair located elsewhere?

Returning to the living room, Rylee plucked a Lee Child novel from the bookshelf, curled up in a big easy chair, and lost herself in another Jack Reacher adventure.

She was in the middle of Chapter Eight when the doorbell rang. She debated the wisdom of answering it, then remembered that the appliances were being delivered today. And still she hesitated. What if they weren't delivery men at all, but people who had been hypnotized by Lycon?

Reluctantly, she went to the door. "Who's there?"

"Delivery for Miss North from Henderson's Appliances."

Should she let them in? Or ask them to come back later, when Andreas was awake? She was still trying to decide what to do when Andreas

                        Amanda Ashley

appeared beside her and opened the door.

"Come in, gentlemen," he said.

Rylee stayed in the living room while Andreas accompanied the men into the kitchen, then stood in the doorway while they unwrapped the refrigerator and the stove and hooked them up. When they finished, he showed them out.

"I guess I'm getting paranoid," Rylee said. "I just didn't know what to do."

"Not to worry, my sweet. It was my fault. I should have arranged for the delivery to be made after dark."

"I'm sorry I'm so much trouble."

He laughed softly. "You are the most delightful trouble I've ever known."

"Do you have to go back to…?" To what, she thought. Bed? Sleep? Death?

"Not if you'd like me to stay."

"I would."

He glanced around the room, his brow furrowed. "I think tonight I'll have to take you shopping again."

"It isn't necessary I have enough groceries to last several days."

"I was thinking of something more in the way of entertainment. A TV, perhaps. A stereo. A computer. Whatever you'd like."

She shook her head. "I can't pay for all that."

"Nor would I let you. It's my house. I've been meaning to add a few modern conveniences." He nodded. "I'll take you out to dinner tonight and then we'll go browse the stores."

* * *

He was as good as his word. As soon as the sun went down, they drove to town.

He took her to dinner at an Italian restaurant, relaxed with a glass of wine while she ate.

"The garlic doesn't bother you?" she asked, reaching for a slice of bread. "I thought it was supposed to repel vampires."

He shook his head. "The whole garlic thing is a myth."

"Oh. Do you ever miss eating?"

"Not really. I scarcely remember how food tasted, although now and then when I see something that didn't exist when I was human, I find myself wondering what it's like."

"What happens if you do eat something?"

"Nothing pleasant."

She tilted her head to the side, her eyes filled with curiosity.

He laughed softly. "It was years ago. I went to a fast food place and ordered a hamburger. Of course, people have been eating beef and bread for centuries, but not in its present form. I took a few bites and was violently ill for days. That was my first and last attempt at consuming human food."

* * *

After dinner, they went shopping. By the end of the evening, they had a big screen TV with a state-of-the-art sound system, and a new computer with a twenty-four inch monitor.

"I'll set it all up in the den later," Andreas said when they returned home. "First I need to talk to you about something."

"That sounds ominous." Sitting on the sofa, Rylee kicked off her shoes. She gasped in astonishment when, with no more than a look from Andreas, a fire sprang to life in the hearth.

"Sorry," he muttered, dropping onto the sofa beside her. "I should have warned you."

"You have a lot of unusual talents," she remarked. "What did you want to talk about?"

"I want you to drink my blood. Just a little," he added, seeing the look of horror in her eyes. "It will strengthen the bond between us, and weaken any link that might be formed by another vampire."

"You're talking about Lycon, aren't you?"

Andreas nodded. "We are fated to meet sooner or later. The odds are that only one of us will survive. But there's always a chance that he might somehow make you his captive before the two of us meet. If that happens, our mutual bond will make it easier for you to defy him. And I will always be able to find you."

That was both reassuring and a little creepy.

Rylee stared into the fireplace, her mind racing. What he said made a

 Amanda Ashley

kind of sense, but drink his blood? The thought was beyond repellent, yet she couldn't help feeling a kind of morbid curiosity. What did vampire blood taste like?

"Are you ready?"

"You want to do it *now*? Tonight?"

"Yes."

Her gaze darted to his neck. She had never bitten anyone.

She was still trying to visualize herself biting into his skin when Andreas bit into his wrist, opening a pair of shallow wounds. Dark crimson oozed from the tiny punctures.

"You need only take a few drops," he said, holding out his arm. "The taste is pleasant, I'm told."

Rylee didn't believe that for a minute, but curiosity drove her to take hold of his arm. She took a deep breath, then bent down and lapped at the blood. It was thick and hot on her tongue and it went through her like liquid fire. After one taste, she wanted another. And then another.

She didn't stop until Andreas withdrew his arm. Embarrassed, she looked away.

And wished for more. She watched as he licked his wrist, noting that the punctures closed immediately.

"Amazing," she murmured. "Do all your injuries heal that fast?"

"Pretty much."

"Can I ask you something?"

"Fire away."

"Where do you spend the day?"

He regarded her for several moments.

Rylee felt him probing her mind and knew he was seeking the reason for the question. She supposed the location of a vampire's resting place was something he didn't share. "Sorry, it's none of my business."

"My lair is here, in the house."

"Really?" She had explored the place from top to bottom, seen every room. Hadn't she?

He shook his head. "The door is well-hidden and veiled with vampire magic."

Vampire magic. It sounded so mysterious, so intriguing. Sometimes, being a vampire sounded kind of awesome.

"Awesome?" He lifted on brow. "Really?"

"Stop that!"

"Why? You read my mind a few moments ago."

"True, but I have no idea how I did it."

Neither did he. "Do you *want* to read my thoughts?"

Rylee started to say yes, then hesitated. What secrets might he be hiding behind those fathomless dark eyes?

Andreas laughed softly.

And Rylee blushed.

"You're right to be cautious," he said. "But if you want to read my mind, all you have to do is concentrate. I'll block anything I don't want you to see."

"So we can read each other's thoughts because we've shared blood? Is that how it works?"

"Usually. Except in your case, you read my mind *before* you drank from me. I've never known that to happen before, but I suspect it has something to do with your unique heritage." When he drank from her the first time, it had made her stronger. Perhaps it also allowed her to read his thoughts.

"Can you read anyone's mind?"

"If I'm so inclined."

"Can I?"

"I don't know."

Rylee shook her head. Sometimes she felt like she was a character in the Twilight Zone. Some legendary woman whose birth had been foretold. A vampire who had showed up in her life like some knight in shining armor to save her from the evil villain.

"A knight?" Andreas asked, amusement evident in his voice. "More like a less evil villain, don't you think?"

"Isn't there some way to keep you out of my head?"

"Yes, although it will probably take you a while to master the technique."

"So, how do I do it?"

"You need to erect a wall around your thoughts. Something impenetrable. It takes a lot of concentration and practice." He caressed her cheek with his knuckles. "It will help you pass the time." Leaning forward, he kissed her lightly. "I need to go out. It's getting late. You should go to bed."

Rylee nodded, her lips tingling from his touch.

     Amanda Ashley

"Remember, don't open the door for anyone tomorrow, even if it's someone you know."

"I won't."

His hand cupped her nape and he kissed her again, his tongue dueling with hers.

Rylee twined her arms around his neck, her whole body yearning toward his.

She let out a little moan of regret when he put her away from him and stood.

"You are one hell of a temptation, Rylee North," he muttered, and vanished from the room.

She stared after him. Later that night, lying in bed, she imagined him there beside her, his arms around her, holding her close.

Sighing, she turned onto her side and stared at the darkness beyond the window. It would nice if she could see into the future, she thought.

Nice to know where their relationship was headed. And if she would survive to see it unfold.

Chapter 11

Andreas prowled the night, his thoughts not on prey but on the beautiful young woman in his house. He wanted her. All of her. Heart and mind, soul and body. Every thought, every caress. She had been born for him, and he meant to have her. But only if she felt the same. He could mesmerize her. He could compel her to love him, to stay with him. But like most things in life, that which was freely given was always sweeter.

Like her blood. In all his centuries as a vampire, he had never tasted anything to equal it. So warm. So satisfying.

When this business with Lycon was settled, he would beg her to be his, to fill the void in his life that no one else had been able to touch.

Amanda Ashley

CHAPTER 12

Rylee spent the morning thinking about everything Andreas had told her. If she left him, there was a good chance that other vampires would come looking for her. They wouldn't kill her, which was good. But what if Andreas was wrong and it was possible for one of them to turn her against her will, and force her to bear a child. That would be bad. Very bad.

If she stayed with Andreas, he would marry her. She would have all of his powers. And she could give him something no other woman could—a child.

He cared for her, but he'd never said he loved her.

Did she love him? That was, she thought, the biggest question of all.

She was fixing lunch when her cell phone rang. After checking the number, she said, "Hi, Mom."

"Rylee, hon, I have some bad news."

"What is it?" she asked anxiously, alarmed by the fear in her mother's voice.

"Your father is in the hospital in critical condition. If you want to see him alive, you'd better come right away!"

Rylee frowned. Her mother sounded strange, she thought, but maybe it was just worry. "What happened?"

"He was hit by a car early this morning. He's on life support. I'm with him now. At Rockland Memorial."

"I'll be there as soon as I get dressed!" *Please, please let me get there before it's too late.* The last words she had said to her father had been spoken in anger. She had to see him one last time, had to tell him she hadn't meant any of it.

Heart pounding, Rylee threw on her clothes, grabbed the keys to Andreas' car and ran out of the house.

And straight into the arms of a man wearing a long black coat and dark glasses.

Rylee screamed as his arm went around her neck. The keys fell from her hand as she kicked and scratched, then rolled her head back and forth in an effort to avoid the dirty, smelly cloth he pressed over her nose and mouth.

And then everything went black.

* * *

The sound of Rylee's scream roused Andreas from the dark sleep. Springing to his feet, he bolted up the cellar stairs and flung open the front door in time to see a white van driving away.

His first instinct was to go after her, but it was mid-day and the world was bathed in sunlight. Even then he was tempted to follow the van, but he'd made the mistake of going outside during the day once before. It was a day he'd never forgotten. He hadn't gone up in flames, as the fledglings did, but that would have been a blessing. The sunlight burned every inch of his body, blinded him for weeks. The pain had been excruciating. As badly as he longed to go to Rylee, he'd be no help to her weak and blind.

Too restless to sit still, too concerned for her well-being to rest, he paced the floor with quick, angry strides. As soon as the sun slid behind the horizon, he would go after her.

He comforted himself with the fact that Lycon would not be able to turn her. It was the only thing that kept him inside. Lycon might be able to drink from her. But that was all.

* * *

Rylee woke in a dark place. When she tried to sit up, she discovered

Amanda Ashley

that her hands were tied. There was a nasty taste in her mouth. Her head hurt.

Where was she?

And then she remembered. Her mother's phone call. Her frantic haste to see her father before it was too late. She hadn't taken time to think it through, just ran out of the house, ignoring all of Andreas' warnings and her own common sense.

She frowned, remembering how strange her mother had sounded on the phone, as if someone was telling her what to say. Was her father really in danger or had someone forced her to make that call? And how was she to know?

Rylee struggled to her feet, then, hands out in front of her, she walked slowly forward until she reached a wall. She turned left and followed it, searching for a door. She found one—locked, of course.

Andreas? Are you there?

Rylee! Are you hurt?

No.

He breathed a sigh of relief. *Where are you?*

I don't know.

What happened?

As quickly as possible, she told him how she had been kidnapped. Andreas, please call my mother and see if my parents are all right.

I will, love. Just sit tight. It'll be dark soon and I'll be on my way.

How will you get in?

A damn good question, he thought. Lycon had undoubtedly warded his lair against intruders. *I'll think of something. Remember, he can drink from you, but he can't turn you.*

Are you sure about that?

As sure as I can be. Stay strong, Rylee my love.

Do you?

Do I what?

Love me?

More than my life.

She was about to say she loved him, too, when the door banged open, hitting the wall. A tall man stood there, his hair brown and lank, his face and eyes devoid of any emotion at all. He wore faded jeans and a rumpled shirt that had the name *Compton* stitched on one pocket and the name of a local gas station on the other one.

Rylee?

Someone's here.

"I brought you something to eat," the man said, his voice flat. After placing a covered tray on the floor, he reached to the right and flicked a light switch Rylee had missed in the dark. "The master says you should keep your strength up for later." And so saying, he slammed the door.

Rylee heard the key turn in the lock. With a sigh, she sat on the floor and lifted the lid on the tray. She smiled when she saw the knife. Food could wait. The blade wasn't very sharp, but she managed to saw through the short piece of rope that bound her hands. Tossing it aside, she picked up the sandwich and gobbled it down, drank the soda, and wiped her hands.

Standing, she delved into her hair for a bobby pin and, after several tries, unlocked the door. *Andreas?*

I'm here.

I managed to unlock the door. I'm going to look for a way out.

Be careful. And put your mind at ease. Your parents are fine. Your mother was forced to make that call, but she wasn't hurt. I'll be there in a few minutes.

How will you find me?

Your blood will guide me. Take care.

She opened the door as quietly as she could. She seemed to be in a basement. A set of wooden stairs led upward. After taking off her shoes, she tiptoed up the steps, walking on the outer edges in hopes of avoiding any squeaky treads.

She found another door at the top of the stairs. Taking a deep breath, she turned the knob, murmured a silent prayer of thanks when it wasn't locked. This one opened onto a short, narrow hallway. She crept along until she came to an arch that led into the living room. No lights were on. As far as she could tell, no one was in there.

Another deep breath and she hurried toward the door. Her hand was on the latch when a voice said, "Going somewhere?"

Whirling around, she saw a man sitting in a chair in the far corner. It was Lycon, though how she knew that was a mystery. Taking a deep breath, Rylee said, "I'm going home."

The vampire rose fluidly, like a snake unwinding. "I think not." In the blink of an eye, he was standing in front of her, close enough to touch.

   Amanda Ashley

Leaning forward, he pressed his face to her neck and took a deep breath. "You smell so good. How do you taste, I wonder?"

Before Rylee could react, his hands folded over her shoulders, holding her in place while his fangs pierced her flesh.

He drank deeply, and then, with a vile oath, he pushed her away.

Reeling back, she slammed into the door, hitting her head.

Lycon wiped his lips with the back of his hand. "You fed on a vampire!"

"Yes," she said, smiling sweetly and blessing Andreas for insisting she do so. "I did." Had Andreas known it would make her blood distasteful to other vampires? If so, why hadn't he mentioned it?

Lycon stared at her, and then, as seconds passed, a slow smile spread across his face. "It tastes vile," he said, his voice thoughtful, "but I can feel its power running through my veins. Perhaps it won't taste as bad the second time. Shall we find out?"

Rylee tried to dart out of his way, but he was too fast for her. Pulling her into his arms, he drank from her again. Drank until she was light-headed and swaying on her feet. Only then did he let her go.

* * *

From outside the house, Andreas cursed long and loud as he sensed what was happening. He had to find a way in there, had to get Rylee out of that monster's hands. He could not, would not, let the woman he loved become Lycon's main source of nourishment. It would weaken her, demoralize her.

He prowled the grounds, his anger and frustration growing with every passing minute.

Lycon was an old and powerful vampire. His wards would be strong, invincible.

Dammit! He had to find a way to get in there!

But how?

* * *

For the second time that day, Rylee woke in the dark. This time, she was too weak to move, to think. She could only lie there, cold to the very marrow of her bones. She felt empty, dead inside, as if someone had sucked the life out of her.

Of course, she thought dully, that was exactly what had happened.

Lycon couldn't drain her dry because he was compelled to keep her alive. But he had taken as much as he dared.

Was this to be her future? Nothing more than prey to a ruthless vampire?

If so, she'd rather be dead.

No! Andreas' voice rang out in her mind. *Rylee, love, don't give up. I'll get you out of there. I swear it!*

She heard him but was too tired to answer, too steeped in despair to believe him. All she wanted to do was sleep.

And forget.

    Amanda Ashley

Chapter 13

Rylee lost track of time. Day and night blended into one endless round of misery. After Lycon fed on her the second time, she had spent the day lying on the floor of her prison, too weak to move. She hadn't seen him since then. Compton brought her food and drink morning and night. He rarely spoke to her.

The only bright spot in her life was her connection to Andreas and yet she couldn't help thinking that, if she had never met him, she wouldn't be in this terrible place now. Then again, there was always the possibility that another vampire would have tracked her down.

She was increasingly grateful for the link she shared with Andreas. At night, when she was most miserable, he told her stories of his youth to entertain her, and always, he urged her to be strong.

Tonight was no different. I'm right outside, he said, his voice tinged with despair. When his man brings you food tomorrow morning, I want you to attack him and then open the front door and invite me inside.

Will that work? This isn't my house.

Not technically, but you're living there.

And then what?

I'm going after Lycon.

How will you find him?

I can sense him. There's another room below the basement. He takes his rest there. But... wait a minute. You said morning. You can't be out during the day.

Don't worry about me. Just do as I said. My car will be in front of the house. Once you're outside, take the car and drive like hell to my place.

But...?

Rylee, love, I can't bear the thought of him drinking from you again. Touching you. I don't like the thought of you being outside during the day.

Andreas wasn't crazy about it, either, but he had to do something. The last two nights had been hell for him, and certainly for her. Thus far, Lycon had remained indoors, out of reach. With Rylee as his prey, he had no need to hunt.

Andreas had considered mesmerizing several men, arming them with stakes, and sending them in after Rylee, but Lycon would sense their presence as soon as they stepped on his property. All master vampires could function inside during the day, if necessary. Andreas didn't want to be responsible for sending innocent men to their deaths, and he had no doubt that Lycon would rip out their hearts before they knew what hit them.

Aside from that, destroying Lycon was something he needed to do with his own two hands. Lycon had taken Rylee and the penalty was death.

Andreas?

Get some rest. Tomorrow, this will all be over.

One way or another.

* * *

Rylee scrambled to her feet at the sound of a key in the lock. Heart pounding, she stared at the door. Compton had brought her extra food and drink earlier that evening, telling her, in his flat, toneless voice, that Lycon would be feeding on her tomorrow night.

She backed up against the far wall as the door swung open, felt her heart sink when Lycon stepped into the room. Panic swept through her. If the vampire drank from her now, she would never be strong enough to attack Compton in the morning and get out of the house.

"I couldn't wait until tomorrow," Lycon said, his lips drawn back to reveal his fangs. "I've thought of nothing else since the last time." He took another step toward her. "I know you want to fight me, but if you don't, I'll see about making your prison more comfortable. A bed, perhaps.

Amanda Ashley

Maybe some music or a book to read to pass the time.”

His gaze held hers, his eyes taking on a faint red glow. “Come to me, Rylee.”

Resist!

Rylee looked away when she heard Andreas’ voice in her mind.

“Come to me!” Lycon demanded. “We can make this pleasant or not. It’s up to you.”

“I’ll never make it easy for you!” Rylee spat the words at him. “Never!” Rage welled up inside her. And then she heard Andreas’s voice again. *Rylee, love, draw on my power. You have it within you. Feel my anger and my strength and make it your own. I’m right outside.*

She clenched her hands as Lycon strode purposefully toward her, fangs extended, eyes red as hell. She reached out to Andreas, felt his strength pour into her, sweeping away her fear.

When Lycon reached for her, she fell back on every woman’s first instinct and rammed her knee into his groin. He might have been a master vampire. He might be as strong as ten men. But he doubled over, cursing.

And Rylee ran out of the basement, slammed the door shut and turned the key in the lock.

Compton was waiting for her when she reached the living room. He didn’t try to stop her when she opened the door and ran outside.

She breathed a sigh of relief when Andreas materialized in front of her. He was here. She was safe.

And then a fist grabbed a handful of her hair, jerked her off her feet, and flung her aside. Lycon!

She landed on her back, the wind knocked out of her. Gaining her knees, she watched the two vampires come together. It was a fight unlike any she had ever seen. They tore at each other like two wild animals, fangs ripping and tearing, claws leaving great long gouges in preternatural flesh that healed almost instantly. It occurred to her that the battle could go on for hours before either vampire suffered a mortal blow.

She was distantly aware that Compton was standing on the porch, his expression as impassive as always.

Struggling to her feet, Rylee glanced around the yard, searching for something she could use as a weapon, but it was too dark to see anything beyond the light from inside the house.

A harsh cry drew her attention back to the life-and-death struggle on the front lawn. Lycon was on the ground, bleeding profusely from a large gash in his throat. Andreas was on his knees beside him, his face and clothing torn and splattered with blood.

Rylee started toward him, only to come to an abrupt halt when Compton ran down the porch steps brandishing a long wooden stake.

Rylee let out a shriek, certain he meant to drive the stake into Andreas, but Andreas wasn't his target.

With a shout that was more like a snarl, Compton drove the stake into Lycon's chest. A hoarse cry erupted from the vampire's throat. He shuddered once and then his body slowly disintegrated until there was nothing left but dust.

Compton let out a wail of his own when Andreas' rose up behind him, one hand holding him in place. Rylee couldn't blame the man for being afraid. Andreas looked like death himself.

"Andreas!" Rylee shouted. "Don't!"

His gaze met hers over Compton's head and she knew she was seeing a side of him he had kept hidden from her.

"Please, Andreas. Let him go."

"The kill was mine to make. He took it from me."

"It doesn't matter now. It's over."

He glanced at the ground where Lycon's body had been. A long, shuddering sigh wracked his body and then, abruptly, he released his hold on Compton.

The man took off running without a backward glance.

"Andreas? Take me home."

With a nod, he put his arms around her waist, careful not to let his bloody hands touch her skin.

The next thing she knew, she was standing in the middle of her own living room.

Alone.

     Amanda Ashley

Chapter 14

In the morning, it took Rylee a moment to remember she was in her own bed, in her own house.

Scrambling out of bed, she went looking for her cell phone, intending to call her mother. In spite of Andreas' assurance that her parents were fine, she had to hear it for herself. And then she frowned. Her phone was still at Andreas' house, along with her handbag.

She bit down on her lower lip, then snapped her fingers. Email! She quickly booted up her computer and opened her account.

Hi, Mom. She tapped her fingers on the desk top as she waited for a reply, praying all the while that her mother was home and alive. She breathed a sigh of relief when she received a new message.

Hi, honey. How nice to hear from you. Why are you emailing? Did you lose your phone?

Are you all right?

Of course. Why wouldn't I be?

Rylee frowned. She wasn't sure what she had expected her mother to say, but this wasn't it. *I left my phone at a friend's house.*

Well, at least you didn't lose it. Is everything all right?

Yes, I just wanted to say hi. Is everything all right there?

Same as always. I hate to cut this short, hon, but I'm expecting your father any minute.

Really?

I know, it's a surprise to me, too. Oh, there's the doorbell. He's here. Call me when you find your phone. xoxo

After signing off, Rylee sat there a moment, puzzling over her mother's reaction. Surely, if Compton had terrorized her mother, she would have said something.

Frowning, Rylee padded into the bathroom, took a long, hot shower and washed her hair.

While drying off, she wondered again if Lycon had somehow orchestrated the whole story. But that was impossible. She had recognized her mother's voice. And then she realized that Andreas had probably gone to the house and wiped the memory of everything that had happened from her mother's mind. But surely even Andreas, with all his amazing powers, couldn't reunite her parents.

After pulling on a pair of jeans and a sweater, she went into the kitchen, only then realizing there wasn't much to eat. Before going off with Andreas, she had thrown out everything that was likely to spoil in her absence. She found a can of chicken noodle soup in the back of the cupboard. That and a cup of black coffee served as breakfast.

Her handbag and her wallet were at Andreas' lair, but she had a spare set of keys and a little cash stashed away for emergencies, so she drove to the store to buy the basics and a rotisserie chicken for dinner.

Back at home, she wandered aimlessly through the house. Andreas hadn't said anything last night. After bringing her home, he'd vanished from sight. Before going to bed, she had tried to contact him through their bond, but it was like trying to penetrate a block wall. Hurt and confused, she had cried herself to sleep.

Late in the afternoon, she curled up in a chair by the front window and watched the sun make its gradual descent.

She was thinking about Andreas, as she had all day, when his car pulled up at the curb. Her heart skipped a beat when he stepped out of the convertible, then paused on the sidewalk. Her gaze moved over him, thinking he looked quite elegant in a pair of black slacks, white shirt, black tie and thigh-length black coat. She smiled inwardly, thinking he looked like he'd just stepped off a wedding cake.

She rose when he started up the walkway, had the door open when he

Amanda Ashley

reached the porch. For a timeless moment, they simply stared at each other. She didn't know who moved first, but suddenly they were in each other's arms and she was laughing and crying at the same time.

"Rylee." He whispered her name, his voice filled with such love and tenderness, it had her crying all over again. "Marry me, Rylee. Say you'll be mine now and forever."

"Yes," she murmured, blinking back her tears. "Yes, yes, yes!"

"Tonight?"

"This very minute."

"You're sure?" His gaze searched hers, as if he couldn't believe she meant it, or that, after all she'd seen, all she'd been through, she was still willing to stay with him.

Nodding, she went up on her tiptoes, hands delving into the hair at his nape as she pressed her lips to his.

He kissed her deeply, then drew back. "Let's go, love. The preacher is waiting to marry us."

"Awfully sure of yourself, weren't you?" she teased.

"No, love. Just very hopeful."

"Well, you're dressed right," she said, laughing, "but I can't get married in jeans and a sweater."

"Not to worry. Just wait here."

She watched from the window as he went out to the car. When he returned, he was carrying a large white box and two smaller ones, which he took into her bedroom.

He stood beside her while she opened the larger one. Inside, Rylee found the most exquisite wedding gown she had ever seen, along with a gossamer veil. The first of the two smaller boxes contained a pair of white heels. The second one held a very sexy black negligee.

"I see you thought of everything," she murmured, running her hands over the cool silk of the gown.

Giving her a wink, he said, "I'll pick you up in half an hour. Will that give you enough time to change?"

"Better give me an hour."

* * *

Even though she'd taken a shower that morning, Rylee showered again.

She was getting married! Wrapped in a towel, she spritzed herself with perfume, brushed her teeth, and applied her makeup.

Standing in front of the mirror on the back of her bedroom door, she stepped into her wedding dress and set the veil in place.

When the doorbell rang downstairs, she smiled at the bride in the glass, then ran down the stairs.

She was getting married!

* * *

Rylee's stomach fluttered with excitement as they drove to the church. "How did you get a license so quickly?"

"You don't want to know," he said with a wink.

"And the preacher?"

"Let's just say I persuaded him."

"I can imagine how you did that," she said dryly.

"And you'd be right."

Rylee glanced out the window. She was getting married. Maybe she should have waited a day or two so her parents could be there. "What did you say to my mother? I emailed her today and she never said anything about Compton or… or anything."

"I did just what you're thinking. I wiped the memory from her mind."

"She's going out with my father tonight. Did you arrange that, too?"

"In a way."

Ten minutes later, he pulled up in front of a large non-denominational church. "Ready?"

She nodded. And then placed her hand on his arm. "Wait."

"You've changed your mind?" He sounded resigned, as if he had expected it.

"No. But, we decided this so quickly… what if I don't want to let you turn me?"

"It doesn't matter, Rylee."

"But you want a child."

Turning toward her, he took her hands in his. "I only want you. A child would be wonderful. But it's you I want. You I need. I love you, Rylee, but if you've changed your mind, I'll take you back home."

"Would I ever see you again?"

Amanda Ashley

"I don't know. To be honest, I don't know if I could go on as we have been without making you mine." He took a deep breath. Then, voice shaking, he said, "What do you want to do?"

"Marry the man I love. Let's not keep the preacher waiting!"

CHAPTER 15

They entered the church hand-in-hand. It was a beautiful old place. The pews were dark wood, the windows stained glass, the altar covered with a lacy white cloth. Dozens of candles nestled in wrought-iron wall sconces cast dancing shadows on the white-washed walls.

Three people stood in front of the altar. Two had their backs to the door. The third was the minister. He smiled as they drew near. Rylee assumed the other two were their witnesses. Even from the back, the woman looked familiar.

"Mom?"

Tears filled Rylee's eyes as her mother turned around. Beaming brightly, she hugged Rylee. Then it was her father's turn. "Thanks for inviting us, kitten."

She nodded, too choked up to speak.

One last hug and her father returned to her mother's side.

Rylee looked at Andreas as he stepped into her father's place and took her hand. *I don't know how you did this, but thank you.*

I'm glad I took the chance to invite them. Would have been awkward if you'd changed your mind!

That was never going to happen.

He smiled at her, his eyes warm with love as the minister spoke the

     Amanda Ashley

words that bound them together as husband and wife.

$* * *$

After the ceremony, the four of them went dining and dancing. Rylee watched in fascination as dinner was served. Andreas didn't eat, of course, but her parents didn't seem to notice. More vampire magic, she guessed.

She blinked back tears when her father led her mother onto the dance floor.

"Shall we?" Andreas asked.

Rylee nodded, thinking this was the best night of her life.

$* * *$

It was near midnight when Rylee and Andreas bid her parents goodnight.

"We never talked about a honeymoon," Andreas said as they drove home. "What would you like to do?"

"I've always wanted to go to Italy."

"Then that's where we'll go." He slid a wicked glance in her direction. "But not tonight."

She blushed under his gaze. "There's something else we never talked about," she murmured.

He lifted one brow. "Oh?"

"Do vampires make love like… you know, like everybody else?"

"I don't know how everybody does it."

"You know what I mean."

Trying not to laugh, he said, "I think you'll find I have all the right equipment in all the right places."

$* * *$

Rylee was more nervous than she'd expected when they were finally alone. She'd had only one serious romance and it hadn't lasted long. Jeff was the only man she'd slept with and that had been almost two years ago. She didn't know if the lack of fire between them was her fault or his.

"Hey." Andreas came up behind her and wrapped his arms around her waist. "You look a little troubled. Second thoughts?"

"Oh. No. I was just… never mind."

He nuzzled her neck. His breath, though surprisingly warm, sent shivers down her spine.

"Rylee?" He turned her in his arms so he could see her face. "Tell me what's wrong?"

She contemplated a lie, then dismissed the idea. It seemed foolish when he could read her mind. "I'm just a little…" Her voice trailed off. She loved his kisses, enjoyed being in his arms, but Andreas had never gone further than she was willing to go.

His brow furrowed. "Have you ever been intimate with a man?"

"Just one."

"I won't hurt you." He stroked her cheek lightly. "I won't do anything you don't want me to. And if you're not ready tonight…" He took a deep breath and let it out in a long sigh. "I can wait until you are."

His words chased all her fears away. What was she afraid of? This was Andreas. He had never been anything but protective of her. And he loved her.

And she loved him. "Are you just going to stand there?" She slipped her hands under his shirt, her fingers making lazy circles on his chest, sliding down to stroke his hard, flat belly.

He growled low in his throat and the next thing she knew, her clothing was in a heap on the floor and she was lying naked in bed with an aroused vampire.

He was, she thought, the most amazingly handsome, ripped man she had ever seen. She pushed him onto his back and straddled his thighs and then began a slow exploration of the man who was now her husband. He watched her like a hungry cat watching a fat canary. When he couldn't take any more, he flipped her onto her back.

"Turnabout is fair play," he said with a wicked grin.

Rylee gasped with pleasure as his hands moved over her, carrying her away to a place she had never imagined.

* * *

Much later, lying sated in his arms, she smiled inwardly.

Come Thanksgiving, she would have a lot to be grateful for.

 Amanda Ashley

EPILOGUE

Two years later

Rylee gazed at the infant cradled in her arms. So much had happened in the last two years. Mr. Williamson had welcomed her back and she'd intended to continue working for a while before she let Andreas turn her into a vampire. But it hadn't happened that way. She had asked Andreas to turn her the night of their first anniversary. It had been an amazing experience. A little frightening, to be sure, but mostly exhilarating.

She had quit her job a few weeks before the baby was born.

Rylee sighed as she kissed her baby's cheek. She had no regrets. How could she, when Andreas had given her such a beautiful daughter? Novalie had her father's black hair, her mother's brown eyes, and a cute little nose. Rylee never tired of holding her, looking at her.

She glanced up, a smile curving her lips, when Andreas entered the nursery.

"I thought I'd find you here," he said, dropping a kiss on her brow. "Your parents called. They wanted to know if you're up to having company."

The news that her parents had decided to stay together had been another happy surprise. "Of course."

"I thought you would be," he said with a wink. "I told them to come over." Dropping down on his knees, he cupped Rylee's cheek. "Have I told you how beautiful you are," he said, his voice husky, "and how much I love you?"

"Not in the last hour."

"Consider it said." Very gently, he stroked a finger over his daughter's downy cheek. "Thank you for this."

"I should be thanking you," Rylee said, blinking away her tears. "You've given me everything I ever wanted."

Andreas blinked back tears of his own as her voice poured over him, as warm and welcome as sunshine.

It truly was a day of thanksgiving.

The End

Amanda Ashley

ABOUT THE AUTHOR

Amanda Ashley is one of those rare birds—a California native. She's lived in Southern California her whole life and loves it. She married her high school sweetheart and they have three sons, all handsome enough to be cover models!

Amanda never intended to be a published author. It just happened. She has always loved to read, though. The Black Stallion books, Nancy Drew, Mary Stewart. And then she discovered romance novels. One night when her husband was at work, her kids were in bed and there was nothing on TV, she sat down and started writing a book of her own. And she's been writing ever since.

Amanda and her alter ego, Madeline Baker, have written over seventy books, many of which have appeared on various bestseller lists, including the New York Times list, the Waldenbooks Bestseller list, and the USA Today list. Not bad for someone who started writing just for the fun of it.